NEVER BOUND

EVERLY CLAIRE

Never Bound: The Unchained Book Two
Cover Designer: Qamber Designs
Editor: Emily A. Lawrence
Proofreader: Brianne Matheny

Copyright © 2025 by Everly Claire

All rights reserved.

Published by: Hudson & Hawk Group
New York | Miami | Road Town | Hamilton
everlyclaire.com

To my island found family, whether or not you ever find or read this book. Next year in Anegada, yeah?

WARNING

This series is set in a dark fictional world and contains potentially disturbing and triggering themes. It is intended only for adults eighteen years of age and older.

For a complete list of trigger warnings, scan the QR code or visit everlyclaire.com/triggers.

Please look after your mental health.

PREVIOUSLY

This book is a continuation of *Never Broken (The Unchained #1)*. That book must be read first and is available on Kindle Unlimited. Scan the QR code or visit https://books2read.com/u/3yJBwV.

At the end of *Never Broken,* our main characters were caught on camera together and then blackmailed by the Wainwright-Phillips family gardener. However, they were unexpectedly saved by Max Langer, the charismatic tech billionaire our male main character suspected of holding his recently-freed sister, Maeve, captive. The gardener then disappeared. This was all in between our MMC risking a whipping or worse to impress a dinner party crowd and Langer in particular with his genius and charm, even though he was supposed to be serving. Maeve also told her brother over a secret communication network that she was helped during her captivity by a mysterious woman named Resi, who planned to free all the slaves in the world.

So ... maybe Langer's not evil after all? It's possible ... except that after he left, Corey Killeen, Louisa's humiliated classmate who is also Langer's intern, appeared with what he claimed was a threatening "message" from his boss: Maeve's slave bracelet, intact and streaked in blood, as if it had been violently removed. He also smashed an expensive bottle of bourbon on the pool deck and burned through our MMC's palm with a cigar, in case he didn't get the point ...

1

HER

"Who did this to you?"

I noticed the blistering crater on his palm almost as soon as he entered my room on Monday, mostly because he was trying desperately—and not very gracefully—to hide it. Only one question came to mind, of course. But I didn't ask it.

"It's nothing," he said, awkwardly grabbing a pen in a way that made it clear it wasn't nothing.

But I did let it go. I hated to, but I did. After all, it wasn't the first time someone had hurt him, and it wouldn't be the last. And why the hell was I telling myself that to make myself feel *better*?

The burn would simply join the growing list of things I couldn't ask about, like why he was still convinced Max Langer was the devil incarnate instead of the only guest at that train wreck of a dinner party on Friday who'd treated him with any decency.

And where his sister was. And whether she was okay. And if she wasn't, whether saving her would in any way involve him running away and leaving me forever. Not that I was trying to be clingy or anything.

Besides, I didn't want to know the answer. I already *knew* it. Borrowing more time didn't make the time any less borrowed. After all, we'd just spent the whole weekend in the same house and hardly saw each other at all.

Sunday usually meant some downtime for the slaves, and I was grateful for it on his behalf, though it hurt that we couldn't spend it together. However, I'd really outdone myself on Saturday, when I'd reluctantly let Juliette come over to hang by the pool. November in the Valley was still warm enough to lie out during the heat of the day, and flipping through fashion magazines—or my chemistry notes hidden inside a magazine, a certain someone would be pleased to know—was feasible. What was also feasible was choosing a laughably skimpy black-and-white string bikini I'd only ever worn on spring break—far, far away from my parents and the unceremoniously departed gardener. And waiting until my chosen mark passed by the pool on his way to some quite-possibly-fictional chore. Of course I let the strings casually slide off my shoulders as if I'd simply forgotten to tie them.

My only reward for all that feasibility? Watching how fast his head swiveled. But that was more than enough—and what made it especially cute was that the poor guy probably thought he was being subtle about it.

Meanwhile, of course, I was keeping a running mental list of everything I wanted to do to him and for him as soon as we had some unstructured time. The problem was, we never had any. Even when we *weren't* being blackmailed, the only hours we ever had together were when we were supposed to be doing something else. Plus, we still had five more chapters to review before the exam and only an hour to spare for each, and if you thought sitting at the desk fighting the unbearable urge to touch each other was awkward, try sitting there knowing you *could* touch each other at any time, and why the hell weren't you doing it?

"So I know we've gone over elimination reactions a million times," he began professorially after he entered the room on Monday, after waving off my question about his hand. "But you also have to remember that they look a bit different when it's a modified alcohol like a methyl group, so I want to look over those with you today, and—fuck, that bikini you were wearing on Saturday could fit in a coin purse."

He barely glanced up from the book, just shook some hair off his face and gave the tiniest, coyest glance back to check my reaction.

I collapsed on the desk in relief. "I was wondering when you were going to say something." I glanced longingly at the sunburst-shaped wall clock over my bed. "Ugh, how the hell are we supposed to get by with only an hour a day for studying *and* everything else?"

"Well, luckily for you, I lived in Germany, where they know a thing or two about time management," he remarked, glancing at the clock himself before meeting my gaze with an unspoken proposal. "*Also, mach schnell, Fräulein.*[1] Are you ready for this?"

---

1. So hurry up, young lady.

"Ready? I've only been trying to do this for the last three days. And I still prefer French."

He gave me another teasing half-smile as his hand gently took mine, guiding it the rest of the way over the fabric of his shorts and up his inner thigh. He was already hard.

"With you, it doesn't take much," he whispered in response to my little bounce of surprise. "And if you'd ever paid any attention to what was happening *under* the desk, you'd know that."

"I was trying to concentrate on chemistry, just like *you* were supposed to be," I said indignantly.

"Oh, I was," he assured me. "I'm just saying, there's no reason why our approach to the material couldn't stand to be a bit more ... holistic." He glanced at the clock again and snapped his fingers. "Shit. We're behind. I should have taken it out thirty seconds ago."

I giggled as he immediately reached down and took care of that. After some adjusting under the desk—no peeking—I found my fingers curled around the hard, solid length of him. Time seemed to stand still in the silent room as I let it sink in. And he just let me cup it there as if the weight of my fingers was, for now, just enough to make him perfectly happy. As for what came next, though?

"I—"

"Stop." He put a finger to my lips. He must have sensed something—my hesitance, my performance anxiety, my sexual imposter syndrome. "Is this your first one?"

"Well—" I blushed.

"Yes? No? Sort of?" He tried to help me along.

"Sort of."

He nodded with finality. "Okay. We can work with that."

"But I want to make it good for you."

He folded his hand—his unblistered hand—expertly over both of mine, guiding the movement of my fingers. I flexed and curled them as I brushed up and down that magnificent sculpted shaft that it would be a crime *not* to touch.

"Lou, your hand is on my dick. To me, even the *idea* of that is amazing."

That made me smile, and after he got me started, I began to drum my fingers lightly while pumping with both hands, and his entire body seemed to melt deeper into the wicker chair. "Fuck, you look beautiful like that. Do we *really* have to study today?"

I laughed and twisted lightly as I stroked, brushing my thumb over the tip, pleased by the fluid already trickling out. My hands trailed the wetness up the shaft, encouraged by the strange, beautiful combination of contented sighs and amazed whimpers I was hearing.

"Just a bit more pressure, yeah?" he said through labored breath.

I added my other hand and meditated on the mystery of maybe—if not making up for the blister on his hand—making him feel even half as incredible as he'd made me feel the other day in the basement and pretty much always. We didn't have time to lie down—hell, we didn't really have time to do *this*—but God, he looked happy and that was good enough.

"Oh, that feels so fucking perfect, Lou, you have no idea." His voice wavered.

"As good as you imagined?"

"So much better. And you were *worried*? You're fucking good at this. Just keep going."

I shifted to the edge of my chair for a better grip, hand over hand, keeping to the rhythm he was reveling in and that was making me feel ... powerful? Beautiful? Not useless? Jesus, who knew a quickie hand job could do all that?

"I'm close," he choked out. "But I forgot—"

"On it." Like lightning, I swiveled the desk chair toward the nightstand, just close enough to grab some tissues while still keeping up the strokes. Even as he shuddered, groaned, and exploded into the tissues, my body relaxed. I balled up and tossed the evidence away while he cleanly replaced everything as if none of it had ever happened. I exhaled, cutting the strings of tension in my body. A promise fulfilled.

"What were you so worried about, young lady? You know you always earn your gold star." He motioned me forward with a blissful, contented sigh, cupping my chin and lightly kissing my forehead, my nose, and finally my lips. As he pulled back and let me fall into his golden eyes, the bedroom melted away. Even the walls of the house seemed to topple, the desert crumbled, and for a second, we stood face-to-face, on a hill of wavering golden grass. Somewhere where we didn't ever have to look at the clock.

"So," he said, snapping us both out of the spell. He turned his attention sheepishly back to the desk, scanning the papers and notes spread out all over it before grabbing the chemistry book and frantically flipping through pages. "Should we start studying?"

"Yeah," I said. "I mean, I guess that *is* why we're here."

HIM

It would take a very special kind of asshole to sneak onto the computer of the dirty-minded angel who had just improvised the under-the-desk hand job of my dreams—one I obviously couldn't turn down, or she'd *really* know something was wrong.

And I was about to become that asshole. But a douchebag, a cigar, and a broken bourbon bottle had made it clear that my sister's life may depend on it. And I had to believe it did still depend on it, that I hadn't failed again. After all, she'd replied to my messages, so she had to have been alive when Corey had arrived at the party with her bracelet. That gave me hope that it wasn't too late.

But if it *was* too late, my job was to burn everything and everyone responsible for it. So sneaking onto a laptop shouldn't seem like much at all.

And it wouldn't, if it were anyone's laptop but hers.

There was some good news—other than my orgasm, that is—and that was that so far nobody had demanded to know why I'd been out by the pool all night on Friday with a mop, broom, and headlamp I'd found in a storage closet, cleaning up the liquor and trying to sweep up all the tiny broken shards from every nook and cranny, wondering why continuously splashing my face with pool water wasn't keeping me from collapsing, closing my eyes, and passing out against the bar. Which I eventually did, of course, only to jerk awake a minute later, startled and disoriented, finding nothing but a vast, silent blanket of stars looking down on me.

When I'd entered her room today, I'd stuck one hand in my pocket, clumsily trying to conceal the massive, throbbing blister, which Louisa's aloe—and nothing else—was doing its best to help. I'd accepted a gauze wrap from the housekeeper earlier but ripped it off quickly as it made any kind of manual labor impossible instead of merely painful. How clever of Corey to deprive me of the one and only value he thought I had.

Okay, look. The phone had no search function, okay? She told me that when she'd handed it over. And I'd have to get rid of it soon anyway. If Maeve had gotten caught—or worse—and it was somehow tracked, I couldn't have it on me. And now Louisa was out of the room, caught up in a heated phone conversation with her mom, who had called from the golf course with some incoherent emergency. The laptop was just sitting there. I already had the password. Plus, I'd pored over everything I could find about Max Langer for the past year and found nothing useful except what had gotten me here but now, at least, I had another name to research: Resi. The one who was supposedly saving us all. Typing that name into the search bar—it wasn't like it was a common name around here—was sure to give me a clue, and it would literally take two seconds. And I could delete the search history in less than that.

I leaned back in the wicker chair casually, tapping a pencil against my chin, unable to make out much of the conversation from the hallway and so naturally deciding to think about Max Langer instead. I felt further away from figuring out what the billionaire's game was than when I started, or how closely Corey was involved in it. But I was convinced that saving us from the gardener was just one short move in a long, long game. *Never assume the queen is safe just because she's standing still.*

And as for that game? Well, kidnapping ambiguously enslaved girls to experiment on them clearly hadn't worked, so he'd moved on to frightening and manipulating them into enslaving themselves. And then *that* hadn't worked, so he—

"Okay, Mom, but is there anyone—"

Grabbing the textbook, I shot up straight in the chair, then relaxed and took a deep breath as Louisa resumed pacing the hallway.

Fuck, I should just tell her. I should whip out the broken, bloody bracelet, the one weighing like a stone in my back pocket, and *show* her what happened. Throw it on the desk just like Corey had thrown it at me. *This is what your kind does.* And see how she'd react.

But I knew how she'd react. The same way she'd reacted the last time I'd reminded her what her kind did. Gasp and be horrified and offer to do anything she could to help. Goddamn her, this wasn't how any of this was supposed to go.

Because whatever help she could offer would lead us straight back to her father. And then where would that leave us?

With a choice. One she shouldn't have to make. One *no one* should have to make. But that was the world we were in, even if it was easy to forget while being jacked off by the smoothest, most perfectly manicured hands that had ever touched my dick.

Look, obviously, things had changed. She and I were now inhabiting an entirely different universe than the one we'd met in, one where the impossible had become possible, the untouchable had become touchable. Where strangers had become friends had become

... um, well. A universe I really couldn't bear to contemplate ever leaving, as much as I wanted to be able to.

But other things hadn't changed. Some things could *never* change. And as my eyes darted between the hallway and the desk, I knew I'd have to make a decision soon. And not just about the computer.

About everything.

HER

"See you soon, Mom. Bye," I said, thoroughly embarrassed but grateful that my emergency trip to the country club to pick her up had been called off, thanks to a pitying golf league friend who happened to live in our neighborhood.

I reached for my bedroom door to throw it open but for some reason stopped. Heart pounding, I left it ajar instead, listening for any noise coming from inside, though it was silent except for the ticking clock. I felt sick, but something told me to creep closer to peer through the crack. And when I did, I drew in a sharp breath, my stomach twisting as I spoke.

"What are you doing?"

Startled, he turned immediately away from the window, where he had been standing staring at the mountains.

"Just wondering if it ever snows up there."

2

HIM

"About the other night, boy," Louisa's father boomed at me from the kitchen doorway.

He had been scarce all weekend, so scarce that I had actually begun to hope that Lucky Sevens magic had kicked in again and he was none the wiser to Corey's and my little bonding moment at the party. But now, as I heard his voice float in from the doorway as I leaned over the kitchen counter, that familiar marching-to-my-doom feeling surfaced. Still, I shoved it down, turned around, and slapped on a poker face, aiming to treat him like a pissed-off grizzly bear and refusing to let him sense my fear.

After all, I'd narrowly talked my way out of certain doom in Louisa's bedroom, when she'd almost discovered everything. And yeah, sure, luck never held forever. In my life, luck rarely held out at all. But that's why I had to be good, too. And good was something I could control.

That morning, the housekeeper had informed me that Friday's party necessitated a kitchen deep-cleaning, which for me, meant both scouring the cast-iron grates and using a toothbrush to apply baking soda over all eight burners. So after I'd left Louisa's room, I'd spent my afternoon on that, but what was it now, then? Had her dad figured out the bottle was missing? Had I missed a shard, and now someone was gushing blood all over the pool deck? Or maybe Corey had changed his mind and decided to claim I had attacked him after all because he just hadn't had enough fun with me the other night and because this mother-fucker really was the gift that kept on giving?

I swept some hair out of my eyes, lowered my gaze, and clasped one hand over the other, trying to conceal the blister. However, my problem right now was that the housekeeper had insisted I use some kind of industrial-strength cleaning agent that might as well have been made of pure saltpeter, given how it had steeped slowly and stealthily into the open wound and was currently stinging so intensely I was blinking away tears from the corners of my eyes.

"First of all," Wainwright-Phillips began, "it should go without saying that you are forbidden to speak out of turn the way you did in front of my guests. I'm sure you can appreciate that it was only because of Mr. Langer's intervention that I didn't punish you then and there."

"I'm so sorry, sir. I know it was wrong of me. It won't happen again," I recited automatically. Can't beat the old standbys. I thought I'd nailed it, but this guy really had a way of drawing out the suspense. As the pain devoured more of my hand, I cursed the fact that I'd had to leave the aloe in its usual hiding spot in the garden.

"For now, I'll take you at your word that it won't. If it does, you can be assured you won't escape the consequences."

"Yes, sir." Was that it? *Please?*

"And one more thing. As I believe you know from the other night ..." He coughed as if the memory of his tipsy little performance in the garden with Max Langer was best memory-holed. "The gardener's gone, and he won't be back." Before I could say anything, he forged ahead. "My wife has never been fond of him—nor the other slaves, for that matter—and somebody offered more than a generous price to take him off my hands," he was still explaining. "And even though I may need you to take on some of his former duties outdoors, I won't expect you to take on all of them. I know your skills are best suited elsewhere. On that note, I know I said I would reward you for tutoring my daughter, and I intend to stick to that. By all accounts, it's going well, and since her exam is coming up, I was wondering what suggestions you might have to make it easier on you as you go down to the wire."

Really? Help me help you? That was what this was about? For a second, I wondered whether my master, having apparently regained some of his zest for life since the deal with Langer, had been hitting *The 40 Habits of Highly Influential Tycoons* or some equally cheesy self-improvement tome. It also could be a trick, but we'd been down this road before, and he hadn't shown any inclination for that kind of underhanded, sociopathic shit. So far.

"Well, sir, there is one thing," I said, cursing myself for hesitating, though it wasn't like I got asked things like this on a regular basis—or ever. "It helps if my brain is rested, and with having to be awake at night, well—" I bit my lip. Something told me that adding *I end up sleeping in your daughter's bed* probably wouldn't help my case.

"Say no more," he replied in a benevolent tone. "Starting tonight, I'll have you share it with the maid. You'll get late evenings. She'll get early mornings. Does that sound fair?"

Well, not to her, but I wasn't about to bring that up now—especially since she'd begged off on the kitchen cleaning a half-hour ago, though we were supposed to be doing it together. I suspected she might be starting to loathe me, which wasn't necessarily a negative development. "Thank you, sir."

He reached out a hand, but it froze in mid-air.

Startled, I raised my eyes slightly. He had been about to do something—hug me? Slap me? Pinch my cheek? Pat me on the head? I was blindsided by what free people did to me sometimes just because they could. None of it would surprise me.

Instead, he drew back and coughed awkwardly into his hand as if that had been his intention all along. "You've done well, boy. I'm pleased."

About what, it wasn't exactly clear. The tutoring? The rockets? The dynamic, proactive, paradigm-shifting way I'd been scouring those cast-iron grates a minute ago?

This guy had no idea how to praise me. That was certain. Few people did. Most accepted the notion that slaves, with their inferior, more primitive natures, didn't respond to praise, only punishment. Wainwright-Phillips was clearly of that old school. Did this mean that maybe, like his daughter, he was evolving? No. He was in business with Langer, so that was impossible. But still.

"And I think it's safe to say the engineers at Orbital Dynamics are, too. Mr. Killeen, perhaps, not so much."

Yes. There it was. He was smiling. Well, this conversation certainly had its share of pleasant surprises. Now please let it be over.

"You know—" he began thoughtfully, but stopped. The thought would remain unexpressed. "Well, carry on." He swept out of the room.

Turning with relief, I ran cold water over my hand, yawned, and glanced at the clock for the millionth time. Well then, only eight more hours until I could sleep, instead of twelve. Small mercies.

HER

Quite honestly, his skill in time management was an understatement. He always insisted I review the chapters first; he would quiz me on the parts he didn't think I was solid enough on yet and drill me until he was satisfied. And given how *he'd* been taught, it wasn't surprising that sometimes it took a lot to satisfy him.

"You're worse than Mrs. Atchinson, my second-grade teacher," I said, throwing my pencil down on the desk in frustration when he asked me to practice what felt like the fiftieth elimination reaction. "She made me stay after class and write out the times tables in words 'to help me learn.' God, I hated her."

"Hey, I'm sure poor Mrs. Atchinson would have rather been sucking on your neck, too," he replied. "But like me, she knew how to put her own needs aside for the good of her students."

The mental image caused me to stifle a thoroughly revolted laugh in my hands. This time, it was my turn to yawn, stretch, and rise from my chair.

"What are you doing?" he asked.

"What does it look like? I'm quitting. You've completely worn me out."

"Okay, I'll go." He rose from the chair and pointed with his thumb toward the door, and I wasn't sure whether he was putting his acting skills to use again or whether he actually did, on some level, think I wanted him to leave.

"Slow learner," I said, the mattress squeaking as I bounced to my knees. "You practice innuendo like it's a scientific discipline, and then you don't recognize an open invitation when you hear one?" I grabbed his hand and yanked him toward the bed, rewarded by his surprised smile as he tumbled after me.

He settled himself on one pale pink pillow, his golden hair spilling across it, radiant in the afternoon sunlight. He raised his right arm above his head and I didn't hesitate to take the invitation, nestling myself cozily into the empty space beside the long, hard muscle of his torso as he reached that hand around in front to entwine with mine. I adjusted the comforter and pulled it over us, then turned so we were nose to nose. To my delight, a sweet, spontaneous kiss greeted me.

"Besides," I teased, "I know how much you love these sheets."

"Oh, yeah," he said, settling his other hand behind his head and thoughtfully gazing at the ceiling. "It's definitely the sheets," he said lightly before sighing and letting his amber eyes fixate on something in the distance, always a sign the gears in his head had begun to turn. And this time, I suspected it had nothing to do with science.

"Daddy told me that with the gardener gone, you're going to get stuck filling in for him," I murmured into his shoulder. "I'm sorry. I didn't mean for that to—"

"Lou, it's fine," he cut me off with a laugh. "Hell, I've kind of missed working in the dirt all day. Just like old times."

My heart clenched at the reminder of his past, even though I now knew that whatever was troubling him, it wasn't that.

"He says he's looking at hiring a service for the gardens," I said. "They send a team of slaves over to do the work."

"Well, here's hoping."

"Any idea yet where he went?"

"Not a clue. The housekeeper doesn't know, either. I asked everyone." It was clear he didn't think he'd seen the last of him.

"Do you really think Langer bought him? He doesn't own slaves. He doesn't *want* to own slaves. That's kind of his whole thing."

"So he says," he said darkly. "Look, if he can hold my sister and a bunch of other girls captive without anyone knowing, no doubt he can also figure out how to buy one toothless gardener without anyone knowing."

Now it was my turn to stare at the ceiling. "Still, the guy's gone. And you know what they say about gift horses."

"I was never big on horse-related aphorisms."

"Well, then I'll try to rein them in." His look was priceless, and I collapsed into sheepish giggles. "I'm sorry. I couldn't help it."

"Yeah, well, you should have, especially because that's an allusion, not an aphorism." My work was done, though—his smile had returned. "Am I going to have to tickle you until you learn the difference?"

A squeal was the only answer I had time to give.

3

HER

I nspired by that, we briefly tried migrating the sessions from the desk to the bed, until we both fell asleep next to each other a couple of times. As blissful as that had been, it was also terrifying to wake up disoriented and unsure of how much time had passed, and from then on, he insisted we stay upright until the session was finished.

And then, of course, we were faced with the daunting problem of just how much sex we could get away with having without somebody catching on to the fact that we were having it at all. The answer proved to be: not much. And not nearly enough.

Just to be safe, we made a rule: one item of clothing could be shed per person per day, not more. In case of emergency, *that* could still be explained away—or so we told ourselves. Of course we also had to master the fine art of muffling every noise with my pink faux-fur blanket and cheetah pillows. Those parts fairly hummed with electricity under his practiced touch, and I got better at touching him. He learned to close his eyes and let me not only gently kiss the blister on his hand but even ever so gently curl my fingers up his back and brush them over the healing wounds, even as he would still joke about everything we *weren't* doing yet. And so, in time, *I* got to see his abs up close. And *he* got to see the expression on my face when I finally saw those sublime six-pack abs tapering to a V and disappearing downward in a tantalizing trail of baby-fine golden hair, the abs I'd so far only glimpsed in one stark black-and-white photo on a site displaying them like a valuable commodity—which they were, of course, but not like *that.*

But they weren't just evidence of what nature had given him but what people had taken away. There were switch and lash marks that curled away over his shoulders and back, puckered, snakelike trails of red and white and purple, in various lengths and stages of healing. And there were burns. From cattle prods. Thank you very much, Slavery Studies 101—and let's face it, cattle was all he was to those who had done it. Hell, these days, there were probably animal rights people around to ensure cattle got treated *better.*

"I'm so sorry," I whispered, my voice barely a breath against his chest as I reached his waistband. He inhaled sharply as my lips grazed the scar, his eyes fluttering closed for a moment. "The whip," he said, his voice low and even. "I was seven. First time. Before that, it was always a cane, which doesn't usually break the skin. So it was my coming of age, in other words." He answered my next question before it could leave my lips. "I wish I could say it was for some super-cool act of rebellion, but it wasn't. I was dusting and accidentally broke this ugly china goose they had. And then panicked and tried to sweep it under the rug, literally."

My heart clenched. It was impossible to imagine, and I knew he didn't expect me to try. My fingers ghosted over the raised line. "I'm so—"

"Shhh." He was smiling a little. "They did it," he said, taking my fingers away and meeting my gaze. "And they aren't you, yeah?"

Sure, it was long ago, and it was stupid.

But that didn't make it okay.

Shaking, unsure where to begin, I just started, kissing a trail down his torso, my tongue hot against the sensitive skin, laving the places that lay slack and soft against his stomach, teeth gently nipping at the ones that stood erect. He shivered in response, breath hitching, and he closed his eyes. But it flickered deeply in the amber-gold—the old pain, the old humiliation. What I wouldn't give to have been there. What I wouldn't—

"Does it still—" I began.

"Shh. It's okay now." He quelled my lips with his fingers, then intertwined them with mine, guiding me down, nails scraping gently across my palm, guiding it past his waistband, trembling as they traced the scars together, to a place where there was no pain.

It was there we usually stopped.

Of course I knew parts of him were twitching to go even further, to enter and fill and infuse me with him—hell, I *knew* they were. I felt them. They came alive under my grip each and every time, as eager and excited and savage and wild as a boy who'd never even thought he'd be here, in his castoff clothes and jagged scars and metal chain, lying on a lacy, silky pink princess bed in a room reeking of camellia and pomegranate, with a girl who was actually *asking* him what *he* wanted, instead of trying to *order* him to do what *she* wanted. And then I'd be left hot and heartbroken and hamstrung to have to *stop* feeling them, to force him to roll over again and breathe a little and assure me he was fine, even though neither one of us believed for a second that he actually was.

But with three minutes left on the clock, it was just too risky to go on. Yes, we were young and horny and stupid, and we were self-aware enough to joke about *that*, too. But also, we were scared. Though we tried not to remind each other of it too much—tried to pretend that what we were doing was normal—the prospect of what could happen if the door to my bedroom was ever opened at the wrong time haunted us, and the ever-present ticking reminded us that our time was never our own. So among the many unspoken promises we shared, one was *someday soon.*

But talking—that was safe. Well, *safer.*

Luckily, we were both good talkers—and since we couldn't leave the room, at least not if we wanted to behave normally, we left mentally, instead. He took me to the fairy-tale mists of the Black Forest, Heidelberg Castle, and the Philosopher's Walk. I took *him* to massive gleaming yachts moored on the ancient crystal-blue coral reefs of Eleuthera. And dark matter and string theory gave way to history, politics, religion, art, and music. My slave boy confessed to loving—of all things—neo-impressionism and French jazz.

"I don't get it," I said after he clicked off one of the selections he'd chosen to play for me.

"It's like ... it's like they're inventing their own formula, their own set of rules, and it's up to the rest of the world to figure them out," he said. "You know?"

"Oh," I said teasingly. "You mean like chemistry. Why does it always have to come down to—"

"Actually, I was thinking more like us."

I could have melted. I cuddled back into his arms as he pressed play again on the laptop set up in front of us on the bed, this time, turning up some woman with a husky voice and a French accent, singing about lovers parting on a train platform. But honestly, it could have been about anything. I just loved that *he* loved something that much.

I probably opened and reopened that desk drawer about fifty times before finally getting up the nerve to offer him the pralines, ever mindful of what he'd said that night at the party. *I'm not your pet to feed.* That wasn't what I was doing. I felt it. I *knew* it. And yet as I stood by the bed and he stared speechlessly down at the package and its Luxembourgish printing, I obsessively scrutinized every twitch of his facial muscles, ready to snatch it back and drop it into the wastebasket if need be.

He glanced up. "Every—"

"I'm sorry," I blurted out, regretting everything. "I shouldn't have. I know you're not—"

He laughed. Oh, thank God. "Let me *finish*. Fucking hell, Lou. All I was going to say is, every other time I've had these, I had to do something. Either steal them or con them."

I felt a blush creep up my neck but clung onto the package like a votive. "Well. I'm just offering."

He took one praline and bit into it. I watched him chew, his face melting as if the clouds had just parted on paradise itself. He ate four more. Then five, then six, all with the kind of look on his face that had me thinking I should be paying ninety-nine cents a minute to watch it. When he paused, his half-smile was teasing but not entirely.

"So what's the catch, really, Lou?" he finally asked, stretching his body out artfully and spectacularly across the bed, balancing on one long, lean, muscular arm, the other still holding the box of pralines. "What do I have to do in return?"

"Like I said, anything." I swallowed. "Or nothing."

He quirked an eyebrow. "Can this anything or nothing be cashed in anytime?" he asked casually, though his eyes raked me up and down like he was scanning an entire dessert menu.

"You mean like a time where it doesn't have to be muffled by a pillow?" I flushed hotter than I had been already. "But—" I paused.

"Wow, a choice. That's like Freedom 101."

"Wow, a course I could teach you?" I teased.

"Only if there's a practical exam—I excel at hands-on learning."

He just left it there, damn him, chewing his lip cheekily like he was curious to see how I'd react. Hell, *I* was curious to see how I'd react. How far I was willing to go to be close to him. And God, if he kept looking at me like that, that was pretty fucking far.

In fact, my stupid, self-sabotaging heart was already picking up, his words sizzling through me like live wire. We were so close, yet still so far from anything resembling the reality we deserved. But for now, we had a moment, and it felt so wicked and wrong and perfect and right, all at once. So nonsensical, and yet as logical as the simplest chemical formula. Kind of like everything else about us.

I moved closer to him, the heat of his body against mine, his scent filling my nostrils—sage and sun and soap and pure pheromones.

I whispered, "Do you really want to cash it in now?"

He turned his head so our mouths were mere centimeters apart, tracing one calloused finger—a finger whose touch I could feel on me already—along a stitch in the pristine, silken white duvet. The look in his eyes was enough to singe every thought from my mind and plunge me into some kind of full-body ache I couldn't possibly be expected to resist. "I think you know the answer to that, *professeur*."

And now I was dead. *Here lies Louisa Danielle Wainwright-Phillips. Killed by one word of French.*

Granted, I didn't know how much a corpse weighed, but I'd never felt so light as his kisses started, playful and teasing in a way that said *I so want to do this* but with a hard undertone that said but *we shouldn't*. I knew because I felt it myself. My body twisted wildly beneath him, trying vainly to get closer, *and* to pull away. But before I knew what was happening, he growled low in his throat and pinned my wrists above my head with the kind of strength I knew he had but had yet to feel, his hand sinking into my hair and pulling roughly. I arched again as he used his free hand to slide up my denim miniskirt and between my legs, pressing two fingers into me and eliciting a small gasp from the back of my throat that I forgot to muffle.

I couldn't make that mistake again. But despite everything, despite the hour—and fuck, I could *still* see the clock from where I was—this was what I had craved. What I had ached for. *He* was what I ached for, and I'd do anything to have him and keep him, even if it was just for a moment.

He continued to work his fingers inside me. "You know," he observed, "I'm no expert on this, but it kind of feels like you want this just as bad as I do."

"Shut up. You are *so* an expert on this."

"I know, but I was trying to be modest."

"You failed."

"Only thing I've ever failed at."

"God," I panted, biting my bottom lip to stifle another moan. If he were anyone else—anything else—I'd be saying his name right now. "Fuck, what the hell am I supposed to—"

Suddenly, we froze. He raised his head, the flush in his cheeks so sexy. Voices drifted up the stairwell. Soft footsteps came from the foyer below. The front door shut with a definite click.

"Shit!" I hissed, pushing him off me none too gently, my arms suspended like a cat on her back with paws in the air. Granted, no one in this house had any reason—yet—to burst into my room demanding to know what we were doing or even care, but—well, I cared. A lot. And given his frantic efforts to keep me still, so did he.

"It's probably just a delivery or something," he said, catching his breath next to me, though I noticed his strong shoulders rising up and down more rapidly than normal. "Relax."

"Delivery or not, we can't take that chance," I whispered, scooching off the bed and tugging my skirt down, sighing with a mix of relief and frustration—and bodily need so intense it felt like it was trying to burn me from the inside out.

I managed to get up without making too much noise. But before I could, he grabbed my hips aggressively and pulled me toward him.

"Are you insane?" I asked, trying and failing to keep from shrieking.

"That is one of the many things I've been called in my time," he admitted with a slight laugh.

"Someone nearly heard us! We could get caught!" I hissed, batting his arm.

He paused for a moment, then said seriously, "I'd never let that happen."

Well, if anything was insane, that was. But for now, I was willing to go with just about anything to make sure he started tonguing my neck again. I almost cried out from the sensation it created, fire and ice all at once as he growled into a kiss, his tongue forcing its way past my lips and inside my mouth, tasting of the pralines we'd shared earlier and something more, something like clear autumn skies and green Luxembourgish meadows, like we had all the time in the world. I wrapped my legs around him and moaned into his mouth, feeling him grind against me, his erection throbbing through his jeans.

He wanted to go inside me. And for one single, solitary, unhinged second, I considered letting him. It all surged through me, greed and lust and some other base emotion I couldn't even name, but I didn't care because he was here now. Finally, this beautiful man I wasn't supposed to be touching was in my bed and—

"We can't," I said. *Fuck me.* "We really can't."

"*Tu as raison.*"

You are correct. If we were at the desk, I would have loved to hear that from him. In bed, I just wanted to explode.

Still, he didn't stop, thank *God*. Instead, my beautiful genius seemed to get, of course, an idea. He ground his hips against mine, his hand finding my clit and manipulating it through my panties as he bit my earlobe gently. He pulled away and reached for the hem of my shirt, lifting it slowly, inch by inch, over my head, his cool lips trailing down my neck and across my collarbone. I arched into him involuntarily but kept my hands busy, yanking at his shirt, too eager to see those abs again after all those days I'd had to go without. And all of a sudden it was there, that *body*, so lovely and maimed, a priceless canvas slashed, filling my whole rarefied, limited world, as he traced me through my panties, outlining my folds so gently I wanted to scream. Instead, I only dug my hands deeper into his scarred shoulders.

He sank down between my legs and licked me through my black silk panties, slowly teasing out the wetness with his tongue until I felt like I was floating apart. My hips bucked off the bed and I gasped loudly, feeling the head of his cock as he ground it against my entrance for just a moment through the fabric before he pulled back. And the idea of that—of *him*, the shape and size, the weight of him, and how close I was to feeling it all, so close and so far—was enough to bring tears to my eyes.

"Tu veux que je te fasse plaisir?"

I nodded frantically, unable to speak, and I wondered what Madame Pelletier from senior year French would be more horrified to know: what he was saying, or that my mind had gone too blank to translate it. Though I couldn't answer through the haze of pleasure, I somehow managed to nod again. Then he was tearing my panties off me, tossing them aside along with the *one article of clothing at a time* rule. He innocently tongued his fingers and then two of them were inside me, stretching me open as his thumb pressed against my clit. And then there was his tongue, lashing against me, driving me up the wall, making me arch off the bed once again.

"Fuck," I moaned, my voice strained and needy. "Please."

He pulled his fingers out and rolled onto his back, his golden hair spilling over the pillow, and grabbed my hips again. I straddled him before he could change his mind and he hitched me up and positioned me over his face while he kept moving his fingers in me, in and out, matching the rhythm with his tongue on my clit. It felt incredible, gentle and rough and innocent and dangerous at the same time, a bundle of infinite contradictions, just like him. I groaned again, my knees thrashing from side to side on the pillow. He sucked and inhaled the nub as he pushed them deeper inside me, probing, tunneling, causing a deluge of pleasure so intense it burned through every nerve ending I had. He thrust his fingers in and out of me slowly at first but then faster, harder, until I was clawing at the sheets in desperation, silently cursing and begging and screaming, though no sound left my mouth at all—I was getting good at that—until my body tensed and I shuddered, rocked to my core in a thousand different ways. I clutched his shoulders tighter as my climax shattered me a billion more. And no, I couldn't say his name, but all of a sudden, a name was there just the same, arriving in a silent, unspoken litany in my head and on my lips.

I'd never tell him.

When it was over, I collapsed on top of him, burying my face in the crook of his neck, breathless, spent, complete.

And utterly terrified at the gift I held in my arms.

Down the hallway, a million miles away, the landline in Daddy's office rang. Soft, insistent, and cut off in an instant when he presumably answered.

"We're gonna die, you know," I said, feeling the shoulders I rested on tremble slightly. His eyes flicked up at the ceiling, for a second, then back. He brushed a damp curl from where it clung to my lips. "It was worth it to see you like that," he murmured.

I think for him it really was.

"Oh God," I breathed suddenly, arching into his touch because he was *still* working magic—or science, or religion, or all three—between my legs, even as I shook with the force of all that release. "Again?"

He glanced up at the clock and then back at me like I was crazy. "Of course. We've still got five minutes before the hour is up."

I smiled serenely and collapsed on my back on the mattress.

If anybody knew how to make the most of what he'd been given, it was him.

———————— · ✦ ❤ ✦ · ————————

The next day, I caught him curiously examining my book-shelf—only with his eyes. I didn't think he'd ever actually touched anything I hadn't given him permission to touch. And even though it might have started out as some arbitrary rule about how a slave should behave, it wasn't anymore. Besides, everything I *had* given him permission to touch, he'd ravaged.

Anyway, we started exploring. Though way above average for a foreigner, his understanding of Shakespearean English was not as thorough as mine, though it didn't prevent him from trying to enthrall and horrify me with his dramatic interpretations of *Titus Andronicus* baking Tamora's sons into a pie. But beyond that, he seemed curious about the book of Plautine and Terentian comedies I'd read in my classics course. After he promised me he had a good hiding spot for it, I gave him that to read during his hours off next Sunday, as long as he agreed to read aloud my favorite verses from *Les Misérables*, in the original French, of course. As he did so, I was so absorbed in how beautiful the words sounded coming out of his mouth that I almost forgot to think about what they meant. And if he did—well, he kept those thoughts to himself.

Nous vivions cachés, contents, porte close
Dévorant l'amour, bon fruit défendu;
Ma bouche n'avait pas dit une chose
Que déjà ton coeur avait répondu.[1]

HIM

The day before the exam, Louisa sat in her usual swivel chair, gazing out the window at the distant mountains she'd seen all her life, her body present, but her mind clearly miles away.

"Where are you, Lou? Tell me," I whispered as I leaned in close behind her, brushing her curls gently back from her face. "Maybe I can help."

"Worrying about letting you down tomorrow," she replied.

I'd been afraid of that and equally afraid that all the drilling and quizzing and practice problems in the world couldn't overcome her self-doubt if she chose to let it win. And as much as I wanted to help her conquer it, I didn't know how. I'd only studied chemistry, not psychology. "You could never ever let me down," I assured her.

"But what if I fail?"

---

1. *We lived hidden, content, door closed/Devouring love, good for-bidden fruit/My mouth had not asked a thing/That your heart had not already answered.*

"Then just try again. Find a way to succeed next time. Or do something else altogether. Believe me, if there's anyone who knows about pushing through difficult, thankless tasks that never seem to end, it's me."

"But—"

"Besides," I continued, wondering how she'd take what I was about to say. Maybe she'd just dismiss it as silly, simplistic folk wisdom, invented by slaves for slaves. But I forged ahead anyway. "I haven't taught you the most important lesson yet. The one that will get you through this exam and every test yet to come."

"What's that?"

"Breathe," I whispered.

"Huh?"

"See? You're holding your breath even now, and you didn't even know it."

"I am?" She turned around, clearly surprised to find I was right.

"I notice you doing it all the time," I said, going for the professorial effect as I sat back in my chair. "Never ever hold your breath, even for a second, as much as you want to. When you do, you're just depriving your brain of oxygen. It's like trying to die, basically. And as a future doctor, I think it's safe to assume you're against that."

"Did your professor teach you that?" she asked.

"No." Suddenly, the pencil I was twirling in my hand had become utterly fascinating. "My mom did."

HER

"Funny thing happened at work yesterday," said Corey.

Outside the o-chem lecture hall, his clammy hand—one I'd managed to blissfully avoid coming in contact with since the dinner party—clamped onto my bare shoulder. He physically forced me to turn around and look at his tanned, fine features, which, to be honest, didn't look particularly fine at the moment. Rather, they bore a sort of blotchy, alcoholic bloat, one I easily recognized.

"Langer says he isn't renewing my internship next semester, and it's all because of that fucking slave of your dad's."

I kept my voice calm, though I already didn't like where this was headed. Especially when my nerves were liable to shatter like glass at the slightest rattle. "If Langer's canning you, it's probably because he can't stand the sound of your voice anymore, in which case I'm in complete agreement with him. No slave had anything to do with it."

"That's funny because I would tend to disagree," he said. "Shame what happened to him after dinner that night, by the way."

I felt sick, but I had had an inkling, of course. "What kind of complete monster hurts someone who you know isn't allowed to fight back?"

"So what? He deserved a lot worse for running his mouth like that to free men, and if your dad didn't give it to him, it's because he's a weak, manic-depressive cuck."

"Leave my dad out of this." Was Corey *trying* to ensure I failed this exam? "What he does or doesn't do with his slaves is none of your goddamn business."

"What the hell is wrong with you, anyway?" He pushed. "Ever since that slave appeared, you've been a complete bitch."

"If standing up for people is what you call being a bitch," I said, "I'm sorry I didn't become one a lot earlier."

"People?" Corey scoffed with a dismissive chuckle as if I'd just claimed unicorns were real. "Is *that* what you call—"

"Hey, guys, is everything okay out here?" One of the TAs stuck her head out the door of the lecture hall. Her gaze landed on me. "We're about to start passing out the exam books in a second."

"Oh, right, that one your slave's been helping you study for," remarked Corey.

The TA's eyes got rounder, but she didn't say anything.

But as she stood there, Corey turned up his volume as if twisting a knob, loud enough for startled heads to turn up and down the corridor. "I mean, everyone here already knew you couldn't cut it in college. That you were a stupid, spoiled bimbo only here to snag a rich boyfriend after Daddy went crazy and pissed away his fortune. And this only proves how pathetic you are. You know, you might as well just use that exam for toilet paper and turn it in. You'll probably get more questions right that way. Maybe try using an actual tutor next time instead of a slave."

"Better a slave for a tutor than an asshole for a boyfriend," I snapped, turning around, unable to disguise how violently I was shaking. "Not that that term will ever have anything to do with *you*. Don't talk to me anymore."

"You think I'm blind?!" He caught me by the arm again. I jerked away as everything became a blur. He'd wanted people to stare, but now it was backfiring on him. Heads were turning. A crowd closed in, and he had no choice but to loosen his grip. But he kept shouting as I darted into the safety of the lecture hall. "I know what this is really all about!"

———————— · ✦ ❤ ✦ · ————————

In the back of the freezing hall, I regarded the chalkboard in a stiff, unseeing stare, shaking too hard to even macerate an eraser or two as usual. Exams and answer sheets trickled their way to the back of the hall courtesy of a pack of grim-looking TAs.

Fuck Corey. I could blame him for shattering my confidence, but the fact was, I'd never had any to begin with.

It *had* made sense, for a time. It really had. The lecture notes, the practice problems, the hours and hours my unlikely tutor had spent helping me spin those arrays of infuriating little carbon and oxygen molecules around like cogs and gears until they miraculously reassembled themselves into something that worked for my brain. But now it was gone, collapsed into one terrifying, soul-sucking singularity.

Panic set in. I could see it all laid out in front of me like some tortuous map to hell. After all that had happened, all the work we'd done, I was *still* going to fail, lose my scholarship, and drop out, but now it was even worse. Yes, Mr. Supportive had said exactly what he was supposed to say, and it was very sweet and all, but seriously, how could I possibly ever face him again if I failed? To explain that he'd wasted hours of his life, of which he had so few free to begin with, trying to fix a hopeless dummy? I should have known better than to ever involve him in this mess.

Watching the fear and anxiety seizing my classmates' faces as they stared down at the exams landing in front of them was no help. Helpless, my breathing grew quick and shallow, a sure sign of an impending freak-out. I reached into my leather schoolbag for my study notes, hoping that staring at something familiar to me might at least help get my memory working again in the seconds before the paper landed on my desk.

As I shook out the papers, I was surprised to see something bright and strange flutter to the floor from where it had been lodged in my bag. I snatched it up greedily: a wildflower.

A sprig of blush-orange globe mallow, one of the only flowers that bloomed in the desert in the fall, its petals shedding delicately in my hand.

And on top of the notes, a sticky note with a message in a by-now-familiar spiky scrawl.

Hey, put down the notes and breathe. You got this.

x

4

HIM

As if it hadn't been tricky enough to find a wildflower in the desert in November, I discovered that morning that my "reward" would be spending the next few days building a wire fence around the prickly pears to keep the javelinas from digging up and eating them. The look I must have given the housekeeper when she told me and the little cluck of her tongue in response said it all. What, did His Royal Highness expect that just because he had, against all logic, gotten in the master's good graces with his little performance the other night, he'd never have to do this kind of thing again?

Well, no, of course not, but I'd certainly *hoped*.

"I'm sorry," she'd said over a plate of toast in the slaves' common area that morning. *"But the master says it needs to be done if we want any cactuses left at all. Plus, the gardener is gone, the landscaping service isn't available this week, and heaven knows I'm not going to do it. He expects it to be done by the time he gets back."*

"Back from where?"

"He's had to fly to LA unexpectedly to meet with his lawyers," she said. *"The valet went with him. And if you're wondering why no one told you, it's because I only found out late last night. And by the way, if you're looking at the master being away as an opportunity to get away with murder, forget it."*

It must have been screamingly obvious how rapidly the gears in my brain were turning. But as always, that was nothing a charming smile and a witty remark couldn't fix. *"I promise, no murder. Petty larceny at* most. *"*

I received the standard will-never-admit-to-being-charmed eye roll in return. This was too easy. Hell, there was almost no limit to what the master's absence might offer the opportunity to accomplish. Having as much sex as possible with his daughter, while clearly the most enjoyable part of it was only the start.

Now if only I could figure a way out of building this goddamn fence.

The housekeeper promptly handed me a sheet of detailed instructions on where to place each post. *"Look, if you make solid progress on this, I won't tell anyone if you want to take it easy for the next few nights. The girl, too. I'll take on the evenings myself, and then we can all enjoy a good night's sleep,"* she said. *"If it helps, we had one half-built last year before it washed away in the monsoons, so most everything you need should be out in the shed already. If you run out of wire, let me know and I'll arrange to have some delivered."*

Her words were mild, but her meaning was clear: *Just try to weasel your way out of this, smart guy, I dare you.* Oh well. It didn't sound *too* hard, and I'd certainly been ordered to do similar things in the past. Maybe I could think of it as an exercise in landscape architecture.

The first step—besides finding out just what the hell javelinas were, to which the answer was, no joke, some kind of wild pig—was trudging outside and surveying the garden, where the porcine invaders had already been hard at work, strewing divots and mounds of overturned dirt all along the perimeter of the property.

With a sigh, I grabbed a spade and whatever other useful tools I could scavenge from the shed, then searched in vain for some gloves, though I wouldn't be surprised if the gardener had snatched them when he'd left out of pure spite. I then turned my attention to the stacks of wooden stakes and heavy bales of woven wire stacked against the wall, which, given that the wheel on the barrow was currently broken and needed parts—something else I blamed the gardener for—I would have to drag across the garden individually.

Two hours later, the mercury was still soaring, and my progress consisted of a series of holes dug eight inches into the ground and two stakes, one of them draped with a disorganized and bloody mass of wire, which had sliced into my hands in a dozen places already, the blood running down my wrists in thin streaks. Now I wrestled artlessly and stubbornly to unroll another bale and drag it across the yard, muttering curses to myself in Luxembourgish.

Despite the housekeeper's offer, it looked like I was going to be working overtime if I wanted to make any progress on this thing at all by tonight—when I hoped to make the most of my time with Louisa when she returned from campus after taking her exam, which should be taking place right about now.

And, yes, while there were many fairly obscene things near the top of my to-do list, support and hand-holding—no matter how the exam had gone—were also on the agenda, and, to my surprise, I wasn't looking forward to those any less.

That might have been enough to still keep me upbeat despite it all. Except that after a few more messages last night and again this morning, Maeve still hadn't answered my question about whether anyone had hurt her.

In fact, she hadn't answered at all. And every minute she didn't answer added to my swirling cloud of dread. I knew there was a good chance that someone on her end had confiscated whatever device she was using and was now using it to try to track *me*, which meant the phone was radioactive. I'd *already* kept it a week longer than I should have. Louisa herself had warned me about this. The smartest thing to do would be to start a brush fire out in the garden and toss it in.

But then there was a chance I'd never hear from Maeve again, ever.

And just as I had taken shelter under a paloverde, desperate for even a minute or so out of the brutality of the sun, a tall shadow blocked it all out.

It was Max Langer, standing there in tan linen suit trousers, floral shirt, and aviator sunglasses, dark hair artfully sculpted, looking as cool and breezy as could be, with a bottle of Luxembourg blackcurrant liqueur and two glasses full of ice under his arm.

Fuck, he'd been *serious*. Not to mention that once again, I hadn't heard a car pull up or a door open, but there Langer was, anyway. Just ... there.

"Um, Master Wainwright-Phillips is away," I said as I reluctantly stood up, even though it was already obvious that if that was who Langer was looking for, he wouldn't be *here*.

"Good thing I didn't come to see Keith," he replied, whipping off the expensive shades to reveal calm but maddeningly inexpressive blue eyes. "I came to see you."

It was official: he was here to cash in the chip he'd won by getting rid of the gardener and not turning us in, exactly as I'd predicted. So much for Lucky Sevens magic. My hot streak was as dead as I was no doubt about to be.

Let's review: he knew about me. He knew about Louisa. He almost certainly knew about Maeve and probably was the one holding her captive himself, assuming she was even still alive. He had wealth that rivaled the GDP of small nations and influence to bend the will of kings. And here I was, trying to go up against him armed with nothing but hope and a garden trowel.

In fact, I think there was a story in the Bible about this kind of situation. Which I now really wished I'd paid more attention to back when the old professor had ordered me to read it, rather than entertaining myself by working out pericyclic reactions in the margins.

Besides, slaves didn't have *guests*. What, was I supposed to show him into the parlor for cucumber sandwiches? I wasn't even allowed to use the furniture, let alone invite anyone else to. Besides, the timing couldn't be worse. Thanks to the reflection I'd caught in the sunglass frames, I knew that besides a healthy sheen of sweat, I had dirt and blood all over my hands, embedded under my nails, and streaked across my face from all the times I'd pushed my hair out of my eyes. The least this guy could have done was wait until I got a chance to spray myself with the garden hose.

But Langer didn't seem to care. He handed me a damp, plush, lavender-scented towel from inside the house—the kind decidedly reserved for guests, not slaves—and watched as I gratefully dabbed it over the bloody streaks.

"Courtesy of your housekeeper, same as the ice," he said, holding up the fancy glasses. "She's a gem. Total efficiency, total discretion. Of course, the box of German chocolates I gave her didn't hurt," he said. He set the bottle behind a boulder, uncapped it, and poured. "Now's our chance to have the conversation we didn't get to have the other night with all the company around. In English, even."

"I don't know, Max," I said. "Are you sure this meeting can't be an email? I've got a really packed agenda today. When it comes to javelinas, time is money." I picked up the spade and gestured behind me, indicating the wooden posts and the chaotic piles of bloody wire.

"Seriously? He's got you digging pig holes?" Langer coolly surveyed the mounds of earth and the chewed-up cactus. "Come on. Forget this stupid shit and walk with me."

"But—"

"You can tell Keith if he has a problem with his pigs, possums, rats, raccoons, or any other species of furry mammal, he can take it up with me. I'll send one of my security guys over with a high-powered rifle, no charge."

"Um, thanks, but then I'm left with a pile of dead pigs to explain."

"I guess you're right." Langer fished out a phone from his pocket, dialed, and probably spoke a total of five words before hanging up. "Fence'll be done by this afternoon. *Prost.*"

I stared at the proffered glass. I wasn't so arrogant as to think a billionaire would choose to waste his entire afternoon driving all the way across town to personally murder a slave in an elaborate poisoning caper, but Max Langer had already proved himself a surprising man.

But since there was no use protesting in the face of the power of the almighty dollar, I shoved the spade under my arm and yanked the glass from Langer's hand, drinking it as we made our way down the stone path into the cooler parts of the garden, weaving in and out of the paloverdes and chollas.

I hadn't been allowed to drink this kind of thing regularly, but there were always opportunities during summer garden parties when, after the guests had been suitably inebriated, I'd been able to slip away easily with Maeve and some of the other young slaves and lie in the grass for a few minutes and listen to the crickets.

Grass. That was one thing I missed. And forests, real forests full of evergreens. Damn, here I was getting nostalgic. Was this part of Langer's plot to lower my defenses so he could strike?

Walking side by side with any free man was surreal enough, let alone a would-be billionaire tech mogul. We were the exact same height, in fact: eye to eye, nose to nose. The rich guy in his spotless clothing, jacket draped over his arm, and me in dirt-covered work clothes. How very appropriate.

"How did that happen?" Langer pointed to the pus-filled blister on my palm. "Accident?"

Your intern. "Let's go with that."

"I had 'accidents,' too, growing up."

I raised my head curiously.

"My dad liked the switch and the belt, but he really loved heat the most. The cigarette; the clothes iron; the stove. He was a true artist. A real Michelangelo of pain. You want to see the scars?"

"I'll take your word for it. Thanks."

"My mother and I were lucky to get out alive. Oh, and besides putting her in the ER on several occasions, he was fucking around on her constantly, and he *loved* shitting where he ate, so it was mostly with his own slaves. Finally, she took me back to her family in Germany. That required punishment, of course, so he made sure she got nothing in the divorce, which meant I spent my teen years in the slums of the most piece-of-shit industrial towns on the Rhine, while he remarried and spent winters in Baden-Baden with his new wife. Never got an invite. Meanwhile, my mom got a job supervising a team of cleaning slaves. At least they got free food and housing. She could barely survive on the wages she made."

"Funny, I hear that a lot from people who have never been slaves."

"I know. And I'm not saying you didn't have it worse."

"Oh," I said, twisting the stem of the glass between my fingers. "Thanks, I guess?"

"Long story short, my mom died, my dad got sick, and I saved all the wages I made at my box factory job—the less said about *that*, the better—for a ticket back. I wanted what was left of his estate.

Better it actually go toward building something than paying for his third wife's fifth facelift, so I took on the role of the loyal, grieving son to much critical acclaim. Of course what I really wanted to do was smother the asshole with a pillow, but I had to settle for seeing him waste away to nothing and lose control of his bodily functions. But it paid off when he changed his will and left everything to me. The house, the money, and the slaves. I freed them, including my half-sister whom I didn't even know *was* my sister. Now she works for me. I used the inheritance as capital to launch FableFlow. You know the rest."

Langer met my eyes, trying to gauge my reaction. He was trying to form a rapport, clearly. I wasn't sure why. I *was* sure I had to prevent him from succeeding. So I said nothing.

"As you probably know, my dad sold and bought slaves. Tortured and/or worked to death several football teams' worth of them. At some point, I decided that wasn't going to be me. Since I took over his empire, it hasn't been."

"Cool story. You're a true humanitarian. Really. Are we about done here?"

To my surprise, Langer just looked at me and took a long, satisfied sip. Not only did being called out not seem to bother this guy, it actually seemed to be something he got a weird *enjoyment* out of. To me, who never called a free person out on anything without first deciding it was worth the grievous bodily harm it would earn me in return, it was a notion as strange as it was impossible to resist.

"Fast forward to this week, when *you*, under threat of a flogging, solved the number one problem of the most valuable company in my portfolio."

I froze in mid-sip. "I did?"

"I got on a call last week with the board at Orbital Dynamics. They were stunned when I told them the where-the-holes-aren't theory. They asked how I figured it out, and I told them I didn't—the slave who served me my cocktail did. They just laughed. They thought I was joking. I haven't checked the ticker, but their stock price is probably tripling right about now, along with my net worth, given I'm the majority shareholder. If there was any justice, you would be drinking champagne in a hot tub surrounded by bikinis full of perky tits and tight pussy, and instead, here you are toiling away covered in dirt."

"At least I have my pride."

Langer chuckled. "Yeah, I have that, too. Plus a ton of other shit."

He drained his glass and lightly tossed it in a wheelbarrow full of clippings, and I did the same, after pouring out the two-thirds I hadn't drunk. The last thing I needed was to get buzzed and let this dude start tricking me into thinking he was actually a decent human being.

He stopped and turned to me. "Let's not mince words, kid," he said. "Here's what I've been able to find out about you: your owner's psychopath son raped your mother, impregnated her, and let her die in agony. You gave him exactly what he deserved, and then you did three years in hell for the crime of having the balls to try to defend your family. And you would have died out there in the fields if you hadn't impressed a chick with your looks and impressed a dude with your brains. In other words, an age-old story: the boy with nothing saves himself using the only tools he has. That's my favorite story in the world because it's my story, too."

"How did you find out?" I asked. The file alone wouldn't have told him all of that. Phoning Luxembourg, or even Germany, maybe. I shuddered to think of anyone from any of my past lives picking up *that* call.

"You aren't the only one who knows how to do detective work."

"What else do you know?"

"Assume everything. We'll save time that way."

"Great," I muttered, slumping against a mesquite.

"Look, the powers that be don't take kindly to a slave who thinks he should still be treated like a human being," he went on. "And they *really* despise the one who's the smartest guy in the room. If you found the fucking cure for cancer tomorrow, they'd toss it in the incinerator, let millions of people die, and ship you off to dig coal, rather than admit that a slave did what none of them could do. Because admitting that would mean admitting they're wrong. That their whole *system* is wrong. And then their goddamn pea brains would explode because of the cognitive dissonance of it all."

Well, yes. Everyone knew it, but no one said it. Even *slaves* didn't say it. I'd bet that abolitionist professor Louisa was so enamored with had never put it so plainly in one of her academic papers.

But just because Langer actually said it out loud didn't mean he believed it. It just meant he had enough fuck-you money to get away with it.

"Oh," he continued. "By the way, I have to hand it to you. Nailing your master's daughter right under his nose. My profound respect."

I'd begun to naively hope he'd forgotten what he'd discovered at the party the other night, or at least would pretend he had for my sake. Right now, though, I could only concentrate on not blushing as hard as I was terrified I was. "Look, it's not—"

"Okay, fine, it's not." Langer just chuckled again. "That said, I have quite a few esoteric hobbies, but blackmail isn't one of them. I don't give a shit what you're *not* doing in her bedroom while you're pretending to tutor her. That isn't the point of this, so relax."

"What *is* the point, Max?" I bristled. "This has been just a great male bonding experience and everything. Very cathartic. But those pig holes, as you put it, don't dig themselves."

This guy wasn't Santa Claus, and he wasn't doing or saying any of this out of charity, compassion, or even friendship. This was a rich and powerful guy keeping his enemies close. I should know. I was doing the same.

"I told you, the holes are as good as done. And there's no point unless you want there to be," Langer said.

"And if I want there to be?"

"Then we keep talking. Yes, I'm giving you a choice."

I blinked. I didn't know what to do with a choice.

"Feels good, doesn't it?" asked Langer smugly. "Like something you could get used to?"

"Yeah. So?"

"So there's something that feels even better. Something you may not have considered."

"What's that?"

"Telling other people what to do."

Look, it wasn't as if the opportunity for power hadn't ever arisen. It had. But for a slave, power was never really power. It was a trap. Free men could be played like free women if you were careful, but you had to keep it close to the vest. If you sold out—if you lost that tiny little sliver of yourself that was yours alone—you'd turn into a rapey psycho like the old gardener, or one of those loathed slaves who would sell out a cohort to be flogged within an inch of his life for the privilege of an extra bowl of gruel. For a slave, chasing power wasn't a formula for success. It was a formula for losing friends and whatever remaining self-respect you had, and worst of all, *still* being a slave.

If that was what Langer was offering, the choice was easy. "I'm not going to be your lapdog, Max. What price do you think I'll sell out for? A place at your feet by the fireplace? Sorry. It's hot enough here already."

"You disappoint me." He stopped and turned, eyes flashing electric blue. "Do you really think if I were after some broken, brainless robot to blow smoke up my ass, I'd be standing out here in this godforsaken heat, wasting my time with you? I could go down to the local auction house and walk out with fifty slaves like that without even putting a dent in my bank account."

"So," I replied, a very familiar feeling spreading in the pit of my stomach. "You want to buy me. That's it, isn't it?"

Three times in my life I'd been bought and sold. Three times it had felt more or less like this. But only one time had I faced the prospect of leaving behind anyone I cared about.

"Honestly? I thought about it. But no. And this is why," Langer explained. "A, I don't want to own a slave. B, I don't need to own a slave. And C, even if A and B weren't true, Keith won't sell you for any price. He told me he already had an inkling of just how good of an investment you might be when he bought you, but the other night confirmed it."

I shrugged and gestured to the holes in the ground behind me. "Funny, you could have fooled me."

"Okay, so your master's a bit misguided. He's also bipolar, on like ten different medications, in debt up to his eyeballs, and if he could spend all his time on the golf course hiding from his shit show of a family, he would. In other words, he's got enough to deal with without worrying about whether his slaves are living their best lives. In the meantime, I'm offering you a deal."

"You're offering *him* a deal. Let's not bother pretending that I get any say in it."

"Wrong."

I looked at him, stunned.

"Listen. You've probably figured out by now that I'm not only in aerospace. I'm also in software and now chemical engineering. Project White Cedar—you may have heard of it. So I need someone who understands chemistry, physics, and math. You know, the hard shit. Your kind of shit. But more importantly, someone who has the balls and ambition to help me grow and scale my companies.

The engineers they keep hiring have all been neutered and/or brainwashed by their pricey, worthless educations, and I'm not getting shit from that tool of an intern who can barely stack a set of wooden blocks—who won't be back, by the way, in case that was something you were concerned with."

Yes. If I were with anyone but Langer, I would have pumped my fist with boyish glee. But I didn't because I could still hear the sound the bracelet made as it fell out of Corey's hand and pinged off the tile. He'd said it came from his boss, but maybe that wasn't the whole truth, considering it was unlikely that his boss would promote him to threatening his enemies while planning to fire him the very next week. Still, Corey was clearly too dumb to have orchestrated that whole thing on his own. It had to have originated with someone smart. But who else was as smart as Langer? Besides me, of course.

"Come with me."

What?

"Work with me. Consult with me. Live with me. My wife moved out two years ago. You could have your pick of ten spare rooms."

I opened my mouth.

"Oh, and just so we're clear, my interest in you is purely professional," he continued. "I don't like dick, and given your extracurricular activities, I'll assume at the very least you can take it or leave it. And if you end up hating me, which you very well might, you can have a whole suite to yourself and never have to see my face outside of work. I don't care. Or we can drink Bordeaux and watch association football like the good Europeans we are."

"Well," I began weakly, not knowing where else to start, "I support Luxembourg, and if you've seen them play at all in the last two decades, you'd know that's not quite the selling point you think it is."

He smirked.

"Look, Max, we both know how this works. If you came here to talk to the guy who decides my future, you're talking to the wrong guy."

"Keith will still own you on paper," he explained. "And he'll see a percentage of the return on investment, but I'll pay *you* in cash money, plus a safe to keep it in that you alone set the combination to, and a stake in the business if you want it. And if you don't want it, fine. It'll be your choice, not his. What do you think?"

I had spent my whole life being talked about as if I weren't there, so I had to marvel at the strange feeling of being offered a say in what happened to me. And not just a say. A *choice*, and not a slave's choice, which wasn't really a choice at all. A real choice. A man's choice. Almost.

But did I think Langer didn't know all of that? That he hadn't planned out the route to this moment step by step, beginning with the moment he'd saved us at the party? Knowing it would be as hard for me to resist his offer as someone dying of thirst to resist a poisoned oasis? I shouldn't bow down just because I'd been offered more than I ever expected to be offered in my entire life. In fact, it was absolutely crucial that I didn't.

Hell, if only he *were* the standard rich asshole who treated all slaves like garbage. *That* I was used to. *That* I could handle. This I had no blueprint for at all. *No plan survives contact with the enemy.* So like speed chess, I'd just have to change up the moves as I went.

"I think," I said slowly, "you think I'm an idiot. In case you forgot, I'm property. I'm not a person. I have no legal identity. You could offer me drilling rights to all of Texas, but how the fuck can I be sure you'll honor it when I can't even sign a goddamn contract?"

"You think I haven't considered this?" he countered. "There are ways. I can issue you bearer shares, which are as good as cash. I can set up an offshore safe deposit box registered to Mickey Mouse and give you the only access key. Hell, I can exchange it for gold doubloons, bury it on some rock in the Caribbean, and draw you a map with X marks the spot. You'll get your money, guaranteed."

"And then what?" I demanded stubbornly.

"After that, I can't promise you anything. But once Keith sees how you can deliver, who knows what might happen?"

We both knew what he was talking about, and I kept reminding myself to breathe. If I let this guy play upon my vanity and pride and my frankly selfish yearning to finally have everything I knew I was worth—let's face it, I'd lose any chance of finding Maeve. My entire trip here, everything I'd done so far, was void unless I found a way to beat Langer at his own game, and needless to say, instantly agreeing to everything he proposed was not that way. I took a deep breath.

"I have a better idea," I said, even as I thought better of it. "How about instead of speculating on what might happen, we talk about what *did* happen? What about the tablet the other night and the sicko gardener you conveniently disposed of seemingly out of the goodness of your heart? What about German? What about, *I'd hate to see you end up right back here*? And what about *this?*"

I dug into my pocket and whipped out the bloody bracelet.

He looked down at it coolly. "I've never seen that before in my life."

"What?" I exploded, more out of shock than anything. I guess I hadn't been expecting that. I don't know *what* I'd been expecting. "But—"

I stopped before I could bring up Corey because Langer was just standing there, rooted to the spot, cool and emotionless.

A creepy feeling crept up my neck.

"Go on," he said, merely waving a hand. "I'm curious to see where you're going with this."

I froze. Fuck, what was I thinking? This wasn't a fellow slave I'd just been sparring with. This was a free man, the richest, most powerful free man I'd ever met, and the old ways came rushing back now—the urge to shrink under his gaze, to curl into myself for protection, to beg for forgiveness. *I'm sorry, sir. I didn't mean it, sir. I'll agree to anything you say, just please don't chain me up and feed me to the rabid javelinas, sir.*

But that would be the slave boy talking. It wasn't the man Louisa saw in me, the one she'd once called brave, and it wasn't the one Maeve was depending on.

"Well, here's my theory, Max," I finally said after a deep breath. "Maybe *I* know something about you. Something that could get *you* thrown in a mine if you're not careful. And hey, you're a shrewd guy, so maybe *you* decided that rather than crushing me like a bug, why not have some fun and flatter my ego? You know, that poor, sad slave boy who's too smart for his own good and wants the girl he can't have—let's fill his head with delusions of grandeur so he drops his guard and doesn't see the cliff coming until he walks right off it?" I finished. "Now tell me, am I getting warm?"

To my surprise, Langer didn't explode with rage. He didn't even move much. Just eyed me with that same disconcerting, icy look. "I'm not an idiot, either, you know," he pointed out. "Sure, maybe there *is* shit I've done that I don't want anyone to know about. Maybe I'm still doing it. Maybe you're the only person alive smart enough to stop me. And if you are, it would make sense that you're exactly who I *want* working for me."

"Enemies close?"

"Exactly. Which is why," he said, "the offer still stands."

"Fuck your offer."

His lips parted in a grin, seemingly more pleased by this than anything all afternoon. "Now we're getting somewhere."

"Maybe I don't want to play by your rules, Max. Maybe I want to play by my own."

"Good. The last thing I would ever do is stop you."

I stuck the spade under my arm and abruptly turned, but he caught me by the shoulder. I turned my face away from the intense gaze, so unused to that coming from a free man.

"One last question, kid," he said. "You can walk away right now, no problem. If you do, this conversation stays between us and the prickly pears. You can go back to digging pig holes and nailing Curly Sue in the pantry, at least until somebody wants a can of soup and it's game over. But ask yourself: when that happens—and it *will* happen—do you really think you're going to get lucky again?"

I stared at a very specific spot on the dusty ground, my vision going all blurry for a moment.

"Wherever they throw you, you're going to die down there, with the bonus of knowing you fucked up *her* life forever, too. And I don't know if it's her eyes, her tits, or that her snatch tastes like chocolate chip cookies, but whatever it is, it's enough to keep you lying to yourself, and worse, lying to *her*, every time you look her in that sweet, innocent face. You *know* you're going to get caught. You *know* this is going to end. And when it does, you won't be playing by anyone's rules but theirs ever again."

The crippling strike, just like the fucking professor while I was off aiming for the king. *You got too greedy, boy,* he'd remind me while smugly sweeping my queen off the board. *And left her vulnerable.*

"Ah. I knew you were smart," he said smugly. As if he thought he'd already won.

"Yeah, I am. Smart enough to tell when I'm being played," I said. With finality, I stabbed the spade as deep in the earth as it would go and turned back toward the house.

He may have the entire board, but I still had one pawn left. And I'd done more with less.

"No deal," I said. "Thanks for the drink. *Sir.*"

———————— · ✦ ❤ ✦ · ————————

At first, I'd been ridiculously smug about the hiding place I'd chosen near the garden shed for the phone, the aloe, and two or three other things I wasn't supposed to have. Sure, it had meant dodging the gardener, but like Langer, I believed in nothing if not keeping your enemies close. And now that there *was* no gardener, you'd think it would be just about perfect.

However, even the best hiding place quickly became a bad one when I insisted on going back there twenty fucking times a day. But what choice did I have?

I still felt disgusting—in more ways than one—and I only had a window of a few minutes to clean myself up before Louisa got home, not to mention decide exactly how little I could get away with telling her about what had just happened, assuming I hadn't dreamed it. But instead, as soon as Langer left, I retrieved the phone and sank to the ground amid a bed of agave plants, drawing my knees to my chest and navigating to the messaging app. But there was nothing from Maeve, and all at once, the image of the mutilated girl in the desert flashed across my mind like images in a bloody slideshow.

The microchips. *Of course.* Because to steal a slave, you had to either disable the microchip somehow—which had never been done—or remove it. But since the chips migrated, removing them usually meant horrific injury if not death for the poor slave in question. And that didn't even take into account what awaited the girls if they survived—and I had a feeling it wasn't freedom.

No, I still wasn't sure what Langer's grand plan was, but I now had some idea of what was happening to Maeve and the other girls.

Disruption. Literally.

But that wasn't even the worst part. No. Because another piece of the puzzle had just fallen into place.

It was only since the party—*when I'd spoken to Langer*—that Maeve had gone quiet.

He knew I knew. He'd known since the party that I knew.

In other words, I had fucked up the whole thing. While I'd been dicking around playing speed chess with Langer, I'd put my sister in even more danger.

Frantically, I tapped out another message, asking if she was okay and pleading with her to respond, even while the image—*the* image—flashed into my mind. The one of Maeve, the purest soul I'd ever known, screaming, pleading, strangled, gagged, restrained, violated, broken. Another family member lost because I couldn't ever seem to use my supposed brainpower for anything other than solving dry scientific equations with no practical use but making rich guys even richer. Fuck, if there was *any* reason to resent the education I'd been given, it was that. At least as an illiterate slave toiling in the fields, I wouldn't be haunted by everything that, despite my gifts, I was still failing at.

After checking the time again, I minimized the messaging app and turned to the contacts. Up until recently, Louisa's number had been the only one saved there, but a few days ago—against all my better judgment—I'd added a second one.

I rose, shielding my face from the midday glare. I now knew where I would dump the phone. But before I did, it was time to make one last call.

5

HER

"You seem to be developing a Jesus Christ-like tendency to hurt your hands," I scolded him, unwinding a length of gauze across his lacerated palms, which I'd already treated with antiseptic and aloe—probably in the wrong order, as my future in the medical profession continued to prove bright.

"Oh, is that what you're going to start calling me now?" he asked. "Just when I was getting used to Albert Einstein."

I groaned as I tried to use some dull scissors to clumsily snip off the end of the gauze. For a pre-med, I sure seemed to fuck up all my attempts to give medical treatment. "Yeah, that's just what you need—to get it in your head that you're not only a super-genius but the Messiah, too. Besides, weren't you just telling me a few days ago that science and religion are fundamentally incompatible?"

"That does sound like something I would say," he admitted. "But weren't you the one who disagreed with me? Besides, science is more flexible than you think. Hell, even gravity breaks down at the quantum level."

I hid a smile and ripped off another piece of gauze. "Oh, so you're happy to defy the laws of science when it benefits you?"

"You know I'm happy to defy the laws of *everything* when it benefits me."

Face to face, we straddled the thick cushions on the sand-colored chaise in an outdoor "room" nobody ever used, which was a shame for something so lovingly landscaped. Red terracotta pots and agave plants, plus a golden paloverde, provided just enough shade from a dusky autumn that had turned his eyes into twin coppery flames and his hair into liquid gold. And it almost matched the color scheme of the trucker-style college hat he'd playfully grabbed off my head and slapped over his sunny locks.

After greeting him, I'd dared to snatch us a stack of fresh-baked raspberry cheesecake bars from the kitchen, which he'd happily inhaled all but one of, despite the tricky relationship dynamics and despite the chance of the housekeeper inquiring why I was suddenly eating for three. I'd hoped to do more, honestly. Earlier, I'd browsed the campus bookstore, not quite bringing myself to admit what I was looking for and pushing aside the thought that he probably wouldn't even accept it. Anyway, I'd given up in frustration. Why had nobody warned me how difficult it was to buy a gift for someone who wasn't allowed to own anything?

However, when I'd stopped at a promotional table on campus to fill out a credit card application—mostly, I admitted, to get the fifty-dollar nail salon voucher they were offering—the hat had appeared as a bonus gift. In perhaps the least shocking revelation of the day, it looked much better on him.

"Keep it," I'd said. "I don't do hats. Not with this hair. But you know the brim goes in the front, right?"

Well, the effect was very "foreigner trying to look American," but it didn't matter when the light here seemed to want to make love to him. Hell, the light *everywhere* seemed to want to make love to him. I myself wanted to paint him, even though I hadn't picked up a paintbrush since seventh-grade art class. The bright sunset colors contrasted with the soft white T-shirt that clung lovingly to his biceps the way his shirts always did no matter what size they happened to be. The worn-in pair of jeans he had thrown on, sitting low on his hips, was even *more* distracting. And it hadn't been *his* idea to straddle the chaise, but I was glad we did, even if it meant I had to keep looking away from the space between his legs to keep from blushing crimson myself. And he knew it. Good God, of course he did.

Upon arriving home, I'd been instantly amazed by the freedom that came with having three fewer people in the house. For one, I could breathe, and for two, I could run immediately out to the garden, into the shelter of the velvet mesquite tree, and see *him* before anyone else, his eyes as hungry and relieved as if we'd been separated for years instead of hours. And then my fingers were arched over his powerful shoulders and *his* fingers were softly brushing across the back pockets of my denim shorts, and all the trials of the day seemed to melt into nothing much at all.

"Thank you," I'd whispered, pressing a featherlight kiss to his lips. The exam results would show up soon enough. For now, nothing more needed to be asked or said.

In the meantime, his hair was still damp from the outdoor shower behind the shed, and I breathed him in, soap and rainwater and the desert itself, as if it had finally taken in this foreign boy as one of its own. But why, if *I'd* been tested that day—in more ways than one—was *he* holding on to me like it was the last chance he thought he'd ever get?

Then I saw the blood. Vermilion streaks trailing down his wrists like tears, and I immediately threw down the bags I was carrying and went for the first aid supplies. Shouldn't I put my rudimentary medical skills to use helping the only person who was working as hard as I was to make sure I passed my course?

So far, he'd been an uncharacteristically quiet patient, watching as I clumsily struggled to unroll and wind the gauze. Whatever his mind was dwelling on, it was very far from the cuts on his palm.

And so was mine. I recalled how utterly deranged my ex-wannabe-boyfriend had sounded as he'd hurled abuse across a river of baffled students. I'd seen now that Corey was petty, jealous, vindictive, and cruel, but not, to my knowledge, dangerous. However, the proof that he *could* be was now staring up at me from the scabbed and bloody palm I held.

And why? Because Corey felt his rival had not only stolen—for lack of a less offensive term—*me*, but his job. But how? It wasn't like Langer could fire Corey and replace him with a slave. But if Corey somehow thought he could, it didn't matter. Booze-bloated wreck or not, Corey still had power over both of us. And as long as the world was what it was, it would stay that way.

But the boy in front of me, his forehead almost touching mine, already knew that.

"You need to be more careful," I whispered, unwilling to let the mention of Corey ruin a moment I had been waiting all day for. "Not just about your hands, I mean. About everything."

He looked down at his wounds, his eyes flicking back up to meet mine. "I know."

I snipped off the end of the gauze and struggled to affix it in place, mostly succeeding in only taping my own fingers together. "Sorry, but I think it might be hard for you to hold a pen for a while."

"After today, I might not have to," he said. "It might be gardening from here on out."

"Well, you are going to keep tutoring me, aren't you?" I asked. "I still have the final and a whole second semester of o-chem ahead of me. Unless you think I'll fail and Daddy will take it out on you, and—" My mind was going places it shouldn't.

He looked at me seriously. "That is not going to happen."

"Which one, me failing or—"

"Any of it," he cut me off. "Don't talk like that. Anyway, gardening isn't a total waste of time. We got rid of the javelinas."

I blinked. "Javelinas?"

He seemed startled as if afraid he'd gotten his facts wrong—for him, a fate worse than death, I suspected. "Javelinas? Wild pigs? That is a thing here, isn't it? It wasn't just some delusion my feverish brain conjured up while I was passing out from blood loss?"

"No, of course they're a thing," I reassured him. "I just didn't realize that was what the fence was for. Those things are the stuff of nightmares, I swear. They have ridiculously sharp teeth and when we had our dog, they used to chase her out of the garden and she wouldn't come back for days. And that's on top of tearing up the yard and shitting everywhere."

"The desert really is a magical place, isn't it?" he remarked.

"I saw the fence," I said amid a giggle. "You got all that done in one day?"

The fence, with all of its precise spacing and neat angles, had looked like more than the day's work of one person. Even one who had been forced to learn a thing or two about building things over the years.

"No. Just some of the holes and wire," he admitted. "Langer's guys did everything else."

My insides churned at the sound of the name of the man who seemed to have his hand in everything these days. "Langer's guys? *Why*?"

"Because he likes me," he said, dropping his eyes and absently picking at the edge of the gauze. "Which I understand, naturally," he remarked. "Or I *could*, if I liked him. But I don't."

"So what does he want with you?" No, Langer couldn't hire him. But there was one thing he could do. My heart skipped. I almost couldn't bring myself to speak the words. "Was Langer here? Did he say anything about—"

"No," he said quickly, though I wasn't exactly sure what question he was answering. I didn't want to know. "Does—does he want to buy you?"

"No."

At first, I relaxed just a bit when he said, "No."

"Worse," he continued. "I think he wants to adopt me."

He was smiling somewhat, but my shock must still have been clear.

"Look, this is for me to worry about," he said firmly. "Not you."

Fuck. He *was* worried. *That's* why he'd held me so tight. "Why am I never around when these things happen?" I demanded.

"Next time I'll call you up in the middle of class," he teased. "'Help, I cut up my hands, come home and cuddle me.'"

"I didn't mean the cuts. I meant Langer."

"Doesn't matter. The solution's the same."

I shook my head. "Of course it is because your definition of cuddling rarely ever means *just* cuddling."

He stared down at the results of my treatment, such as it was. "Well, if it helps, this gauze is wrapped so tight, my repertoire will be limited," he said. "Slightly."

I gasped indignantly. "Well, I tried my—"

"Hey, relax. It was very sweet," he said and gave me a forehead kiss for good measure, though he was already prying at the gauze, trying to loosen it. "I can't remember the last time anyone went to that much effort to treat my injuries." He looked up to see my exaggerated pout. "Cheer up. Maybe you can be one of those doctors who just look at X-rays and never have to actually interact with patients. Plus, you can still cuddle me," he said, leaning back on the chaise, the hat making him passable as a frat boy on a spring break vacation. "You can cuddle my brains out if you want."

I looked around frantically, turning back in horror. "Here?"

He smiled slyly, one arm casually behind his head. He wasn't joking, of course. I should have known him well enough by now to know that he was *never* joking about such serious matters as wanton semi-public sex.

"What the hell happened to being more careful?" I demanded.

"You're the one who told me nobody ever comes out here."

And just like that, all my hard work on the gauze was for naught as he peeled it off and immediately dove for the bare skin between the hem of my crop top and tiny shorts, pulling me forward to encourage me to straddle him and push my pelvis deep into the thighs covered by that soft denim, melting bodily into the friction, feeling a soft moan bubble up from the same vicinity. And so my endless curls swung down like a curtain as I kissed the lips I had never stopped longing for even in the most desperate, fragile moments of my day, and I quivered while he kissed my eyes and cheeks and tongued along my jawline, trembled at the ghost of his thumb on the nipple that stiffened under my tight top. His fingers—surprisingly nimble despite their injuries, at least when they found an activity they enjoyed—slid teasingly up the soft skin of my thighs and started working on the buttons of my shorts.

At a sudden vibration, we both jumped, both more on edge than either of us wanted to admit.

"Oh shit," he said as the phone slipped out of his pocket and onto the sandy ground next to the chaise. For a second before he swiped it up, we both looked down at it in shock, then up at each other.

He never carried his phone around. I'd never seen him with it since the day I gave it to him and had no idea where he kept it—I was happy enough to receive the occasional playful message, and out of courtesy, I didn't ask questions. That didn't mean I wasn't wondering what was happening or where Maeve was. But every time I remembered the night I'd given it to him—and the argument that had almost destroyed what we now had before it even started—I chose not to. If he needed more help, surely he'd come to me. After all, he trusted me now. Right?

If I'd had even a moment to think, maybe I would have asked him. But a second later he was gone, and *I* was left sitting on the chaise, mystified and alone, in the shadow of the swaying paloverde, with my pussy naughtily soaking the fabric of my half-unbuttoned shorts and the pristine plush cushion beneath, not understanding just what the hell had just happened but aware that something was very wrong. Wronger than Corey; wronger even than whatever he suspected Langer of being up to.

Because I knew the number I'd seen flashing on the screen. And I knew there was only one place he could have gotten it.

HIM

Okay, *two* last calls. The house was emptier at the moment, but it was still a bitch to find someplace with decent reception and where I wouldn't be seen, overheard, or suspected of being somewhere I shouldn't be. The garden shed was pretty much the only place on the property that met those requirements, even before the gardener's unceremonious shitcanning. So that's where I went to take the call, knowing that any explanation I could possibly offer the wet, purring, half-undressed vision on the chaise would only make things worse, not better. Hell, I might need *another* shower—an icy cold one—before I was in any state to be traipsing through the garden, either.

The biggest tragedy of all was that I probably had mere minutes before the housekeeper tracked me down, started asking questions about the fence, and bombarded me with all the tasks she wanted me to do before she'd actually let me go to sleep. And then I'd have *no* chance to get back to Louisa that night.

That was until small, faint footsteps approached. Female footsteps.

I hastily apologized and ended the call. "Lou?"

I knew she'd recognized the number, and now she'd probably heard me talking. Talking with a woman I'd never met and only knew about because of her, whose handwritten number I'd swiped off her desk when she was out of the room, without ever telling her about any of it.

When I put it that way, it sounded so *bad*.

But still. I could handle this. I would have to come clean, but we could work through it.

Unfortunately, it wasn't Louisa in the doorway. It was the household's *other* girl.

"So your sister's missing? *That's* what this is about? How awful. Tell me more."

"Goddammit." I ran a hand through my hair in exasperation as I turned around. It wasn't as if I hadn't suspected something like this would happen. But why did it always have to happen at the worst possible time? "Why couldn't the master have taken you to LA, too?"

The maid emerged into the murky light of the shed, sashaying as usual in those hip-hugging jeans, though I only saw the sadness and desperation behind it now. But you could be sad and desperate and still dangerous.

"You know, I asked myself that same question," she said. "I've always wanted to see the ocean. But he didn't, so I'm stuck here with a shitload of time on my hands, and you're still in the hole from the last one." She stepped closer, and my eyes followed as she traced a thin, pale finger along my jawline and cheek, trailing up to the edge of the hat that in my haste I hadn't thought to remove, its brim still twisted to the side. She grabbed it off my head and stuck it on her own.

"So if you want me to stay quiet about all this, you're *really* gonna have to make it worth my while."

6

HIM

As my lacerated fingers groped a pair of heavy pruning shears hanging on the wall behind me, I couldn't help thinking how tempting it was to grab them, knock her out cold, and dash to safety. Of course that would just create more problems than it would solve, but one of these days, I hoped to get to use pure brute force instead of coming up with clever, elaborate plans all the time. It was becoming exhausting.

"Go ahead and say something," I said, calling her bluff. "I don't care."

She wrinkled her nose and mouth in a way she probably thought was cute. At one point, I might have agreed, but at the moment, the effect was slightly demented. "So you really don't care if I walk right in and tell the housekeeper what I just heard, and she calls the master? You'd be fucked six ways to Sunday."

"Wait, what?" That was a new one for me.

Her green eyes flashed in annoyance. "Never mind. It's an American saying. You're telling me you don't care."

"Nope."

I glanced warily over her shoulder and out into the waning lavender light of the gardens. I could do this. Just con her long enough to buy another day. No, I didn't even need a day. Just a night would be enough. Hell, a few *hours*. Not to mention, I had to extricate myself from this situation before Louisa came looking for me because the shed would be the first place she'd look. And yeah, maybe I would have been able to explain away the phone call alone. But *this* situation would require a level of finesse beyond that of mere mortals, and I could not, much as it pained me to admit it, actually turn water into wine.

To my relief, though, she had started to look somewhat disconcerted that her plan wasn't working. "You're playing games with me."

"You know me. I don't play games."

She scoffed. "Oh, right, Mr. Chessmaster-rocket-scientist-brain-surgeon-whatever-you're-claiming-to-be-today," she said. "Well, in that case, you should have no problem explaining just why you don't care whether I tell anyone."

"Because by the time you tell anyone, I'll be gone." I swallowed. "And I want to take you with me," I blurted out. "Baby."

I cringed. Really? *That* was the best I could come up with? I was disappointed in myself. But it was too late to do anything but double down.

"What?"

"You heard me," I said, making my first small attempt to wriggle out of her shadow. "I'll take you with me. Tomorrow morning, when I go to find my sister. The master's away. It's our best chance."

"What about the chips?" Her voice gave nothing away.

"I know how to deactivate them," I lied, ducking past her. "Someone showed me how. Someone from the SLA."

"I thought the SLA was gone," she said, blocking me with a hand on my chest. She couldn't physically prevent me from leaving, but *if* I left and she chose to run to the housekeeper, where would I go to escape *that*? "I thought they all got arrested and sent to the mines years ago. Or they're in hiding."

"Not all of them."

"You're shitting me." The surprised expression was a new one for her.

I shook my head and smiled reassuringly. "I'm not," I said softly, moving closer and lightly touching her hand. Was this laying it on too thick? "I know what I want, and I want you with me when I go."

For a few seconds at least, it seemed to work. She appeared momentarily captivated by my words, her hardened gaze softening and her smirk replaced with curiosity.

A second later, the smirk was back. "Well, then you'll have no problem showing me," she said, shaking some dark hair out of her face and tilting her lips up toward mine.

Well, shit. I had to get out of this. I might be able to charm the birds right out of the trees, but she was now less a bird and more an angry, buzzing horsefly, nimbly dodging whatever I tried to swat her with.

I turned to push her aside, but in a second, it didn't matter, anyway.

Louisa stood in the doorway, where the fiery light of sunset had at some point been replaced by the violet twilight, and almost would have been beautiful if her eyes when I met them hadn't been utterly, terrifyingly blank.

The maid spun around, sizing up the situation instantly. Any idiot could have.

I should have known it all along. She'd had no intention of telling anyone about anything. She'd just wanted to fuck things up between us, plain and simple, and her work here was done. Little did she know that hers was just the icing on a fucked-up multi-layer cake.

"Well, good luck," she told me lightly, reaching up to pat my cheek. "You know where to find me if you need me." She turned to Louisa in the doorway. "Thanks for the hat, miss, but you can have it." She handed it to Louisa, who took it robotically before dropping it in the dust, her eyes glued to *me*.

"I'm not really a hat person, either," the maid whispered conspiratorially before slipping away.

Ironically, I'd wanted to buy myself some time. But it only took one terrifying second for Louisa's eyes to fill with tears, another for her face to crumble, and a third for me to watch helplessly as her silhouette disappeared into the gloom.

———————— · ✦ · ❤ · ✦ · ————————

"I didn't," I said to Louisa's back as she sat in her pink velvet swivel chair, writing something out in a notebook. She didn't turn around.

I hadn't been able to avoid the housekeeper, who seemed convinced that I was up to something, which, of course, I was. I *always* was. So I told her this, which seemed to put her off for a second while I disappeared upstairs. After all, it was either risk her wrath or Louisa's if I didn't at least attempt to explain myself, and the choice was obvious. I took a deep breath.

"I know," she said. "But you would have."

"Maybe," I admitted. "But only to get out of the situation." Like that made it any better.

She spun her chair around so suddenly it startled me.

"Oh, you mean the situation where she saw you calling *my* professor, with a number that you took off *my* desk, in an attempt to save your sister from a supposed kidnapper who you think is *my* dad's business partner?"

And I thought I'd been speechless in the shed.

HER

"Maybe I haven't stressed this enough," I began, channeling my father in the way he peered down at people from behind his massive desk. If he insisted on treating me like an idiot. "I may not know as much as you do about chemistry, or physics, or calculus, or metaphysics, or epistemology, or French post-gypsy jazz, or whatever other highfalutin Eurotrash art forms you think are really cool, *but I am not an idiot.*"

"I know you aren't. But—"

"That day I saw you at the window looking at the mountains," I said. "You found that piece of paper with Erica Muller's phone number on it, in that little pink box on my desk. You had to grab it fast and shove it in your pocket, and then you put it back when I turned away."

His shock was evident. But all he asked was, "How come you didn't say anything then?"

"Because I was willing to give *you* the benefit of the doubt," I said. "But you weren't willing to give *me* the same. Instead, you looked like you were about to kiss and do who knows what else with a chick I'm pretty sure you don't even care about—stop me if I'm wrong—just so you could continue to sneak around."

"You're not wrong," he said quietly and seriously, in a way that was breaking my heart already. "I don't care about her. I never did."

I bit my lip. To my surprise, I believed him. Maybe because I already knew him well enough to know that if he ever betrayed me, it wouldn't be by doing something so cheap and lazy and stupid as kissing some slave girl in a toolshed. It would be smart, calculating, and deeply, deeply deceptive.

Just like him.

"But what I don't understand is how I was supposed to give you the benefit of the doubt." He seemed genuinely confused.

"*How*? Do you really think I wouldn't have just given you the number if you'd *asked*?"

"I know you would have," he said quietly, coming farther into the room. I backed up a bit, but I didn't prevent him from entering. "And then you would have asked why. And then we'd be right back here. With you asking me to choose."

I leaped out of my chair. "Don't you understand, you absolutely infuriating idiot? I'm not *asking* you to choose. I'm asking you to let me in and help you. That's all I've been asking this entire time. Why don't you get that?"

"I do get it. I just can't do it."

"Why not?" I demanded.

"Because your dad's involved!"

Now it was my turn to be speechless.

"*Nondikass.*" He took an angry swing at the back of the swivel chair I had just been sitting in, sending it spinning toward the bed.

Whoa. What was *that*? He had never exactly shied away from profanity in English, but in his native language, it sounded downright scary, and quite jarring to observe in someone who had been raised, albeit unsuccessfully, to be submissive.

"Why did you make me say that?" he demanded. "Why did you push me?"

"How about, why did you *lie to me*?" I demanded back. "I think that's the real question here."

"I never lied," he said. "And if there were things I didn't tell you, it was only because I was trying to protect you."

"You've known this whole time, haven't you?" I asked quietly. "Since the first time you tutored me."

He tried to calm his tone to match mine. "The real estate title for the place where Langer is keeping her and other girls, too, is in your dad's name. I found it in his file cabinet."

"*What*? By accident?" *As if that's even possible, dumbass,* I scolded myself.

"No." He was unapologetic.

"God," I said, shaking my head. "But how did you know he and Langer—"

"I've known for months. Since Germany. It's ... well, it's kind of the reason I'm here."

Another piece of the puzzle filled in. "The warehouse," I said. "That was it on the map the gardener was waving around at the party, wasn't it?"

"He was trying to blackmail me with it."

"After you printed it off *my* computer," I concluded.

He cringed and nodded.

I threw my hands up. "Unbelievable."

"But I never lied to you," he insisted.

"Oh, yeah, no, sure, of course you didn't lie." I was shaking now. "You just misled me about *everything*. Did you ever even *want* to be in here with me? Did you even—did *we* even—" I bit my lip, a sob building.

Slowly, tentatively, he approached me like I was a scared baby animal who might bolt. He touched the tip of my elbow, but I snapped it back from his fingertips. "The first time I came into this room, it was for my sister," he said. "But every time I came back, it was for you. If you don't believe anything else I say, believe that."

I closed my eyes. I believed him. I almost wished I didn't. "And yet, despite all we've been through, you still don't trust me," I said softly. "And apparently I can't trust *you*, either."

"Lou, your dad is loyal to the guy who's going to make him rich again, and you're loyal to your dad," he explained. "Can't you see how I couldn't risk putting my sister in more danger when I came this far just to find her? They're doing horrifying things to her. Maybe as we speak."

"Like what?"

"What do you think?" he asked. "It's slavery. Do I have to draw you a diagram?"

He reached into his pocket, a slow, deliberate movement, and pulled out a small, blood-stained bracelet—Maeve's. He handed it to me. The metal was cold, the reality colder. Because what I noticed immediately, besides the blood, was that it was totally intact—it hadn't been cut off or smashed or even torn from her wrist by force. The implications made me gag.

"Corey gave it to me. He said it was courtesy of his boss."

"Langer." I recoiled, the bracelet dropping from my fingers and onto the carpet as if it were electrified. "Oh God." Horror churned in my stomach. And amid my trembling body, an eerie chill surfaced. I looked up at him. "You're going to go after her, aren't you?"

He paused as if this were the hardest admission so far. "Yes."

My knees turned soft, and I sank onto the bed, head spinning, eyes a blur.

"If I don't, no one will. I was hoping Erica Muller would help me come up with a plan to do it without getting myself or my sister killed."

I wasn't sure which was worse—the deeds he was accusing my father of, or that he was planning to run away forever in an attempt to stop them.

And all he could say was, "You can't say I didn't warn you."

He was right. He *had* warned me. He'd warned me not to poke, not to prod, not to search, not to get involved. I'd done it anyway. Why? For a lark? To give my life meaning, to get a gold star in compassion? Or because I cared, and never in a million years had ever thought it would blow up in my face like *this*?

"How could you think so little of me?" I demanded, not daring to look at him. "You're literally standing here telling me my dad is a kidnapper and a rapist, or at least helping someone who is. And assuming I'm going to *defend* him."

"I don't have to assume. You *are* defending him."

"I'm defending him because he's innocent!" I cried. "Daddy's a lot of things, but he is *not* a rapist."

For a second, his expression changed, and I knew he was taking in the information. "If Langer is doing what you say he is, I can guarantee you he's lying to Daddy, too." My voice teetered on the edge of breaking. "And if you'd only bothered to ask—if you'd only bothered to trust me, instead of going behind my back, I could have *told* you that. Say what you will about what a complete fucking mess my family is, but nobody in it has ever done *that* to a slave. Ever."

His voice was cold. "Then you're blind."

"How *dare* you?" I screamed. "This is my *family*!"

"Yeah, I had a family, too, once," he said. "Now one of them is dead, and the other is being held captive by a sicko because of people like *your* family. And you wonder why I have trust issues? You know, I never realized how easy it must be to forget your family owns slaves," he continued, "when you have the privilege of *not being one of them*."

"Oh yeah, 'privilege.' I've heard that before. What privilege? The 'privilege' of having the shittiest, most dysfunctional family of anyone I know? The kind where I spent my entire senior year counting down the days until I could get myself the fuck out of here and then being told I couldn't go? The kind where I had to stop having friends over because I'm so fucking embarrassed by them?"

"Right, you're just so embarrassed that you're stuck in your ten-million-dollar mansion with slaves serving your every whim. Yeah, I feel just really fucking terrible for you. Will you listen to yourself?"

"That is so unfair." I was crying now, for real. "You of all people should know that what I have—my status—whatever label society gives me—is *not* who I am."

"Except in this world, it's all the same in the end, yeah? Because what you forget is that not only do they have power over me, they have power over *you*. They can take all this away from you in a second," he said, waving to the room around us, the refuge in rose gold, where we'd spent so much time exploring and learning and sharing the wonder of our young bond, all going up in smoke now as if someone had taken a match to it. "And then where would you be without your designer clothes and pink furry pillows and brand-new computers and country clubs and pool parties and your overpriced college education that you'd be flunking out of if it weren't for me, by the way? And meanwhile, you're feeding me cheesecake and letting me sleep in your bed but only as long as I'm a good boy and do exactly as I'm told because if I don't and you tell anyone, I'm off to a mine tomorrow. And you know it. Maybe you even *like* it. Because deep down, you're all the same."

I just stood there with my mouth open like a fish. Neither one of us said it, but we both knew who he meant: the free women of his past. The ones who, with one false word, held the power of life and death over him.

I wasn't controlling; wasn't dominant; wasn't cruel. But right now, I was full of the kind of anger and pain that could make even a rational girl do something irrational; something monstrous. The kind that could relate to *them*.

"If you want to go?" I said through gritted teeth before a sob tore out of my throat. "Go. See how far you get once I tell Daddy."

"Oh, I'll get as far as I need to get, chip or no chip," he said, stalking toward the door as my vision blurred.

This was happening. He was walking out. In seconds, he'd be gone.

Time. How had it come to this?

Fiercely, I turned my back to stare at the window to keep him from seeing the tears pouring down my face. I yelled over my shoulder, "Well, for your sake, you'd better because I'm telling him everything!"

I regretted it as soon as I'd said it, but it was too late.

"Then you *are* all the same."

· + ❤ + ·

We went a day and a half without communicating, long enough for me to see my B-plus pop up in the university's online portal. And when I came home, there was no one to tell—just my empty desk with the wicker chair still pulled up next to mine, the dusky afternoon light swirling around it weakly. I fell asleep on top of my chemistry book, tears running down the pages of the wordy volume I used to hate and that had now become the most cherished one on my shelf because it was the only one with spiky boyish handwriting in the margins and globe mallow petals pressed into the pages.

Really, I just wanted to press the intercom and start all over again. But I wouldn't be asking for coffee this time.

I had threatened to punish him. But I should punish *myself* for thinking that someone so hurt and abused could ever learn to trust anyone, let alone the daughter of the man who owned him and had the power to destroy him. Even a man innocent of the accusation, as I knew my father was.

Still, in a way, he had been right. I *had* wanted to find a way to keep him with me—let's face it, forever if I could. It was why I had threatened to call my father and why I still *wanted* to, to the point of grabbing my phone every time I was seized by the grief and rage of him turning his back on me. It was an instinct that deep down I was afraid was horrid, that made me fear maybe I *was* the same as all the rest.

But the fact was, I didn't really want that. I didn't want to own him, or command him, or violate him, or punish him. After all, having the rarest, most beautiful bird locked in a cage, no matter how much you petted and adored it, wasn't like letting it fly. If it had to fly, you *had* to let it fly. And let it be enough to know it was somewhere out there, wings spread, a tiny, glimmering flash against the massive sky.

The bird could still choose to stay, of course. But for that to happen, you had to accept that it had to be free to fly away, and the bird, that the cage door would always be open.

———— · ✦ ❤ ✦ · ————

My phone vibrated, jerking me awake. Papers flew off my desk as I scrambled to wipe off the sticky combination of hair and saliva pressed into the side of my face. The sun was much lower in the sky, and the room was gloomy. What time was it?

The display showed four new messages from Corey, but the call was from Erica Muller, and needless to say, that seemed far more important. I raised the phone to my ear in a daze.

"Where is he?" My professor's voice blared out of the earpiece.

"Who? What? I don't—"

"You know who I'm talking about. You have to find him, Louisa," she continued. "Immediately. Normally, I would never betray the confidence of a slave who came to me like this, but I can't reach him now, so he must have burned the phone. He's in danger, and so is his sister. Make sure that whatever he does, he does not go to that warehouse."

"What? Why?" I sputtered incoherently.

"I don't have time to explain now." My professor sounded alarmed, her voice so unlike the cool, dry, pedagogical tone she used in the lecture hall.

"But what do I tell him?" I'd be lucky if he'd listen to or believe anything I said, after the words that had been exchanged. Words we could never take back.

"Tell him I can help him and that I know other people who can. But he cannot handle this by himself."

"What should we do?"

"You both need to come see me as soon as possible, and we'll take it from there. Can you get to the mirror telescope building on campus today?"

"I think so, but—" There were several "buts," the first one being that we had both more or less vowed to never speak to each other again. But I had a feeling that Erica, if I tried to explain *that*, would slap us *both* upside the head and tell us to get over ourselves. People's lives may be at stake.

Except there was another, even bigger "but."

I'll get as far as I need to get, chip or no chip.

A shroud of dread unfolded slowly over me from head to toe. Because there might be a reason, *other* than the fight, that I hadn't seen him all day.

My father was 400 miles away physically, my mother was 400 miles away mentally, the other slaves were understandably slacking off, and I was avoiding him.

If he was going to take off, this was the best, and maybe the only, opportunity he would ever have to buy himself enough of a head start to succeed.

"Good," said Erica, whom I'd forgotten was still on the line, and who had apparently already decided that there were no "buts" acceptable. "When you get there, look for one of the volunteer guides with a name tag reading *Milagros*. She'll be expecting you."

7

HIM

At dawn, under the barest glimmers of stars, as I dumped the burner phone in the exact spot I'd planned to dump it all along, I stared up at the red-gold mountains that were at last mine to see up close and thought about how running away wasn't supposed to feel like this.

It wasn't supposed to feel like anything.

I'd never told Louisa, but this wasn't my first plan to run. Like most fifteen-year-olds, I'd been as stupid as I thought I was smart, and almost as soon as I'd won over the farm owner's wife enough for my liking, I'd started conning her into helping me slip out. Of course I'd gotten my arm nearly lopped off before the plan got very far, and I'd been thankful every day since that I had. I'd have been caught within hours, and if I were *lucky*, I'd still be at the farm. More likely, I'd be in a mine, or dead, and as terrifying as that was—yes, I admitted it, there were things that scared me, okay?—the worst part of it was that there would be no one here now to rescue Maeve.

Have you ever heard the name Resi? I'd asked Erica Muller when I'd got her on the phone.

Yes, she'd said after a pause.

And? I'd prompted. *Is there—?*

There have been whispers, she'd said. *People talking. But people always talk.*

So Maeve was right: there was something happening. But at the same time, Erica was right: there was nothing slaves loved more than talking about freedom while refusing to give up whatever minimal safety and security they'd achieved to try to get it. And the few free people who claimed to want to help us were often even worse: armchair activists who spent their days attacking their pro-slavery opponents in online forums in place of actually doing anything concrete.

Maeve was different. She'd started out a dreamer, sure, but by the time she was eleven, the last time I'd seen her, she'd already started talking more and more about rebellion. Real rebellion. She'd just been sold off and abandoned before she'd had a chance to actually rebel.

And as for me? Well. I'd studied history. I knew what happened. The successful rebellions were outnumbered ten to one by those that had ended with all the rebels' heads on pikes at the city gates. Forgotten names dying for forgotten causes, the ones you never read about in textbooks. And sure, dying for a cause is inspiring and all, but those who die for a cause are still as dead as anyone else. I would bet that even all those failed SLA bombers—Erica's friends who had gotten thrown in mines, if any were still alive—would now happily sell out all of what they once believed for one more chance to hold the people they loved, or hell, to see daylight.

So where Maeve had ideals, I had facts and figures. In fact, I'd always thought the goal of a good scientist was to be a force of pure logic, to be *above* ideals. That way, you could never be compromised. And less likely to ever be wrong.

The problem was that reality had already proven it didn't work like that. I was already compromised. My mother and Maeve had compromised me. If I hadn't cared about my mother, maybe I'd still be in Luxembourg. If I hadn't cared about Maeve, maybe I'd still be in Germany. Or maybe I would have accepted Langer's offer or someone else's. Maybe I would have gone on to become a billionaire rocket scientist under some genius's wing. Maybe in time, I would have even figured out a way to disrupt slavery for real. To free not only Maeve and whoever was trapped with her but myself and every other slave. And all because I wouldn't be hobbled by feeling anything for any of them. But maybe then, I wouldn't even care enough to try.

And, of course, if I hadn't been compromised by someone in the ten-million-dollar mansion I'd just walked away from, I would have been gone from this place hours ago. The girl who had no stake in the revolution. The girl who shouldn't care, and if by some miracle she ever did, it should be from an armchair like all those other useless so-called activists.

Instead, she did care. She cared so fucking much that it scared me. Because I didn't know what to do with that. Because I didn't understand why. Because it felt like a trap. Because no one was *supposed* to care. And because it wasn't supposed to feel like this. It wasn't supposed to feel like anything.

So I was running away to just do everything on my own, like I always did.

Except I wasn't. Instead, I was hearing Maeve's voice. A voice I heard a lot, and that I probably would have listened to a lot more often if it weren't for all the rainbow unicorn stuff.

Our lives are so shit we have to make up happy endings or we'll never get them, and here you are throwing away your chance for a real one.

So down in the valley on the other side of the pasture, the ever-distant mountains red-gold amid the rising sun, the matching college hat pulled low over my face, the entire desert laid out before me, I did what I should have done a long time ago: I listened, and cursed the fact that sometime in the past few weeks, I had become worse than compromised. I had become human.

HER

When Erica hung up, I turned to the messages. But all I needed to see was the first one from Corey before I shakily bulk-deleted the rest as if they'd been splashed with toxic waste. In the two seconds it took to read it, the idea that I'd once considered dating him had gone from embarrassing to downright sickening.

Still shaky but doing my best to shove the messages out of my mind, I headed downstairs. Erica Muller had only been my professor for a few months, but I already knew she was the type where if she said something was important, she wasn't fucking around. And I'd better not, either.

The maid was clearly aware someone had entered the kitchen, but she didn't even turn around, which meant she knew it was me and had deemed me beneath her notice. Bitch.

"Hey." I hated the way that sounded. "Turn around. I need to talk to you."

She made a big show of violently jamming the knife back into the wooden block before turning to face me, hands clasped like a good little slave, staring down at her scuffed sandals, but even a submissive pose couldn't hide her disgust as I fired off questions about a certain person's whereabouts.

"I really don't know, miss," the maid replied with that infuriating lopsided little grin of hers. As if this bitch hadn't caused enough trouble for me today, now she was deceiving me for no good reason. Was that just what slaves learned to do when they knew they'd be punished either way?

In any case, it felt familiar.

"If you're lying to me—" I didn't exactly know how to follow through with that. If you weren't willing to go for the whip, there weren't a lot of other good options, and she knew it.

"I wouldn't cover for him, miss," she said. "The fact is, he still owes *me* a few favors he hasn't repaid."

"For what?"

That lip continued upward. She was *enjoying* this. "Why, some favors I did for *him*, miss." She outright smirked, though her eyes were still trained on the marble tile. "Not that I didn't enjoy them, too."

Whore. Humiliation mixed with rage boiled over inside me. If it weren't bad enough that I might be about to lose him forever, now I had to contend with knowing *that*.

I had never hurt a slave, ever, but at that moment I was ready to slap the maid's face so hard it would leave a mark for days. And why shouldn't I? She deserved it for talking to me like—

No. I took a step back.

Look, either those days were over now, or they weren't. Either all slaves were human beings who deserved dignity and respect, or none of them were. Either I was the girl who would call her father and accuse my boy of something he hadn't done, or I wasn't.

Even if I never saw him again, *this* was what he would leave me with. This was about my soul, and ironically all because of someone who insisted he didn't believe in souls.

Instead, I breathed and looked again at the maid.

She wore two items I could vaguely recall owning once upon a time—an oversized oatmeal-colored top with the sleeves rolled up, and a pair of faded ripped jeans that had shrunken and conformed perfectly to her body over the years. Since I was curvier, they were one of the few things I'd ever given her that fit her right. No wonder she never seemed to take them off.

I thought back further. The maid had arrived when we both were around fourteen. My family still had money back then, and young, pretty slaves were a must-have status symbol—to touch or just to look at, depending on the owner's whims. My father, always with an eye toward the bottom line, had decided that a young teen would be a better investment than an older, better-trained slave, so one day, he bought the maid back from a high-end private dealer and set her in the kitchen like a gleaming new appliance: shiny, attractive, and quiet. I had never bothered to ask where she had come from before that. If I thought of her at all, it was to lazily order her around, throw her some of my old clothes, or resent her for her effortlessly smooth, dark, glossy hair, alabaster skin, and slim figure—all so unfair at a time when I had still had baby fat and braces and acne and a wild tornado of curls that I hadn't yet found the right methods to tame. In fact, at least twice, I had invited crushes over to swim, and instead, they spent the whole time trying to grope the maid. Of course, instead of blaming the boys for being disgusting creeps, I had blamed her, as if she could have done anything about it. But beyond that, I had never asked about her day, solicited her opinion, learned her story, or considered that she must have had someone she had to leave behind. It had never occurred to me that she must have things she hoped for, things she dreamed of. Just like *him*, she must have seen darkness upon darkness, must spend many nights dwelling on things that had been done to her loved ones and been done to her.

I took a deep breath. "I'm sorry."

"Excuse me, miss?" The girl looked as bewildered as I felt. The teasing lip had fallen.

"For anything I said or did, or didn't do—I just, I'm sorry. I know it doesn't make up for anything. And that you probably hate me."

"It's okay, miss. I don't hate you," she said, much to my surprise. "You've never hurt me or been mean on purpose. You were actually kind of nice to me." Then her sour expression reappeared momentarily. "Once or twice."

Okay, so we weren't exactly BFFs yet. I ran a hand continuously down one of my curls as I continued to speak. "It's just that things have changed recently, and I—"

"I know, miss," the maid said.

"You do?"

She shrugged. "Well, excuse my saying so, but you're absolutely shit at hiding it. He's better, though not nearly as good as *he* thinks he is."

I opened my mouth in a silent plea.

"Don't worry, miss." She must have seen the tears in my eyes as I ran away from the shed earlier. And she wasn't totally devoid of compassion, as much as she had the right to be. "I'm not going to tell anyone. I'm not *that* much of a bitch."

I closed my eyes.

"Also, that stuff with me and him? It all happened right after he got here. And it was never like *that*."

Just think: if I'd given in and slapped her, she wouldn't be telling me this. "He does owe you favors, though, doesn't he?"

"A few." The submissive pose was long gone now. She had crossed her arms casually, absently scratching a scab near her elbow, and for some reason, I was glad.

"Well, maybe I can take on some of his debt. What do you want?" I asked. "Um, from me. So I guess there are *some* limitations." Not that I really thought the answer would be "sex," but who knew?

"Well, I told him I wanted to see the ocean, and I wasn't kidding."

"Done," I said quickly. "Well—"

She rolled her eyes, clearly having expected to be screwed over, although perhaps not this fast.

"Not right away," I hastily clarified. "I have to finish out the school year. And, uh, get some money. But this summer we're totally going. I promise."

"I believe you," she said. "And for what it's worth, I saw him put the phone in one of the yard waste bags this morning."

"Was it still working?"

She shrugged. "And I'm fairly sure he was planning to go out the back way, through the neighbors' horse corral. After that, I have no idea. He didn't tell me," she said. "Really."

It wasn't much to go on, but it would have to do. I should have ripped that warehouse map right out of the gardener's filthy hand, but I'd been an idiot and hadn't. Nor did I have time to sneak back into my father's file cabinets and figure it out that way. Besides, even if I did figure it out, it would be too late. It might *already* be too late. If the phone was still intact, my best hope right now was that he'd left something on it that would help me trace him.

Because the only solution after *that* would be to call my father, tell him he had run, and get him to trigger his chip.

Better whipped than dead, right? I kept telling myself that.

Meanwhile, she had turned back to her work. I knew she didn't really believe me because why should a slave ever believe anything she was promised? Not to mention, what the hell were the two of *us* going to do at the beach? Slather on luminescent mineral sunscreen and commiserate about how the campus smoothie bar kept running out of organic kale?

But I hoped that didn't matter. I hoped the apology was the key. Frankly, the chances that no free person had ever apologized to her before and actually meant it weren't zero.

The garden shed was predictably empty. I sank down in the dirt, already weary, in the shadow of the four thick paper yard waste bags that had been lined up next to the shed. I pulled out my phone, aware that it was likely the last time I'd ever dial Albert Einstein—at least with any hope of him answering. Of course no vibration sounded from anywhere, and a monotone voice informed me that the number was no longer in service.

I growled and attacked the first bag, then the second, pawing through cactus stems and paloverde trimmings, their thorns piercing the delicate skin of my fingers until they were almost as bloody as his had been earlier. At last, I found it, a brick of broken plastic that I scooped up, knowing before I even brought it into the light that it was too late. The case, smashed, the guts and wire hanging open like an eviscerated animal. All of Maeve's messages, and all of mine, gone into the ether.

I sank down into the dirt, too spent even to cry. It didn't matter how long I kept the cage door open. After what I'd said—after what I'd done—the bird would never fly back.

I picked up my own phone and selected a contact robotically, knowing the only way I could get through this conversation was by dissociating from my body, and hopefully my mind, too. "Hello, Daddy? It's about the boy."

But before I could finish, a sound from behind cut me off: sneakers crunching on fallen leaves, and a tall shadow blocked out the afternoon sun. I spun around to see him standing frozen a few steps from the shed, still in his sunset-colored college hat, straightened now. His chest heaving, exhausted golden eyes darting in disbelief between my face and the broken phone in my other hand.

"Louisa? What is it? What about the boy?" My father's voice crackled through the line again.

I lowered the phone slowly, my mind making a million calculations a second.

"Loulou? Are you there?" His alarmed voice was barely audible now.

I raised the phone again. "Daddy, I ... I made a mistake," I said rapidly. "Everything's fine. The boy is fine. I'm sorry for bothering you. I gotta go. Love you." I ended the call before my father could mount any response, shoved the phone shakily into my pocket, and turned.

Even though I knew he was already gone. Again.

8

HIM

When I spotted her, crouched in the dust, hands streaked with blood and dirt and pulverized leaves, limp, sweaty curls curtaining her face, staring down at my broken phone and her intact one, exhausted and defeated, I forgot everything. That she was a spoiled brat. That she hadn't seen my side. That she'd threatened me. That she was one of *them*.

I just saw her—Louisa, *my* Louisa—lost and scared and heartbroken. And for a second, I was glad I hadn't left, even if it meant joining Erica's cause. Maeve's cause. Louisa's cause. *Anyone's* cause. Maybe as glad as I was to have once almost lost an arm.

Of course that was before I overheard who she was talking to. And about.

When I did, my entire face went up in flames, adrenaline coursing through my veins, still bleeding from the barbs. I yanked off the hat and threw it to the ground. So what if I got a sunburn? It was better than taking even a single thing from the girl I'd been stupid and weak enough to think was different. To think cared. To think considered me a fucking person.

Blinking, I raced across the lawn, vaulting over the low fence and into the neighbor's property. The horses whinnied and stamped nervously as I ran past them until something as tight as a shackle on my ankle pulled me back. I gasped and turned to see my leg had snagged on a coil of barbed wire coming loose from the fencepost. I tugged frantically, my fingers slick with sweat and panic, but the wire only dug deeper into my flesh, blood soaking through my jeans as I fumbled with the glinty barbs. And now Louisa's footsteps were pounding across the grass behind me.

"Wait!" Louisa's desperate voice floated across the yard. "Please, just listen to me!"

"Fuck." I yanked my leg again, gritting my teeth against the searing pain as the barbs ripped free, taking bits of flesh and denim with them. "Off."

"Stop! Don't move!"

She flew into the pasture, her long curls flying behind her like a white flag of parley. But when she got up close, I couldn't decide if the tears in her gray eyes were sadness or anger. They were still goddamn beautiful, though. Fuck her.

"Oh, for fuck's sake, stop *struggling*, you idiot. It's just going to make it worse."

I said nothing, heaving like a trapped, angry animal afraid to die. Louisa took a tentative step toward me, her hands raised as if to signal that she wasn't a threat. When I didn't move, she reached me and began methodically untangling the barbed wire from my clothes and skin, wincing as it tore at her own hands. "What were you thinking, trying to go through here?" she growled.

"Fuck, I don't know," I panted, my voice dripping with the combination of pain, anger, and sarcasm I prided myself on having perfected. "Maybe that I'd rather take my chances with a bit of barbed wire than stick around here, waiting for the cops to show up and cattle prod me before shoving me in the back of a van?"

"I don't know what you're talking about," she said through gritted teeth.

"You really expect me to believe that you *didn't* just call your dad and tell him I ran away?" I decided not to mention the other thing she'd threatened to report.

"Yes, I do," Louisa said with another twist of the wire, finally allowing me to free my leg with a vicious yank that tore my already raked skin, blood seeping through fresh tears in my clothes.

I stumbled to the earth, picked myself up, and brushed myself off with basically zero dignity. As if I'd ever had any. "What do you mean you do? I fucking *heard* you! And you call *me* a liar?"

"Okay," she said. "I called Daddy. But—"

"No shit you did. You always run to Daddy every chance you get, like the spoiled, selfish—"

"Shut up and let me *finish*," she growled, and if my goal was to turn her clumsy compassion back into anger, I'd succeeded. But it wasn't my goal, so I'd failed. "I was trying to save ... to save Maeve," she finished with a tight swallow. Ignoring the fresh rivulets of blood dripping down her fingers—whether mine or hers, who could tell now?—she straightened up and met my gaze.

"What?"

"Follow me," she snapped in a way that couldn't be less inviting. She swiped frantically at her eyes and left a streak of blood on her cheek, and I had the strangest urge to gently wipe it away, but instead I just petulantly shoved my bloody hands in my pockets as we made our way back through the pasture through a gamut of curious snorts and flicking tails.

Why *was* I following her, anyway? I was free. Well, free from the wire at least, and if I stayed here any longer, I'd lose the almost-zero-but-maybe-not-entirely-zero chance I had to get free for real. Not to mention that the cynical part of myself that I hated told me this could be a trap.

Spotting the hat I had thrown in the dust, she grabbed it and heaved it toward my chest. I caught it, but instead of putting it back on, I just spun it around on my finger childishly, deciding that if there was any chance Louisa knew a way to save Maeve that wasn't a suicide mission, I could afford to take a second to find out what it was. I watched her as she started around the side of the house, heading for the four-car garage with its floor-to-ceiling glass display window. She glanced back to see if I was following her, gritted her teeth, unlocked the door, and jabbed her finger toward the passenger side. "Get in the Cadillac. There's a first aid kit under your seat."

"Where are we going?" I asked.

"To my overpriced college that I'd be flunking out of if it weren't for you," she snapped. "And before you say anything, this is *not* about us or whatever happened the other day. This is for Maeve, and only Maeve, and if you give a shit about her, you'll get in the car."

"If *I* give a shit about her?" I opened the door and slumped reluctantly into the creamy leather seat of the vintage luxury car, then reached under the seat for the box full of antiseptic wipes and flimsy bandages, while she wedged herself behind the wheel. "That's fucking rich that you've now appointed yourself the undisputed expert on *my* family situation."

If we'd been behaving normally instead of like bickering arch-nemeses, I might have taken this opportunity to confess that I'd always been secretly fascinated with cars. I'd driven exactly three times in my life—each time in the south of France, where the professor had a country home, a vintage Citroën, and was pretty much constantly drunk, which provided the perfect opportunity. My mind naturally had a feel for machines and how they worked, and driving was freedom. I'd in fact enjoyed it more than—for liability purposes—I generally liked to admit enjoying anything other than sex. I'd already admired this sprawling American classic, having washed it several times and even poked around under the hood once or twice when no one was around. I might even go so far as to say that I wanted one like it someday, although, judging by the storm cloud on Louisa's face, I should've learned by now to stop wanting things. Look where it kept getting me.

"Oh, I understand the situation perfectly," she seethed, blood-streaked fingers fumbling clumsily on the seat belt as she buckled herself in. "The situation where I tried over and over again to prove that you could trust me enough to help, but you wouldn't let me. But then again, I guess *no* mere mortal could possibly understand the unfathomable depths of your vastly superior brain, the one that gives you the right to go around conning and misleading people with no consequence."

"Oh," I said. "Speaking of misleading people, aren't you afraid to get in a car with the slave who brutally violated you? You know, the one you're going to tell Daddy all about?"

Fuck, what was *wrong* with me? She'd just wrenched bits of jagged wire out of my bloody flesh by hand and was now voluntarily driving me somewhere to help my sister, and I was still too much of a stubborn fucking asshole to apologize to her. Instead, I was making it *worse*.

She started up the car with a roar, forcing herself to wrap her bloody hands around the steering wheel. If anywhere, we should've been headed to the fucking ER.

She backed out of the driveway with a lurch, then slammed her foot on the gas pedal, then the brake, sending both of us flying forward and the first aid kit smack into the dashboard, its contents spilling all over the passenger side. "Don't you understand that I *never* would have threatened to say that if you hadn't left me feeling completely humiliated?"

At the first intersection, she braked violently again, this time forcing me to brace myself with a bloody handprint on the dashboard. "*Humiliated*?" I repeated incredulously. "*You*? Before you go around claiming that, you might want to consider who you're talking to."

"Given how this conversation is going, who I'm talking to is unfortunately the last person I'd *like* to be talking to," she shot back.

"Oh, in that case, right back at you. You know, you were *so* close to having me convinced that you weren't a spiteful, vindictive brat."

"Yeah, well, you had *me* believing that you weren't a pretentious, manipulative dick!"

"Oh, but I thought this wasn't about us."

"Shut up," she growled. "Just shut up. I don't want to hear anything else out of you for the rest of the drive. And before you ask, yes, I *will* whip you this time."

"The hell you will." I leaned back in the seat defiantly. "You don't have it in you."

"Wanna bet?" She gritted her teeth and prodded the accelerator further, her eyes in tunnel vision. The car fairly leaped forward as we flew down the highway on-ramp. She stayed in the far left lane, weaving her way around slower drivers as if daring them to try to pass her.

"I'm pretty sure I've won every bet we've ever made, so, um … yeah?"

"Ha. You just fell for the gambler's fallacy!" she said, hair whipping in her face as she turned to look at me in demented triumph. "Surprise! I'm more logical than you are."

"Oh really?" I scoffed. "Because there's not a whole lot of logic in the way you're driving right now."

"Then stop fucking stressing me out! Do you *want* me to crash this car?"

"You know, at this point, I—"

"Fuck!" we both exclaimed. She'd missed her turn and overcorrected, whipping the Cadillac violently across two lanes of traffic and toward the side of a grocery delivery van. Just in time, I reached over and grabbed the wheel, veering us out of the shadow of the van driver, who angrily laid on the horn as we sped away up the exit ramp.

"Do you even *know* how to fucking drive?" I demanded.

"I do when I don't have someone in the passenger seat *screaming* at me!" She tried to get her breathing under control as we rolled off the freeway and onto University Boulevard. I was doing the same, though not as loudly. "So if you value your life, shut your goddamn mouth!"

That did the trick. I gathered up the antiseptic and bandages from under the seat and passed a handful over to her. We cleaned ourselves up as best we could, riding the rest of the way to campus in silence.

HER

If we'd been capable of communicating in any way but screaming, I would have taken the opportunity to explain that the Cadillac used to belong to my brother—one of his two most prized possessions, along with his guitar. When he left, he'd initially taken both, but in some drug-induced haze, he'd abandoned the car in a washout in the desert. The police returned it to my father, whose name was still on the title. Ethan knew where it was but hadn't been back for it. And even though the car had been mine by default for over a year, driving it still reminded me of him.

And after that, I would have explained that as soon as we stopped, I planned to call my father again but only to explain that I was bringing my boy to campus to meet a professor who was "interested in his background," which wouldn't be a lie. My plan was that my hopefully judgment-impaired father would then call the housekeeper to explain the situation, meaning we wouldn't have to worry about being missed. For a while.

As it was, though, we pulled into the campus in silence, while I gripped the steering wheel like a vise so he wouldn't see my hands shaking as I wedged the Cadillac into a spot in the top-tier parking zone that matched the sticker on the windshield I'd convinced my father to pay for as consolation for disallowing me to live on campus.

As usual, throngs of backpack-laden students trudged to class or zoomed by on bicycles. Still more swarmed in and out of the student center, juggling sandwiches and smoothies, or spread out on picnic tables or in the grass under the shadow of the lane of towering date palms standing like soldiers on either side of the campus mall. If I'd been alone, it would have been so mundane as to be beneath notice.

But with *him* next to me, it was like landing on Mars. The biggest tragedy was that I wouldn't have any idea what he was thinking, other than that I was a spiteful brat and slightly insane, which wasn't too far off the mark after *that* drive.

"Shit," I muttered without looking at him. "We've got a problem."

"Yeah, we do," he said without looking back.

One-third of the people on campus were slaves—the grounds and cleaning crews and most of the service workers. But they wore uniforms, which was helpful in letting students and faculty know from a distance that they could ignore them, abuse them, or simply shove them out of the way. Personal slaves got brought to campus, too, and allowed to stay with their owners in classrooms, sitting or kneeling as per the owner's preference, but there were rules governing their behavior, too—starting with always walking a couple of steps behind.

I sized him up out of the corner of my eye. If only he hadn't tangled with the wire fence. In his college hat, T-shirt, and jeans with rips in the leg that could almost pass for deliberate, he'd otherwise be indistinguishable from the crowd of other college boys milling around, except for one thing, of course. We'd either have to hide it and pray no one noticed, or show it, have him behave the same as every other slave on campus and pray he didn't slip up. Sure, there were a few Erica Muller-type radicals, but there were far more rich snobs coasting through college on their parents' dime, and if some pro-slavery asshole caught on and made a scene, we were fucked no matter what.

Hiding it would be easier. I threw open the trunk of the Cadillac and scanned the space until I found a potential solution balled up in the corner: an old denim jacket of Ethan's, with a shearling wool lining. It had at one point been luxe-looking, though it was now stiff and wrinkled. I tossed it at him. "Here."

"Do you know how hot I'm going to get walking around in this?" He glanced at the jacket warily, then up at the sun.

"Yeah, well, tough shit," I said. "It's either that or play the good slave. I don't care either way, but it will cost us time that I don't think *you* want to waste."

We glared at each other until he gave in, shook it out, and slipped it on. Immediately, my face flushed rose-red. God, those broad shoulders looked *incredible* in clothes, the few times anyone gave him anything decent to wear. And now all I could think about was ripping the damn thing off him. I jerked my head away before he noticed. *Not now.*

And anyway, he was already halfway down the sidewalk.

"Hey, it's—what are you doing?" I exclaimed, chasing after him. "You're going in completely the wrong direction."

"Maybe it would help if you actually *told* me where we're going."

"Maybe it would help if you'd listen to anything I said!"

He crossed his arms impatiently. "Well?"

"The Harris Mirror Lab," I said. "To meet someone named Milagros."

To my shock, his whole expression transformed. "Wait. Mirror lab? As in the mirror telescope? The *Zenith* telescope?"

"Yeah, it's made out of liquid—"

"Liquid mercury in a paraboloid shape. Yeah, I know," he continued eagerly. "It's the biggest in the world outside of the Himalayas. They're now testing the same technology in microgravity to see if they can build one like it in a crater on the moon. Hell, when I started researching Phoenix, it was the only thing about this place that sounded halfway interesting."

If I weren't still so angry, I might have actually smiled at how his eyes were glimmering like the binary stars of Sirius. Instead, all I asked was, "Is it still?"

He opened his mouth, but before he could answer, I spotted a figure frantically waving from the other side of the mall, long platinum-blond hair unmistakable.

I groaned. "Shit. It's Juliette."

"Oh, great. Is it safe to assume she's a typical friend of yours?" *A rich, slave-abusing jerk,* was what he meant.

"She's one of the better ones, though I know that doesn't mean much to you after the examples I've provided. Also, she knows who you are. Well, *what* you are."

"Thanks for that."

"But she's also a girl, so just flash her a smile and she won't ask too many questions."

"Oh, that's the plan, believe me," he said, watching Juliette trot toward us across the lawn.

I rolled my eyes. "Isn't it always?"

"Hey, I—"

"Hey," said Juliette, blissfully interrupting our sniping. We both said "hey" back. But only one of us, when he smiled at her, made Juliette flush, stumble over her words, and completely forget to demand what the hell was going on. "What—what have you heard from Corey?" she finally asked me. Her tone was concerned.

"Nothing repeatable," I said grimly. I'd almost forgotten the vile message I'd received from him this morning, with everything else going on. Of course it had made me momentarily ill to see such disgusting things written about me by someone I used to consider a friend. I'd blocked him immediately and decided not to tell my boy, even though he'd been mentioned in it, too.

As for Juliette, she might not know precisely what the problem was with Corey, but she probably had her suspicions. After all, she had just fallen into a pair of amber-gold eyes and barely made it out alive. "The last time I saw him, he was stumbling out of yet another bar on University with some sketchy characters I'd never seen before. Then he sent me a message today. Tomorrow is his party, by the way. I hope you don't mind that I gave him your regrets."

"Not at all."

"Then I got his response."

I felt as ill as Juliette looked. "I don't want to read it, do I?"

"I wouldn't. It was really disgusting, Lou. I'm not telling you this to cause drama. I just want to warn you." She glanced quickly at him again. "Both of you."

So it wasn't just a suspicion then. Shit. This needed to be addressed. But so did a lot of things, and I wasn't even sure where to start with most of them. In the end, I just thanked Juliette and told her we'd catch up soon. We both knew it was a lie.

"And to think I was planning to leave without even saying a proper goodbye to my old buddy Corey," he said carefully after we left Juliette and bounded up the stairs of the mirror lab. "How insensitive of me. Poor guy sounds devastated."

"Yeah, sounds like he's really weeping into his beer," I replied just as carefully as he pushed open the door.

"Can I help you?" interrupted the balding male volunteer behind the front desk. A question I had noted was rarely offered with any intention of helping.

In a second, I saw the problem.

His haste to gape in wonder at the ten-meter-long disc of rippling liquid mercury suspended on the wall was understandable. However, entering the building, he had inadvertently pushed up the sleeves of his jacket. I couldn't blame him, since he must have been boiling after the rapid walk across campus in the blazing sun. But the world *could* blame him, of course, and did.

"What are you doing?" I hissed. I pushed his arm down, which was totally pointless since it had already been seen, and the fact that I was so freely touching him would just get us in more trouble. Would the guy kick us out? Would he call the campus police? Would it get to my *father*? Panic settled quickly in. I could see it on his face, too. Right now, it was looking like our best shot was to make a break for it. But then what about—

"I'll deal with this, Teague," broke in a woman with petite, delicate features, freckly ocher skin, and tousled hair dyed in cotton-candy streaks of aqua and electric blue.

Milagros—so her name tag said—continued to stare at Teague politely but pointedly until he disappeared into the back office as if he'd never been there. She waited to speak until he had closed the door. "I used to do that, too, when I got distracted," she said, nodding toward his wrist. "My neighbor used to take me to campus with her, but she threatened to stop if I couldn't learn to hide it better. But I just wanted to go to the planetarium to learn about black holes and quasars, and I didn't care whether anyone knew I was a slave. To me, it was easier *not* to hide it. She wanted me to be her equal, and I didn't know how."

Well, *that* got his attention away from the telescope.

Normally, the last thing a former slave would ever bring up in conversation was *being* a former slave—that's why I hadn't met many of them, at least knowingly. *Blend in and keep quiet* was the name of their game. In fact, of all the things Milagros could have turned out to be, that hadn't even been on the list. Maybe it had been on his, though.

"In the end, she had the right idea, though," Milagros continued.

"Why?" he spoke freely now, his attention riveted.

"Because I'm now a graduate student in astronomy. And she's now my wife."

For the first time in over forty-eight hours, he and I met each other's eyes in something other than white-hot rage.

"Your wife?" I asked.

Milagros nodded serenely. "Erica Muller."

9

HIM

"We had four years together—in secret—before Erica's family moved and I got sold," Milagros explained during the four-block walk between the campus and Erica's and her house. She'd said it was the safest place to discuss what we had come to discuss. "My owners only spoke Spanish at home, so not only was I illiterate, I couldn't speak English, either. Erica taught me everything—I taught her Spanish, too—and they allowed it, as long as she didn't take up too much of my time. When you're both girls, nobody really worries that you might fall in love. They just thought she saw me as a charity case, you know?"

But, she explained, Erica's father's job transferred him back East and Milagros' owners lost a fortune in the recent recession, and—despite Erica's fruitless pleas to her own family to buy her—sold her off cheaply to a service that sent teams of slaves to do housekeeping for lower-income families who couldn't afford their own.

"I probably don't need to go into detail about what it was like," she said, looking at me meaningfully.

No, she sure didn't.

Erica, she explained, distraught at having had to let the love of her life go, fought back the only way she could—by joining the SLA, which at the time had been infiltrated by a faction that saw violence as the only way forward. But their plan to blow up every police car in the state failed, of course, and many of Erica's old associates were tracked down, convicted, and made slaves themselves, sent to toil in mines, farms, and factories. Everyone else went underground. Erica and Milagros kept in touch—for five years—over the same communication network that Maeve and her brother had used.

"She kept telling me she'd come for me," Milagros said. "I believed her, but she was a wanted fugitive, and I couldn't let her put herself in more danger for me. I don't know which of us spent more sleepless nights." Their luck, so to speak, changed when Milagros had been injured on the job and sent, much like me, to a discount auction, for a reserve price that Erica could almost afford. One of the richer remaining members of the SLA put up the rest of the money and found a proxy buyer to close the sale. Milagros was soon freed—but they'd had to spend another full year in hiding, together, before Erica's family lawyer managed to convince a court to drop the terrorism charges in exchange for turning herself in, pleading guilty to a lesser charge of vandalism, and paying a fine. "And here we are, right where we started—the campus science department," finished Milagros. "And soon, I'll become Dr. María de los Milagros de Ulloa y de la Torre-Giralt-Muller, partially after the Spanish explorer who discovered Ulloa's ring, but mostly because I'm amused by the idea of some pompous dean having to read all of that out loud at the graduation ceremony."

Objectively, I found this last fact hilarious, but in reality, I barely heard it. Because at some point in the last hour, I had realized I wasn't angry anymore. Not at Louisa, anyway. Maybe it was her genuine panic near the telescope when it looked like we were in trouble, grabbing my arm without a thought. Maybe it was my guilt over the fact that the biggest asshole I knew was now terrorizing her with literal death threats, which I blamed myself for—and which wasn't totally off, given that Corey apparently held me personally responsible for ruining his life, instead of just, you know, looking in the fucking mirror. Maybe it was that even if I technically hadn't lied to her, it didn't fucking matter because she still felt betrayed. Or maybe it was the fact I *knew* she hadn't reported me to her father and never would. I'd known it the whole goddamn time, really. But like the stupid, stubborn, arrogant motherfucker I was—as stupid as I'd been at fifteen—I *still* couldn't apologize. Couldn't admit I was wrong.

Because if I was wrong, I didn't have shit. The only thing that had ever made me special—the only thing that had ever made my sad, pathetic life worth a damn, in my own eyes or anyone else's—was being *right*. Was being smarter and cleverer and wittier and *better* than everyone else, even if they never acknowledged it. My childhood had taught me that, and my teen years with the old professor had cemented it.

Although now, I was kind of *glad* to be wrong. About Louisa's betrayal, anyway. But only that.

Anyway, much as I enjoyed being in a car, the idea of actually walking somewhere had me even more captivated. Since I'd arrived, my only trips out had been shopping with the housekeeper, to vast retail parks full of big-box stores and fast-food chains, only making me long for the compact, narrow streets of European cities. There, being sent on solo errands meant stealing time to explore the city. Here, it seemed like you had to drive for twenty minutes to get anywhere, and even then it was nowhere worth seeing—except for the mountains, but they never seemed to move any closer. *This*, however, could pass for a proper city, with its narrow sidewalks and bicycle lanes connecting artisan bakeries and art galleries.

But I didn't have the wherewithal to care. I was too busy figuring out how to stop the girl in front of me—whose hair and eyes had turned a misty rose, reflecting and refracting the low sun in the shop windows—from drifting out of my reach for good. It wasn't helping that she jerked away every time I came near. Society not allowing me to touch her was bad enough. *Her* not allowing me to touch her was an infinitely more painful kind of torture.

Even worse, here Milagros was bouncing along beside us, joyfully emphasizing that sometimes it works out, with no way of knowing that I'd already made such a mess of everything that she might as well have added, *except not for you, you irredeemable fuckup.*

"Do you speak Spanish?" Milagros asked me as she led us up the walk to a one-story white adobe house set on a quiet side street, the landscaping in its front yard a curated riot of cactuses and palms and a wrought-iron iguana.

"I'm still learning it," I finally said, like it was embarrassing to speak only four languages instead of five.

"Miracles," chimed Louisa suddenly, just loud enough for me to hear.

I turned away, pretending to be fascinated with the fishtail cactuses by the steps.

"Your name means 'miracles,'" she added as Milagros opened the door.

HER

The deceptively large house felt like a living, breathing organism, dense with lush and growing things. Pots hung from every conceivable space on the ceiling, bursting over with stringy vines of all shapes. Umbrella and bird-of-paradise trees curled up from urns on the floor, competing for space with jumbled Southwestern art and towering bookshelves. The airy, sunny indoors flowed into the outdoors, with swings and hammocks among the white upholstered chairs, in whites and tans and other neutrals. The very air felt infused with oxygen.

Out of the corner of my eye, I observed him watching the room out of the corner of *his* eye. Even here, in Erica Muller's house, probably the safest space for a slave for 200 miles, he still couldn't drop his armor. After throwing off the denim jacket, he hovered right inside the door, scanning the place like a computer. I knew by now what he was doing—taking in data on everything and everyone, trying to figure out what he was and wasn't allowed to do. It was a skill he'd had to hone over many hard years. Milagros helpfully took the jacket and opened a bottle of wine, which seemed to help him relax. And fuck, he *deserved* to relax. Nobody should have to spend their whole life having to guard against somebody jumping out and punishing them simply for existing.

His gaze, which I wasn't supposed to be returning, said all of that, and more, and before carefully following Milagros into the kitchen, I looked away, blushing, reminded of our first few encounters when eye contact was a sinful treat to be stolen, squirreled away, and devoured in secret.

"If I were you, I'd need a drink after that," said Milagros, possibly having noticed that he had also stolen a glance at the impressive wine rack. "It's before five, so Erica wouldn't approve," she said lightly. "But she doesn't own me."

I could swear I heard sarcastic laughter from the other room.

"You guys seem to have some kind of weird reciprocal stigmata going," Milagros said, looking back and forth to the similar puncture wounds on our hands, which had almost stopped bleeding at this point. "I don't know if it's a religious thing, a sex thing, or what. I won't pry. By the way, I hope you don't mind Spanish white."

"Verdejo?" he asked.

"Sí."

Really? For someone who claimed not to speak Spanish, he seemed to be doing okay. His eyes were also now popping over the floor-to-ceiling bookshelves, especially Milagros' collection of astronomy books. Then I followed his gaze to the piano. Was I dreaming? Was this really going to happen right now?

"It's been a while, but may I?" he asked, all scrupulously polite as if he still expected to get his hand slapped, even here.

"Mi casa es tu casa," said Milagros.

"Gracias."

Milagros was looking at him skeptically now.

"What?" he said. "I said I was learning Spanish. I learn fast." He put his glass down, sat on the bench, and in an instant, had a gorgeous-sounding jazz arpeggio pouring out of the keys. "Sorry, I'm kind of rusty," he explained over his shoulder.

"They say science and music use the same part of the brain," remarked Milagros idly as he kept playing, a clever, complicated jazz arrangement that I, miraculously, recognized.

And that was because it was "Stardust." One of the tracks he'd played for me during that mostly futile but desperately cute jazz appreciation crash course he'd put me through, without ever mentioning that *he* could play just as well as anyone we'd listened to. For a second, I stood there with my mouth open. What the fuck? Where? How? And what would I have to do, who would I have to pray to, what would I have to sacrifice, to be able to stay here forever, listening to him play that over and over again? Because if I could, I was pretty sure nothing would ever be wrong again.

"If you don't mind my asking," I asked Milagros after she jolted me back down to earth to accept a glass of wine in my awkwardly bandaged-up hand. "How was it? After you were together, I mean."

"Awful," said Milagros, probably expecting the shock on both of our faces.

"Oh." Scratch the thing about the sacrifice.

"We fought all the time. Given that I just got out of slavery, it should come as no surprise that I was constantly accusing her of being controlling. But I was just as hard to take. I was like a rebellious teenager sometimes, testing the limits. But deep down I was just scared of losing her. After all, she let me go once, and I couldn't bear the thought of it happening again."

"Same here," called Erica from the other room. I stretched my neck to see where she was seated, which appeared to be a wrought-iron patio table strewn with papers, scrolling on a laptop. Behind her, doors opened to reveal a white brick wall covered in overgrown leaves and vines, walling off a garden that looked like it could have contained a deck and maybe even a swimming pool, tiny as it was.

Erica rose from the table and entered the kitchen, eschewing the wine and pouring herself a glass of lemon-infused water. "She had the world at her doorstep for the first time in her life. Why would she stay with me when not only was I a fugitive who was keeping her from the free life she deserved, but I'd already abandoned her for the five years when she needed me the most? Worse, I knew that if I tried to force her to stay, I'd be as bad as her former owners. After all, I *had* been complicit. My family owned slaves, too."

"But the great thing is, even though she came from them, she *wasn't* them," said Milagros, shooting Erica an unmistakably loving gaze. "She learned and grew and changed. She had a pilgrim soul."

"So did you, you know," chimed in Erica again matter-of-factly. "And I hate to interrupt couples' therapy, but I think—among other things—I just found out what happened to your former gardener."

HIM

Pilgrim soul. I didn't believe in souls—or pilgrims, for that matter—and yet I thought about that phrase as I surreptitiously watched Louisa chew on a curl, observed purple hummingbirds flicker between the flowering vines, and tried to shake off the weirdness of drinking wine at a table with three free women. Oddly enough, it was the second time in my life I'd been invited to do that, but it was the first time I'd done it without being ordered to, and without the women in question clearly being more interested in tasting *me* than what was in their glasses.

For a wide variety of reasons, I decided that likely wasn't the case here. Which was why I could still devote part of my mental energy to figuring out where I'd heard *pilgrim soul.* It was probably in one of the dense volumes the professor had ordered me to plow through after he was satisfied that my literacy was up to par—and that usually only left me longing for chemistry and physics again. Either the Bible or Shakespeare, I decided. Didn't that account for like half of English literature?

"According to this, he's no longer a slave," Erica said.

"The *gardener*?" I practically spat out a mouthful of Spanish wine, much as I hated to waste it. "Are you fucking kidding me? Someone freed that disgusting psychopath? Unbelievable. Well, it's official. There's no justice in this world." But as outraged as I was, it was worse to watch Louisa shudder to think of the man who had taken delight in terrorizing her—for years, from what I'd gathered—unleashed on the free world. And to not be able to do anything to ease her worry.

"Well, to be fair, I don't know if he was freed, necessarily," said Erica calmly. "He's just no longer being actively tracked by the slave database."

"Wait a minute," I said. "Does it say 'location unknown'? Like my sister?"

Erica peered at the screen. "As a matter of fact, it does." She looked back at me. "You said you thought they might be physically removing the microchips, which is a solid theory, given what we know about the girl found in the desert here—according to my well-placed source in the medical examiner's office, the injuries to her arms and back would be consistent with trying to locate a chip. By the way, do you have the bracelet?"

I'd told Erica about Maeve's bloody bracelet over the phone, but I hoped she wouldn't make me produce it again. It had been bad enough to have to show both Max *and* Louisa. I knew the hope was in vain. I'd examined it a little since then because I had to, though it made me sick to look at. But so far, it was the best physical "evidence" we had. I produced it from my pocket and placed it in the center of the table. Exhibit A.

Erica leaned forward, her eyes narrowing as she examined the bracelet closely. "Look at this," she murmured, fingers tracing the grooves, unflinching. She wasn't like Louisa, I realized. In her years in the underground, she'd seen worse, no doubt. "The blood ... it's somewhat fresh, isn't it? This wasn't done with surgical precision but in haste." She lowered her voice slightly. "Possibly during a struggle."

I turned to her sharply. "Is she—"

"I think she's still alive," she said quickly, and I believed her. I had no doubt that sparing my feelings was fairly low down on her list of priorities, if it was there at all. "The fact that this was done hastily suggests they were interrupted or rushed."

Louisa still looked concerned, though she didn't say anything.

"They wouldn't need to hurry if she weren't alive to resist," I explained cautiously. "And believe me, Maeve, for someone who loves fairies and unicorns so much, is a hell of a fighter when she wants to be."

"But we do need to act," broke in Erica. "This kind of violence, it escalates. We don't have much time if we're going to get to her before ..." Her voice trailed off. All right, so maybe my feelings weren't *totally* unimportant to her. "Anyway, to regrettably bring us back to the gardener, if it's the same people, it's not unreasonable to think they might have given *him* a similar treatment."

"Well, if that's the case, at least we can take comfort in the fact that he suffered horribly," I remarked, hoping the dark humor might coax a smile out of Louisa as if it could possibly be that easy. "Wait," I said. "Who was his last owner? Please say Max Langer."

"I hate to disappoint you, but it wasn't a 'who.' It was a 'what,'" said Erica.

"Damn," I said wistfully. "I thought we had him."

"Specifically, a company that doesn't seem to exist anywhere. Except for one place."

"Where?" I asked.

"Here." She turned the screen to face us.

"Two-eleven Cholla Avenue?" Louisa read aloud. "Whose address is that?"

"According to real estate records, up until his death, it belonged to one Gerhard Langer."

"Max's father?" she asked.

Erica nodded.

"Oh, fuck yes," I exclaimed.

Milagros smiled from behind her wine glass.

"For what it's worth, many of us in the abolitionist community have also been suspicious of Max Langer for some time."

"Really?"

Erica pressed her lips into a firm line. "Let's put it this way. He wouldn't be the first corporate bigwig to loudly espouse progressive values while secretly undermining them at every opportunity," she explained. "Now about that warehouse that was transferred to your father."

Louisa slumped low in her chair in shame.

"It doesn't mean he's involved," I said quickly.

Louisa's eyes immediately snapped toward me. *What?*

"He's a slave owner," said Erica. "That's not meant to be a reflection on you, Louisa, but it puts him under suspicion."

"Not necessarily," I spoke up. Louisa was still gazing at me, lips parted in unconsciously sexy surprise, and it made me suddenly frantic to keep her attention. As if I'd lured a shy chipmunk out of her burrow and was now desperately throwing out nuts and seeds in her path to win her over before she scurried out of my reach again. Even if one of the seeds had to be defending the guy who owned me, whipped me, and granted me roughly the same level of personhood as his programmable kitchen appliances. "That is to say, um—what's to prevent Langer from lying to him about what's going on? Maybe Langer thinks that with all his debts, he's so desperate for a big score that he won't look that closely at what his partner's really doing."

Both women looked skeptical.

Erica cleared her throat. "Look, Louisa, I know he's your father, and you love him, but—"

"This isn't up for debate," I cut her off. "I know Louisa, and she knows her dad. If she says he's not involved, I believe her."

The girl across from me was still hunched low in her chair as if she were in a plane that had been nosediving into some mountains—but someone had just pulled up on the throttle.

Keep going, keep going, keep going.

"Besides," I continued more energetically. "If Langer bought the gardener, he owns at least one slave, so at the very least, he's a liar and a hypocrite. It's not much of a stretch to think he's not being honest with her dad, either."

If you'd only bothered to ask, I could have told you that.

Of course Louisa could have told me that. The problem was that a week ago, I wouldn't have believed it. I believed it now.

Erica, for her part, looked from me to Louisa—two equally determined expressions daring her to disagree—and reluctantly gave in. "Well, we don't have any substantial proof that he's involved, so for now, we'll operate under the assumption that he's not."

Louisa heaved a sigh of relief.

"However, I'll have you note that any slave can be looked up by typing in their number, which you know. What you may not know—because the pro-slavery lobby doesn't want you to—is that there's a reverse lookup, where you type in the owner's name and it gives you a list of which slaves, if any, they own. And I'm afraid Max Langer isn't listed in that database. Either personally, or through any of his companies. However."

"However?" Louisa asked. She was leaning forward now. But she wasn't looking at Erica. She was looking at me in an almost normal way.

"However," Erica continued in a tone that would have sounded at home in her lecture hall. "We've known for some time that people with the means set up shell companies offshore and purchase slaves using those. That way, the owners won't be publicly associated with slavery when doing business in places where it isn't legal or popular. So the fact that he isn't in the database isn't the final word. But of course, those accounts are untraceable, so for now, we've hit a wall there."

"What about this Resi that my sister mentioned?" I pressed on. "The one she claims is going to free us all? You said you found something on her, too?"

"I'm getting to that," Erica replied. "You told me you zeroed in on Langer because he and some of his executives were in Brussels when your sister went missing. I contacted one of my colleagues in Europe to comb through some news items from around the same date, and I'm going to show you what he sent over. Let's see if the same thing jumps out at you that did at him."

I scanned the screen. "Tresa Hahn," I said finally. "Felony sexual assault and soliciting a minor."

"Tresa?" Louisa asked.

"It's German," I explained. "Resi is a nickname." I sighed. "I *knew* it sounded too good to be true. Turns out Maeve's valiant rebel leader is actually a sexual predator."

"You'd be surprised at how often that turns out to be the case," remarked Milagros.

"The case never went to trial, let alone made headlines," Erica went on. "She paid a fine and left the country a week later. Somebody pulled some major strings for her. You probably don't need three guesses as to who. However, what's even more interesting is the home address she listed on the police report."

"Two-eleven Cholla," I said. "Same as the late, unlamented Gerhard Langer."

Erica nodded. "My guess is that if your sister is anywhere, it's *not* at the warehouse. It's at that address. The warehouse may just be another stage in whatever the grand plan is."

"Grand plan? So you think Resi is actually working with Langer? Why would she have helped Maeve and the other girls, in that case? Unless that's also part of the grand plan?"

"Will you two stop saying 'grand plan?'" demanded Louisa. "We don't even know if there *is* a grand plan."

"Oh, there's a grand plan, all right," I said confidently.

"Your guess is as good as mine as to why she helped them, or at least let them think she was helping them," continued Erica.

"So you think there's no rebellion in the works? Maeve was lied to?"

"I didn't say that," said Erica neutrally. "But we'll know more once we check."

"Check? We?" I asked.

Erica rolled her eyes. "Yes, we. *That's* what I was going to explain on the phone before you went off all half-cocked, if you'll forgive the expression."

Milagros, who so far had mostly observed, turned to Louisa with a thoughtful sip of her wine. "Your boy here seems to have a real problem with accepting help," she said.

"He's not mine," Louisa said automatically.

That didn't sound good.

"He's his own."

That sounded okay, actually.

Erica continued, "If you'd stayed on the line long enough, I would have told you we have people who specialize in these kinds of things. Free people, who have better methods available to them than those available to you and your sister," she said. "Such as running away and going into permanent hiding." She peered critically over her glasses.

"I don't recommend life on the run," Milagros remarked. "It may sound glamorous, but you can only dye your hair in a gas station sink so many times before it loses whatever appeal it once had."

Erica continued, "If we can locate her, we can get her somewhere safe where you can still see her. In the best-case scenario, we work with lawyers who might even be able to prove that she was freed. Either way, no one will hurt her again. You have my word."

It all sounded incredible. Better than I ever could have hoped for, frankly, and more help than I ever expected to be offered.

I turned to Erica and took a deep breath. "I appreciate everything you're offering. More than I can say. And the information. But actually saving her is something I have to do myself. Maeve is my sister. I tracked her this far, and I'm the one who needs to find her."

Erica sighed, exasperated. "I don't know how else to put it, but this isn't about your pride. We're talking about your sister's safety. Her life."

"I know that better than anyone." Selfish, ungrateful bastard. I'd be lucky if Erica didn't snatch the wine out of my hand and kick me over the back fence. But I didn't stop. "Which is why I can't just sit back and let someone else handle it, no matter how capable they might be." I pushed back my chair. "Look. I need to be the one to look her in the eyes and tell her she's safe now. That I'm here for her, and that I'll always be here for her. I failed her once before. And I can't—I won't—let it happen again."

Milagros, however, looked at Erica with an expression only the two of them understood. She placed a gentle hand on my arm. "This isn't just about Maeve, though, is it? It's about you too."

"Well—"

"No one's saying you can't be involved," Milagros continued. "But let Erica and her team help. They have resources and experience that could make—"

"I think I can explain," said Louisa.

Three heads turned to look at her instantly.

"Look, Erica, I know you're the expert on this stuff," she continued with a quiver of stage fright in her voice that reminded me why I was the supposed actor and not her, "and I'm just an ignorant college girl. Before I met *him*, the most rebellious thing I ever did was skip school to go stand in line at a designer sample sale. I-I don't know what all this might involve, or what we'll need to do. And I know that just by allowing us to be here at all, let alone helping us, we already owe you more than we could ever repay. But this is something he's got to see through—for Maeve, yeah, but also for himself. The weight he's carrying around since he lost her—it's heavy. It's really—" She paused to suck in a delicate breath, her shoulders shaking. I mean, knowing her, it didn't surprise me that she was crying. But it did kind of surprise me that she was crying right *now*. Okay, maybe that didn't surprise me, either. But I did wonder why it seemed to be suddenly coming from someplace very personal, and I did feel like shit for not being able to comfort her. But I didn't dare. Not yet. "It's really heavy. I'm sorry." She looked up like she was afraid Erica was going to kick *her*.

But she didn't. Instead, she nodded. "I completely understand," she said.

"You do?" Louisa squeaked in surprise.

"I do, and I'm sorry. I was blinded by my own privilege. I wasn't listening."

I pushed back my chair and stood. "Lou, can I talk to you in the kitchen?"

HER

"I shouldn't have said anything," I said immediately, thinking he was about to scold me.

As if he weren't always the one *getting* scolded by everyone. "I'm sorry," I said. "I didn't mean to say—"

"It's not that," he interrupted. "I'm glad you did. It's just—why are you here?"

At some point in the last hour, I realized I wasn't angry anymore. It wasn't about him coming back. It wasn't about him sticking up for my father. It wasn't about whether he meant what he'd said. Though whatever his other opinions on the man might be, I suspected he did. It wasn't even that when I heard him talk about his sister like that, I suddenly understood everything he'd done for her and why.

It was about the fact that he was trying. And now—if I couldn't make it right, if I couldn't put the shattered smithereens of whatever we'd had back together again—I could at least try, too.

Too bad it was looking like I'd fucked it up. Again. "What?"

He stood there, in the shelter of the trailing vines hanging from wicker baskets, speaking in a slow, dark voice. "Seriously, Lou, *why are you here?*"

I hadn't been expecting that. Ridiculously, I felt embarrassed. Denuded. Disarmed. Like maybe I *shouldn't* be here. "I ... I thought it was obvious?"

"No, it's not obvious," he said, absently fingering the heart-shaped leaf of a curious philodendron vine that had drifted in front of him. "And here's why. My mother was raped and left to die. My sister was abused. Their innocence was stolen. They didn't get to be children. They weren't even considered people. Their lives were thrown away like garbage, and I couldn't stop any of it," he said. "Meanwhile, you had the opposite. Everything in this world was designed to make your life a fairy tale. From your birthday cakes to your prom dresses to your college education to your fucking furry pink pillows, as much as I hate to bring *those* up again."

I opened my mouth, but he cut me off.

"Which you could be lying on right now, doing your nails or something. But you're not. You're *here*. You're in the last place in the world you have to be, and it could ruin your life if anyone knew why. And none of this is an excuse for why I said what I said, or why I did what I did, and after this, I'm going to start apologizing like a motherfucker the way I should have done two days ago, but for now, I'm just saying this so maybe you can help me understand the crazy question that keeps running through my head. The one I can't get over. *Why are you here?*"

He flicked away the vine in frustration. And the hand in the hair; I knew that was coming. And I also knew this wasn't rhetorical. He was genuinely demanding an answer. He looked baffled, almost stricken, trying to comprehend that one scientific equation that just didn't compute, no matter how many hundreds of different ways he tried to write it out so it did.

"I don't know," I said, shaking my head. "I just am." Which was true, although it wasn't the whole story about why I was here, or why I'd been crying in front of Erica. "Does everything have to make sense?"

"Yes," he insisted. "Everything does."

"Oh, please." But I knew he meant it. And my tutor couldn't be argued with when he got like this. When he found a problem that needed solving, nobody was allowed to give up until it was solved. I'd learned that the hard way.

"No, I'm serious," he continued. "According to science, everything has to make sense, and if anything doesn't, it's only because we don't yet know the exact theories that explain it. But that doesn't mean they don't exist," he finished. "Someday, when you're a doctor and someone is suddenly healed and they claim it was a miracle, are you just going to take that at face value?"

"Well," I said thoughtfully. "Yes."

"Oh, *come on.*" He turned away in exasperation as if this personally offended him. "Slow learner, have I taught you nothing? You're an intelligent person, Lou. How could you possibly—"

"But I would, okay?" I interrupted. "There *are* things that can't be explained by science or anything else, and I'm not going to stand here and try to explain them because *they can't be explained*. Hell, maybe science *is* a miracle. Or maybe miracles are just another kind of science. But it's not your job, or my job, or anyone's job, to have it all figured out this second, as much as we would like it to be. And fuck, if you want to talk about logic, why do you think it doesn't make sense that I'm here?"

"I don't know," he said. "Maybe because it doesn't make sense that you're here?!"

I sighed. "See, there you go. The gambler's fallacy again. As smart as you are, you keep falling for it."

There was a bit of curiosity on his face now, amid the confusion. "What do you mean?"

"Look, as humans, we all want things to make sense, so we invent patterns where none exist. We convince ourselves that past events affect the probability of future events, even when they don't. Like thinking that just because you've lost the last five hands, you'll keep losing," I said. "In other words, just because nobody was ever here before doesn't mean nobody was ever going to be."

He swallowed, obviously thinking about it in a way he hadn't in the car, given that we'd both been watching our lives flash before our eyes.

"Okay. Okay, but—" He didn't finish his sentence, and I was close enough now to see that the sleek muscles in his neck were taut, shoulders and chest moving up and down arrhythmically; the whites showing around his beautiful eyes. Strayed far from home, into territory he didn't understand. But he was trying. Oh, he was trying so *hard*.

"Because, listen," I continued, my voice gentler. "You think there has to be a reason for everything. I know you, and I know how you are, and that's fair. But I think that *you* think, like the gambler you are deep down, that the reason is secretly because I want to own you.

Because with people in your past, that's *been* the reason. That they want to punish you or control you or hurt you, which would in turn leave your sister hurt. And I fucked up because I made you think that I did want to do those things. But I don't. And I know I don't. I didn't know it before, but now I do. And I'm sorry, and now I guess it's my turn to make a whole fucking embarrassing apology speech."

"You don't—"

"Yes, I do. I'm apologizing because I was wrong. Too."

He actually smiled at that.

"Anyway, that doesn't answer your question because that's not the reason I'm here. And I may not know what the reason is, or maybe neither one of us is ready to hear it, but I do know this. Yes, you stupid fucking idiot, I want you. But I would never *ever* want you like that. And that's why you get to fuck up. You get to fuck up with me. You get to be a complete fucking dick in every way imaginable, rather like you were today, *and I am not going to punish you.*"

"You're not?"

"No. I'm going to get angry, of course. I'm going to scream and yell and call you a stupid idiot and tell you to get your fucking act together, but I am never going to punish you, trap you, or cage you. Because I'm not your owner. And I never will be. And I never *could* be. And if I ever try to be, call me the fuck out on it, okay? Because the only way I ever could own you, *you* could own me just as much."

His voice was shaky when he finally got out a complete sentence. "The world doesn't say that."

"Fuck the world. I'm saying it. Okay?"

"Okay."

"Now kiss me."

A smile, at last. "Is that an order?"

"You're damn right it is."

Laughter. Actual laughter. "Do I have to call you out on this one?"

"Nah, I'm calling mys—"

"Good enough." His kiss cut me off. I melted into it, never so grateful to be able to finally stop talking.

His relief matched mine. I could feel it in the way every muscle of my body seemed to uncoil as he clutched me. It took only seconds for his mouth to be everywhere, pressing behind my ear, tonguing my throat, nibbling on the upper part of my spine, and for his hands to be up completely under my bra, straining at the elastic, not even yet having *reached* my nipples, and yet still sending every follicle of skin leaping to attention after having been asleep for days. And the happily tearful, quivering wetness between my thighs only echoed it all.

"You make one hot detective, by the way," I whispered in his ear, fingers tugging gently at the strands of golden silk brushing his neck.

"So do you," he whispered back. "Do you know what I would do to you right now if we weren't in your professor's kitchen?"

Just as I was about to tell him to go ahead and do it anyway, a gentle knock on the doorframe prompted us to separate immediately because dammit, habits were hard to break.

"Hey, it's been half an hour. Have you guys made up yet?" Milagros popped her head in, looking from one flushed, well-kissed face to the other. "Okay, that's a yes. So can I interest you in a taco, a joint, or both?"

We exchanged glances. "I've never—" he began.

"Had a taco?" Milagros supplied.

"How did you know?"

"Wild guess," she said, patting him on the shoulder. "Well, you're in for a mind-altering experience."

10

HER

"So the consensus is that there are no safe choices," he said. "Either I stay and Maeve is in danger, or I go and we're *both* in danger."

He was stroking a very satisfied black long-haired cat named Millie—Milphidippa, formally—who had just the barest sprouting of red hairs on her paws. *A tortoiseshell in disguise*, Erica had pointed out, after which he'd observed that must be why she was named after the cunning maid from Plautus' *Miles Gloriosus*.

So he must have read at least *part* of the book I'd given him. And for some reason, that made me happier than anything yet.

We lay side by side on the woven double hammock. My body was curled into the curve of his arm that Millie didn't occupy, my head on his chest, rising and falling with the rhythm of his breathing, while his fingers traced star shapes on the soft strip of skin between my top and shorts.

Ironically, I had the same model of hammock by my own pool at home. But *that* I'd never shared with anyone, since there'd never been anyone with whom I'd both wanted to and been allowed to. Of course this pool was about one-sixteenth the size and unheated, meaning it was already too frigid to use, according to Milagros. But still, I liked it better. It seemed wilder, in a way, draped in palm fronds and liana vines and surrounded by agave plants, and a turquoise light that shimmered up from somewhere below like the glow from the underside of an iceberg. Also, when we'd arrived outside and I'd remarked that I'd forgotten my bathing suit, he'd said that he failed to see the problem, and I'd replied that I'd really walked right into that one, hadn't I?

But the conversation had quickly taken a more serious turn, since the question about what to do about Maeve and who would do it still lay unresolved.

"Almost by definition, this isn't the kind of situation that *has* safe choices," said Milagros now, her bare feet tucked up beneath her in a wooden deck chair identical to the one in which Erica was sitting.

Although Milagros had now had three glasses of wine and Erica had had none, I sensed that they spent many nights here just like this, smoking, drinking, being couple goals, and thanking whoever that things were no longer shit.

"But it might not always be that way as I've sort of spent all afternoon not-so-subtly hinting to you," Milagros continued. "If you stay, at least you have a chance. Running away all but eliminates it. I know nobody asked me, but I say, why not at least give yourself the chance? And give Erica's people time to do what they do. If they aren't making progress or you don't like the way things are going, you can always regroup." Her freckled face and blue-green hair were lit only by the torches and the light from the joint she had rolled immediately after she'd served us all a platter of tacos dorados, filled with pork carnitas—mushrooms for Erica—that she had spent all morning slow cooking.

I had thought he and Milagros had been joking, but it was true: he seemed far more familiar with weed than he did with tacos, despite having eaten about a dozen of them.

"What? University towns aren't always about studying as you well know," he'd said earlier in response to my surprise.

"Right, but you're not supposed to—"

I cut myself off because he was holding the joint away from his face and laughing. "I'm not supposed to do a lot of things I do. Or hadn't you noticed?"

And then I was laughing, too.

Now, with my head on his chest, nestled in the hollow of his neck, I not only saw everything as he saw it but felt every slight movement his body made—the deft click of his finger on the lighter, the soft orange glow that resulted, the inhale, the motion of his arm as he held it away from his body, and the slow exhale, the fragrant herbal smoke swirling around both our faces. The mention of studying had jogged something in my memory, but it had slipped away just as fast.

"You know what going back means for me," he said to me. "It's not just you in that house, you know. If only it were."

"Yes. And going back to the status quo is not what any of us wants," I whispered, my hand moving soothingly up and down his torso. "But at least we'll know that the wheels are in motion. I think it's Maeve's best chance. And yours. And yes, it also means I don't have to say goodbye to you yet. But you know that's not why I'm saying it."

"I know," he said, dropping the lighter in the netting and inhaling again. "But even if you are, it's okay." He turned his face toward the stars. "Still, do you know how much easier this would have been back when nobody cared what I did?"

"I sure do," I said. "But those days are over. Sorry."

"Erica, how soon did you say you can have someone looking for her?" he asked.

"Tomorrow," Erica replied. "Early. I've already made the calls."

As he stared up through the smoke, a shadow crossed over his eyes, just for a second. But it was gone before my brain had enough time to register it was there, and now it was just his familiar clear gaze staring back at me.

"You know that if it gets to the point where only I can help my sister, I'll go," he said. "And I won't think twice about it."

"I know," I said.

"But for now?" he said, giving me a slow, hopeful smile. "I'll stay."

I closed my eyes, relief flooding my body. There would be more time, which was all I was asking for, anyway. All I *could* ask for. Sure, we didn't know how *much* time, but when had we ever?

"If you go, I want to come with you."

He recoiled. "Over my dead body would I *ever* let you do that. And it's not because I don't want you with me because you know I do."

"I know," I said. "And I never expected you to agree. But I still want to. And I thought you should know that. In case it, you know, helps."

"It helps. It doesn't change anything, but it helps."

"You know, Louisa," Erica spoke up. "If you want to help the cause, I can find other things for you to do. I already have some student volunteers working with me on various initiatives. Even a few from the medical school. We meet here every Wednesday afternoon."

"Really?" I raised my head. "I'll do anything. Well, I mean—" I backtracked, recalling some of Erica's previous "initiatives."

"Don't worry," my professor said drily. "We're not recruiting suicide bombers at the moment. These are all above-board, university-approved projects."

"I'll be there," I said to Erica, motioning to him. He placed the still-lit joint gently between my lips. The more I smoked, the more I found it soothed my anxiety, though I knew I had to be careful. My family didn't exactly have a good track record with this kind of thing.

I inhaled and exhaled thoughtfully before handing it back to Milagros, trying to recall the thought that had slipped away. "The exam!" I exclaimed, sitting bolt upright in the hammock and sending it swinging wildly, while a shocked boy and cat clung desperately to the rope.

"I can't believe I never told you, considering o-chem is kind of the reason we—well, it's the reason we're here," I said. "Obviously, when I found out, we weren't exactly on speaking terms, but still."

"Wait." Now it was his turn to sit up, nearly flipping the whole thing over. That was game over for Millie, whose paws landed on the tile below with a tiny little *meow* of protest. "You mean you passed?"

"Yes!"

"Lou, that's amazing!"

And here I was enveloped in the much-delayed hug and kiss of congratulations, the one I had imagined a million times. But never in Erica Muller's hammock.

"Not that amazing. It was only a B-plus."

"Are you kidding me? Do you remember when we started? You didn't even know the difference between ether and ethanol."

"Hey!" I protested. "I did, too."

"Ah, that's not the way I remember it," he said. "Then again, I also remember you being naked most of the time, so maybe don't rely on my memory. Anyway," he added. "I'm proud of you."

"You are?"

"Of course. And I always have been. And since I'm not running away, I can promise to say that more often."

An hour later, I was feeling rather relieved and pleased and buzzed and high all at once, so it was only when I heard more jazz arpeggios drifting out of the living room that I realized he had disappeared with no explanation. Rather a habit he had. I wandered back in, but he had already left the piano. Instead, I found him standing at the bookshelf with a volume open in front of him. Glancing up, he slammed it shut hastily.

"You don't have to look so guilty, you know," I said as he slid it back into its place on the shelf. "You aren't in trouble."

"Not this time."

I bent down to glance at the title: *The Collected Works of W. B. Yeats.*

"Poetry? You?"

He looked sheepish. "And in English. And nobody's getting dismembered or baked in a pie and fed to a family member or anything," he said. "See what you're doing to me?"

From the doorway, Erica cleared her throat. We both turned around.

"It's getting late," she said. "And everyone here is on their way to being too tired, drunk, and/or stoned to take you back. So to quote another famous poet, if you've got to go, go now." On her lips, the professor wore the knowing little smile I had first glimpsed during her office hours all those weeks ago. "Or else you've got to stay all night."

—————— · ✦ ❤ ✦ · ——————

"You know, I'm off duty right now," I hinted, gazing past Louisa's shoulder and out the kitchen window again, to find the moon still blanketed by clouds.

Well, shit. After all, it wasn't too often I got a chance to lie back in a hammock with nothing to do but gaze at the wonders of space. Let alone with a beautiful girl relaxed and undone—and willing?—in my arms, one who miraculously didn't hate me despite my having been a complete asshole to her for the past two days. And who just might have a future as a doctor, after all. And who was currently risking everything, up to and including that future, to help me find my sister.

And yet.

Do you think you're going to get lucky again?

Louisa had said I had a gambler's soul. She must be right because here I was doubling down on a losing hand, again. What else could explain my delusion that what we had in that hammock, in this house, could ever be real? As if my agreeing to stay meant some kind of happily ever after when literally no part of it involved happy, or ever, or after?

There are no safe choices. Well, no shit. The choices were between being a slave and (probably) being dead.

In my experience, days that started off shit didn't improve with time. But this one was only getting better.

So maybe I wasn't losing as badly as I'd thought. And here she was, standing there with crossed arms, brow furrowed unreadably. Was she annoyed? Scared? Disgusted? Aroused?

Was it time to raise the bet again?

I figured I had about ten minutes to figure it out and make my case before Erica would be back in the kitchen wanting to know whether we wanted a lift back to campus—or seven hours in heaven.

"I mean, I'm never really 'off,'" I clarified. "But I'm not doing late nights. No one is. The housekeeper has been staying up for a few hours in the evenings, but that's it. She's probably already in bed."

"Are you saying you think we should stay?" she asked. "And do what, exactly? Hmm?"

"Well, um—" Was there any way to explain this that wouldn't make me look like a complete perv?

"You should see the look on your face," she said with a giggle, coming closer. "Here, I'll do it for you." She reached up with both hands to smooth the stray locks back from my forehead, where my own hand had been about to go. "Of course I want to stay. And Daddy isn't back until the day after tomorrow. But we need to think about this carefully."

I closed my eyes, leaning into the feel of her cool hands running through my hair. Even with chips in her manicure and cuts on her fingers, it felt better than any touch in recent memory. I leaned my elbow back against the counter. Her posture mirrored mine as we racked our brains for any possible roadblocks.

"Daddy said he would tell the housekeeper that we were going to campus."

I looked up at the clock. "At this hour, though? From what I've observed, nothing happens on a university campus this late except drinking and sex, and we haven't exactly disproven that."

"But if she's already in bed like you said, she won't notice. Until early tomorrow, anyway. And we'll be back by then."

"All right," I said, like I was going to argue with her about this. "But your mom—"

"Won't be an issue, either. Not at this hour," she said, glancing at the wall clock. "Trust me."

"And the maid—"

"Also won't be an issue."

"Oh, shit." Speaking of issues. "You didn't kill her, did you?"

"No," she said huffily. "Not that I didn't briefly want to. But she informed me I don't have any reason to."

"Did you believe her?"

"Yes. But I never really doubted it." Her reassuring smile obliterated my brief nervousness. "At any rate, I think I've defanged her. So if there ever was a night—"

"It would be tonight," I finished, and the silence hung there, infused with meaning.

She nodded. "But there are still no guarantees."

"Look," I said, taking one of her hands, my scabbed-over fingers caressing each one of hers, slowly and languidly, each one the reminder of the promise we'd made when we'd agreed to only shed one article of clothing at a time.

Someday soon.

"I know you're used to guarantees. But my life doesn't have any. It never has. So it's your call. Whatever you choose, that's what we'll do."

Her eyes—gray as the cloud cover beneath their long lashes—looked down at the floor and then flicked up. One little word was starting to feel as strong as the force of gravity.

"Yes or no?" I asked.

But the decision was already made. It had been made weeks ago, at her bedroom desk, over that complex matrix of chemical reactions, in the microscopic interplay of heat and light, in the pull of a subtle glance, the friction of an accidental touch. It had been made in those moments when I would patiently wait for an answer, listening to our hour ticking away, until she got her head together and gave me one.

And so she did. "Yes."

The smile broke over my face. I'd never say it, and I hoped I hadn't pressured her, but I also hoped she knew which word I'd been praying—praying? Okay, praying—to hear.

"Oh," I said, glancing up. "There's one problem. They only have one spare bed. Don't worry, though." I nodded with resignation. "I'll take the sofa."

She stood there, dumbstruck.

I laughed as I gathered her into my arms. "You should see the look on your face."

11

HER

Despite how relaxed the various substances I'd ingested had me feeling, I couldn't help the growing knot of anxiety in my stomach and the tingling at the back of my neck as I watched Milagros down her last swallow of wine, put out the burning end of the joint, and rise from her deck chair. There was about to be no turning back, and as much as I wanted it, wanted him, wanted *us* in every single way we had coming to us, the idea of how things might change still scared me a little. It scared me like the beginning of a journey into a strange, savage, and beautiful wilderness, one I'd waited my entire life to take. I wasn't a virgin, technically, but I sure did feel like one.

Erica, meanwhile, was almost disturbingly businesslike as she went inside, pointing us toward the spare bedroom, which was across from the bathroom. "Everything you need should be in the cupboard there," she said with absolutely no trace of embarrassment, even though everyone knew she wasn't talking about towels.

"Thank you," we said, almost in unison, though our gratitude was beyond anything worth trying to articulate.

Erica just smiled and went to bed.

And then we were alone, sitting across from each other in the chairs the other two had just abandoned, the vintage jazz record he had put on Erica's equally vintage turntable, the torches burning low.

I took a frantic gulp of wine, twisting the stem of my glass.

"Well," he said matter-of-factly.

I looked up in a way I wished hadn't been so obviously startled.

"I guess the only thing left now is for you to get naked."

"What? *Me*?" I sputtered, all my awkwardness replaced by outrage. "Why don't *you*?"

He shrugged. "Okay." He grabbed his shirt and started to lift it over his head.

"Wait, wait, wait!" I said. "What are you doing?"

He looked genuinely confused. "What you just asked me to do."

"I *know*, but why are you so eager to take your clothes off?"

"Well," he began, "A, in my life, I've found that trying to preserve my modesty has not generally been a good use of my time. And B, as you've probably noticed, being naked generally makes it easier to have sex. Next question?"

"Damn," I said. "In that case, if we hadn't been so afraid of getting caught, I would have asked you to undress ages ago." I looked behind me again, confirming we were alone out here. As if there weren't zero chance that our hosts didn't know exactly what was going on and had vacated the pool area exactly for that reason. "That being said, I suggest we do it at the same time."

"Count of three, then?"

I nodded, although I waited until his shirt was over his head—wanting no false starts—before grabbing the bottom of my tank top and peeling it off, then unhooking my black lace bra, heart already racing. My fingers fumbled on the hooks, trying not to look as clumsy as I felt as I removed it by a strap and dropped it on the nearby chair.

Neither one of us had been wearing many layers of clothing to begin with, so it didn't take long to strip off the rest. And after a month of caution and anxiety and clock-watching and cold showers and half-clothed longing, there we both stood, bare in the (lack of) moonlight, lit only by the glow of the torches and the wavering turquoise light coming up from the bottom of the pool next to us.

And suddenly, inexplicably shy, I directed my eyes everywhere but where it seemed most obvious to look.

And hadn't I just been thinking he looked good *in* clothes?

The complete body in front of me—*his* body, revealed to me and for me—was so much more than the sum of the parts I had seen. So much more beautiful than my imagination alone could have ever supplied. I didn't know what to allow my eyes to drink in first: the broad mass of his square shoulders, the toned abs rippling under the skin of the narrow torso, the line of light, baby-fine hair that formed a trail down to the end of the inverse triangle, in an exercise—he'd be pleased to know—in classic Euclidean geometry. And below *that*, well. I'd felt the weight of his hard cock before, my finger muscles having memorized its dizzying mass and density, but in its natural state, it was stunning in a different way. Baser, rawer, more elemental.

And then. I'd seen the scars on his chest—seen the scars just about everywhere. But here, all at once, it too was pure and raw and unrefined, a reminder of who he was and what he was. That I could claim his body, and he could claim mine, but there were other claims that would always, *always* come first. And they'd carved their initials into him long ago, with blood.

Well, fuck. He'd just caught on to where my attention had turned. My eyes must have been like dinner plates.

"It's official," he said, tearing his gaze away from me to glance down at himself. "You're prettier."

"Well, yeah," I said. "But you're not far behind." In case there was any chance he actually thought that any of the scars made him any less beautiful in my eyes. *That* had never crossed my mind for a second.

"I must not be," he said, "given how hard you're blushing right now."

Mortified, I covered my face. If only I hadn't also been inflamed everywhere else. "Oh, yeah? Well, you're blushing, too!" Actually, he was, but there was no chance he was even half as red as I felt. Though the desert night wasn't all that warm, I could feel my temperature rising even as I spoke.

"Well, whatever you do, don't smile. Smiling while naked is not allowed."

Obviously, it was too late. I was laughing. And so was he.

"You're still glowing red, young lady," he said. Hell yes, I was. Not only could I feel myself blushing, I could feel my pupils dilating, my breath quickening, my body preparing. The entire beautiful and complex machine of my body was shifting into overdrive for him. "In fact, I think you're in danger of overheating. We're gonna have to do something about that."

"And just what would—oh, shit." I should have seen it coming. And I'd seen no better evidence of his reflexes *and* strength than the way he, all in one swift motion, snatched me up and tossed me into the tiny, frigid pool like releasing a handful of flower petals. I shrieked as the icy surface of the water shattered like broken glass all over the goose bumps already covering my skin. I came up gasping and shivering.

"Shhh. You'll wake up Erica," he scolded me, standing at the edge of the pool with his arms casually folded and a smirk engineered to infuriate me. He wasn't even *wet*. "And if she has to come out here, given what I've seen of her, I have a feeling you won't be coming back up for air."

"Fuck you," I said, flipping my hair back in one smooth motion, my limp curls falling in ropes down my back. I made a desperate grab for his leg but didn't even come close. "Now get in here and help me warm up again."

"Nah. Not until you say it."

"Say what?"

He only had to raise an eyebrow.

"Oh, for—fine," I ground out. "I'm overheated. I'm glowing red. I'm on fucking *fire*."

"And why might that be?" He gestured lazily.

"Uh, because you're standing over me naked and I'm not blind?"

"And?" His infuriating smirk had graduated to a full-on grin.

"And also because your cock is the single most beautiful organ I've ever seen and I want to climb it like a flagpole?" I mumbled, my cheeks on fire. "Satisfied?"

"Hey, I just wanted you to tell me you think I'm cute," he said, shaking his head with a sigh. "You *always* have to take it too far." He plunged in with hardly a splash. In fact, the cold didn't seem to bother him at all. He'd grown up above the 50th parallel, after all. "But yes, I'm satisfied. Or, at least," he added with a tilt of his still-dry head, "I will be soon."

I growled and directed as large a wall of water at him as my two hands could manage.

"That's pathetic," he said, grabbing me and dunking me under the water again. I responded with another shriek—Erica or no Erica. The second time I surfaced, though, instead of retaliating, I stopped. Stopped just to look at him in the blue light. Now, at last, the splashback had sent water streaming down his broad shoulders in rivulets and his thick strands of hair adhered haphazardly to his face. And that blue light shot up from some untraceable place below, turning his entire body a shimmering silver-blue. Quite honestly, so far, I was aware of no light that had ever touched him that didn't seem to adore him. If only the rest of the world would catch on.

He managed to shake some of the strands out of his eyes and pulled me toward him to keep me from floating away, while I wrapped my legs around his waist tightly, our girl and boy parts jammed right up against each other, noses nearly touching, chests heaving up and down in perfect rhythm as the droplets rained down. Enveloped in all the heat and strength of those gorgeous, sleek muscles now in relief, I was convinced there was no way I could ever feel the cold again.

"Up close, am I still prettier?" I teased.

"Even prettier than I imagined the first time I saw you," he whispered.

"Thank you. And now just why were you imagining me naked the first time you saw me?"

He gazed at me with no trace of irony. "Because my imagination was the only place I thought I'd ever see it."

"Oh." This conversation about hardcore nudity had just become unexpectedly touching.

"And to tell you the truth," he added, "it was even before I saw you."

"The intercom," I said, not quite ready to admit that our brief conversation had caused me to wake up the next morning to a throbbing, gushing river between my thighs. The very thighs that were currently anchored right up against his hipbones, the ones that seemed to pulse electrically in response to the memory.

"Your voice was so sexy," he said. "I had it in my head all the next day."

"I threatened to have you whipped!"

He laughed. "Yeah, but even then I knew you'd never do it. And as usual, you're proving me right. So far, anyway."

"But why did you think I wouldn't do it?" I pressed. I knew he was really thinking about it.

"Because I could tell you had a good soul," he finally said. "There. Happy? I said the S-word."

"But you—" I couldn't help it. I glanced down at his body again.

He sighed. "Do you remember giving me any of these scars?"

I shook my head.

"Because I sure don't. In fact, I even remember a few times when you could have but chose not to."

"But my whole life, I've seen so much that was wrong," I whispered. "And I never questioned it. I never said a thing."

"How *could* you have said a thing?" he said, squeezing my fingers gently, stilling them where they landed. "You were a kid. You didn't have a choice, any more than I did. You think radical ex-fugitive bomber Erica Muller would let you darken her door if she thought you were part of the problem?"

I shook my head, though unconvinced.

"You have your whole life to do good in the world," he said. "You've already started."

"I have? How?"

"By helping me find Maeve, of course. And by going to Erica's meetings. And if you want to," he murmured, "you can kiss me. Right here." He guided my hand down to brush against the long, deep, pinkish scar slicing across his midsection and poking its soft, tentative edge out of the surface of the water. His oldest one. *The goose.* Like it had a name or something.

"Not because you have anything to apologize for. But because you've never made me feel anything less than amazing. So by all means, continue."

This time, he didn't need to tell me twice. I pressed my lips over the damaged tissue, my tongue cutting through the cold water to his skin, his nipple hardening beautifully beneath my lips as I trailed my warm tongue up his shoulder to where his scar disappeared.

I sped up, suddenly hungry to make this boy who had seen and felt so much pain quiver and melt with pleasure beneath my lips.

It seemed to work. Speechless, he reached up to take my chin in his powerful hand, mashing his lips into mine, raw and unapologetic, exploring my mouth the way he'd done in the kitchen earlier that afternoon. The way he'd done the moment he realized he was going to get another chance to do it. The moment I realized how much I still wanted him to.

Only this time, I felt his erection pressing urgently up against my side.

"See what you're doing to me?" he whispered as it dawned on my face what it was.

"So it isn't just your newfound liking for poetry," I whispered with a smile.

"Not *just* that," he whispered back between kisses, guiding my hand underneath the water to cup it, nearly weightless, my thumb tracing luxuriously over the hard cleft as he continued to nip and nibble, and my collarbone hardened and flexed to meet his lips.

Seeming determined now, he lifted me away from him, propelling my whole body smoothly, weightlessly through the water, setting me on the narrow stone steps leading out of the pool so that only the lower two-thirds of my body was submerged.

And there it was again—that serious expression he gave me in moments like this as if I were some eternal riddle, some divine puzzle, one he would spend all night—or the rest of his life—finding the solution to. Rivulets of silvery water dripped down from his hair and onto my breasts. He palmed one of them with his large hand, exquisitely sculpted and elegantly marred. My nipple had already heightened just above the surface, trembling bashfully under his thumb. My own fingers slipped along his shoulder and back to his nape, squeezing locks of sodden dark golden hair beneath my fists.

His tongue swirled on my nipple, sending the water lapping lazily over my skin, flicking his eyes up again and again as if he couldn't stand to completely look away from my face. I lay my head back on the cement, my insides turning to liquid at the thought of what would come next, my heart already hammering as his hand slid up my thigh, gently coaxing my legs open. Automatically, I slid up one step so I was sitting on the rim of the pool, giving him the kind of up-close view I knew he wanted. All at once, my entire body was exposed to the night air, but I still couldn't feel the cold, not for a second, with him there.

"Still pretty?" I cooed.

"God," he said, like someone on the brink of starvation who had been invited to a feast. "That hardly begins to cover it. Do you know how many times I imagined this?"

"I—I did too."

"When?" His eyes had brightened into the kind of innocent yet vulgar curiosity I knew well, his lips parted in shameless hunger. God forbid anyone ever made him choose between sex and science.

"When you were tutoring me," I admitted. I supposed I should have been embarrassed, but I wasn't. I was so obviously turning him on. "And—and later. In bed."

"Yeah?" he said, his arousal evident everywhere I could see and many places I couldn't, his body a hard mass of rigid, throbbing proof. His hand traced the length of my core, making me moan. "That's so—"

"Yes?" I said huskily, leaning closer, my thighs quivering with need.

"What did you imagine? Tell me." His voice was lower now, darker.

"Y-you," I hesitated. "Touching me. With your fingers, your lips, your—everything. Everywhere," I said, almost hesitant to choke out the words, remembering acutely those cold, quiet nights upstairs, awake, alive with the knowledge that the young man starring in all my dirtiest dreams spent every night in the basement of the same house, in a room with an automatic lock on the door. Almost as if someone had seen this moment coming and tried to prevent it. And really, *really* fucked it up.

"How did you touch yourself, Lou? Show me," he requested, eyes already fixated on where he longed to see my own hand go.

"Just like this." I knew it from muscle memory, from all those soundless, lonely nights, my fingers sliding down my inner thigh, brushing against my swollen lips, massaging my clit gently, just exploring, then more than exploring—then moaning, then stifling screams. *All those nights.* My legs and hips curled and contracted at the touch, wanting more of him there.

"And what else did you think about?" he whispered.

"I thought about—you," I said. "Touching yourself. Thinking about me."

"I did, you know," he said.

"Show me?"

Now he was gripping his cock under the water, which hardened further still under his stroke, even as I watched. I could see better what I'd done to him, that hard, full length under his palm, working up and down the shaft, his eyes glassy and feverish with desire for me.

And for the first time, I thought about what it might feel like. Inside.

"In my mind, I so badly wanted it to be you there, looking just like you are now," he said, leaning over me as I splayed across the pool deck. "Every gorgeous inch of you."

"Such a naughty boy," I said, releasing a sharp moan even at the image of him wanting me that way. "You know, somebody should really whip you for that."

"Well, if it has to happen, I hope it's you."

"I couldn't."

"I know," he said. "That's why. And I promise I did try. Not to, I mean. Because I knew it could never happen. Shouldn't ever happen." He was dead serious, I realized. He *had* really tried. He'd tried to be a good slave instead of a bad one.

"In this complicated modern world, who's to say what should and shouldn't happen?" I whispered, half-delirious.

"How morally relativist of you."

"See what you're doing to me?" I asked. "Anyway, you know what else I imagined? Your tongue—tasting me. Here." I curled and uncurled my fingers shyly.

"Do you want me to taste you now?"

I nodded since my voice was no more than a whimper. But that was all he needed. His hands rounded my thighs, pulling them apart. I lay back, gasping as his tongue rimmed the outer lips of my pussy, followed by a swift motion in a straight line up to my clit, knowing exactly where he was going. But then, he always had, hadn't he?

All I could see, still, was the hand, its wrist chained in servitude, gripping his cock, secretly and guiltily, in some private corner of the basement, liquid trailing out with every stroke, then exploding at the mental picture of me. *Me*, Louisa as I'd been, at the desk, pencil in hand, my camisoles and pajama pants and wild hair and graphite-stained fingers, my haughtiness and clumsy compassion. Little knowing that upstairs, I'd been shattering myself for *him* as *he'd* been, arms and abs, shredded and carved under cast-off T-shirts, the wit, the bold insolence, the absolute refusal to fail, or allow me to. Of us, then so ordinary and so inviolable.

And now.

I drew in a desperate gasp at the thought. Stretched back on the bare concrete pool deck, I buried my fingers in his golden strands, inhaling ecstatically at every staccato dip of his mouth as he played me like the virtuoso he was, in so many ways.

"Can you taste it?" I murmured. "Oh, can you taste just how much I want you?"

His response was not much more than a deeply satisfied hum of his own.

But the truth was, I wanted him deeper. I wanted to open up completely for him, to give him a space where he didn't have to hide his desire, to let him take me like a man deserves to take a woman, wholly, bodily, completely unbowed and unashamed. Something I suspected he had never had.

Yes, in that way, even he was a virgin.

"And I want—"

He raised his head suddenly, his eyes liquid gold in the light of the torch behind me, his rosy mouth blushing beautifully in the torchlight. "What do you want? Tell me, Lou."

"I want to feel you inside me," I burst out. "All of you." My hands snaked desperately up over his shoulders as if I could take in all his massive maleness into me in one breath.

"Knackeg," he said.

"What the hell did you just call me?" I asked with a shocked giggle.

"It's Luxembourgish," he said.

His French always turned me on, but hearing him speak his native language was different—startlingly intimate as if I were gazing into a keyhole at his childhood.

"It means, um—crispy."

"*Crispy*?" I exclaimed in horror.

"I swear to God, it's a compliment," he said. "In the sexiest language there is, *Mäi léift*."

"And what was *that*?"

"Nothing," he said. "Bedroom?"

———————— · ✦ ❤ ✦ · ————————

A month ago, if I had been asked to imagine the room where we'd go all the way—after overcoming the pearl-clutching horror of imagining it at all—I wouldn't have imagined anything close to *this*. I wouldn't have imagined a quaint pink patchwork quilt over a queen mattress, a round gold mirror above the headboard, a vintage hat rack in the corner, or two shelves over the bed lined entirely with ferns, their fronds trailing lazily down the walls.

But a month ago, I wouldn't have imagined a lot of things.

Like seeing his cock. Like *touching* his cock. Or like settling myself dreamily on that pink-and-white quilt, watching his immense erection drift toward me from the doorway like some fantastical dream, still slick with silvery water, cradled in my line of sight by nothing but his slim, strong, masculine hips and that summery, sandy patch of hair it nestled in.

"Was that all me that did that?" I asked, sucking in a breath.

"You know it was."

And I had never imagined his broad hand now curled around his shaft, stroking, turning it to steel, nor the way my body was already responding to how his utterly intoxicated eyes drank me in as my entire form unfolded itself across the bed for him—legs spread, pussy drenched, insides and outsides moaning and clenching with anticipation at what perhaps he had, just like me, hoped and prayed—prayed? Okay, prayed—to get the chance to do.

I squirmed, suddenly thinking about the bathroom cabinet. But there was no need. The condom, far from being out of reach, was already somehow in his hand and half unwrapped. Because of course. But just as he was about to roll it on, he paused. "Hey, do you think she knew ahead of time? Because, well, you wouldn't think *they* would need—"

"Don't overthink it," I said.

"You know me," he said. "Hard not to, but I'll try." He turned to me. "You ready for this?"

"Why do you always ask me that?" I said with a giggle.

"Because I want to be sure," he said, unrolling the condom the rest of the way, and confidently slid himself into a comfortable position over me, the bedsprings reacting predictably to the addition of his mass, his damp golden locks tumbling dreamily over his eyes as I stroked it back playfully to reveal them again. "If you want, we could—"

"Yes," I said, nestling my head deeper into the pillow and briefly closing my eyes. Searching for fear, for anxiety, for doubt in body or in mind—and finding, for the first time, none.

I opened them. And still found none. "I'm ready."

"All right, then. Remember to breathe." And he penetrated me. I gasped, but it was true: I was soaked to the bone and totally ready, in every way, to receive him.

"*Ngh*," was all I could manage at first, nails digging into the flaxen sheets as he pushed with his thickness, stretching me to my limits, every ridge and vein of him caressing my walls as he bottomed out, locking our hips together.

It took a minute of pure animal instinct before I could finally settle into his rhythm. His movements were gentle and slow, giving me time, easing me into the motions, letting my hands run all over the muscles of his chest and back and shoulders, all the cruel souvenirs of a world determined to leave him broken.

But it wasn't them I held. Instead, my imagination had supplied, for my pleasure, the perfect, unmarred body nature had intended him to have if everything hadn't gotten so fucked along the way, and I took a second to hold that body, to hold that man—the one that in some other universe I might have known wholly and completely.

But that didn't last because that boy wasn't mine. My boy was this one, and the scars, too, made him who he was. And now, they rose up unchecked beneath my fingers, insisting on themselves, and his body flexed and unflexed under the pressure of each of my fingertips as though even the touch of me, as light as it was, was unbearably intense. His eyelashes fluttered.

"Need to breathe, too," he reminded himself with a labored gasp, and we both laughed.

"Is this everything you thought about?" I whispered.

"It's everything I dreamed about," he replied, even as he bent down to nuzzle his beautiful face against mine, his voice somehow coming from far away now, a place of wonder. "You're my dream come to life, Lou."

There'd been shocks and revelations that night, but none more than that his shoulders were shaking, that powerful body now aching and vulnerable, his voice shot through with the kind of emotion I didn't expect to hear from him or any man, on this night or any night. His rhythm continued slow, deep, languid, musical. I was silent for a moment, my breathing in time with his breathing, my body expanding and contracting in time with each thrust as I sipped from the cup of this moment, of this limited yet timeless present.

"God, do you have any idea how good you're making me feel right now?" he half-murmured, half-moaned. "The way you're taking me like you were made for me."

"Maybe I was."

He paused as if he couldn't believe that a maker, even one he didn't believe in, would make *me* for *him,* but like a lot of things tonight, he was willing to go with it.

"You're *good* at this, you know, Lou. You really are. How do you do it?"

"When I met you, I was starting to think I wasn't good at anything," I whispered. "Anything that mattered, anyway."

"You're so wrong, Lou," he said, shaking his head. "You're *so* wrong. If I could only give you one thing in this life, it would be to give you the chance to see yourself the way I see you. Now and always."

I blinked, a screen of mist across my eyes.

"You're good at the *only* things that matter. So much more than numbers and formulas. Things I can't comprehend. Maybe I never will. Maybe I *can't*."

"If I can get o-chem ..." I trailed off.

"What you're good at is harder, Lou," he said with a sigh. "So much harder. For me, anyway."

"I know it is," I said, my hands loosely gripping his arms, sliding down to where his hands balanced on the mattress on either side of my body. "But you're smarter than I am."

"Let's call it even," he said with a smile. "How does this feel? Because I'm going to speed up. Unless—"

"It feels wonderful," I said, arching my back as if I might accept even more of him, as if this image, this scene, hadn't been somewhere in the back of my mind from the very moment I saw him—from the very moment I *heard* him. "Do it."

I wanted it. I wasn't afraid anymore. Of anything. Of darkness, of abandonment, of punishment, of pain. Tomorrow would bring what tomorrow would, but in this moment, at least, it was all conquered already. And after he arched down and kissed me again, there was nothing left to do but take his advice and keep breathing; through the hammering of his hips and the incredible noises he was making, through the frantic increase in his tempo, through his pinning me down against the bed with the incredible strength of all his wanting, through his coming with a quiver, one that seemed to squeeze his body from the inside out, then let him go.

Withdrawing, he bent to kiss me but hovered over me, just for a second, just to look. Damp strands of golden hair brushed my face. I reached up to push them away from his forehead as I had earlier. He'd leaned into it then, but now he just closed his eyes, collapsing into my touch and my lips.

He removed the condom and returned immediately to me, tiredly reaching for my curls, bunching them together in his hand, then letting them fall gently over my breast. A boy running his hand down the snowy, heaving flank of a unicorn. Something he still couldn't believe was real.

"What do you want, Lou?" he whispered. "What can I do to get you to come for me?"

"Just kiss me," I breathed. "And touch me. You know that's all you ever have to do."

And he did, his lips and tongue featherlight and gentle on my lips, neck, and ear. He knew all the places. After only a few weeks, they belonged to him. *I* belonged to him, in all the same ways that he belonged to me.

His kisses and his fingers sweeping over my clit were enough for me to yield again and forever. I moaned softly, ready for it; nothing needed in my mind but the wonder on his face moments ago, feeling exactly how a man should feel. Exactly how I'd wanted to make him feel. *You're my dream come to life.* And it took a few more seconds only before I was up, up, floating far above the earth, far above the cruel ruin men had made of it, and then I came like falling, like snowflakes drifting down to cover it all in white.

12

HER

I fell asleep in his arms, but I woke up in darkness, alone in the bed.

He was gone.

I pawed the cold sheets. *No.*

Panic. Terror. Paralysis. He said he was staying. I hadn't dreamed that. I *couldn't* have. There was time. He said there was time. There *had* to be time.

Then from the bedside came a voice. I collapsed bonelessly into the soft mattress, my heart rate returning to normal.

"Wake up, Lou," he whispered, flicking on the bedside lamp. "I need someone to come stargaze with me!"

I relaxed further when I was greeted by the soft glow of the bulb reflecting in his wide-awake, eager eyes. "What time is it?"

"Four a.m."

I recognized that excited tone, which made him sound not more than ten years old. It was way too early in the morning for a boy to be this cute.

"It's a few days too early for the Leonids, but maybe we can catch one or two," he explained.

"I think Milagros is your girl for that," I teased him, giggling as I covered my head with a pillow.

"Oh, come on," he said, grabbing my wrist and almost bodily dragging me to the edge of the bed. "How could anyone sleep when there's astronomy happening?"

He was already partially dressed, and he handed me my shorts and tank top, helpfully gathered from where I'd shed them by the side of the pool. I rubbed my arms. "It'll be freezing out there."

"Here," he said, handing me the fleece-lined jacket I'd given him earlier.

I shook my head.

He looked around, grabbed the quilt off the bed, and threw it over my shoulders, then put the jacket on himself. "Better?"

I nodded.

"Then come." Outside, he grabbed a padded lounge chair and pulled me, rolled up in the quilt, down to his lap. I settled the quilt around us both. We were both momentarily startled by movement in the foliage, but a pounce told us it was just Millie the cat, prowling on top of the wall.

"Shit," he said, looking up. He started laughing.

"What's so funny?"

"It's just—I was kind of thinking this would be romantic," he said sheepishly. "The list of things I like about the desert isn't particularly long, but one of them is the clear skies. But not tonight. With these clouds, we can't even see the moon, let alone a meteor."

"Hey, we're not in the basement, the pantry, or the garbage," I said, secretly melting at the fact that he'd even been thinking about that. "Which already makes it the most romantic night we've ever had." I added a kiss for good measure, and he seemed to relax.

"Maeve was the only one who'd ever do this with me," he remarked idly. "Stargaze, I mean."

My ears pricked at this spontaneous reveal about his past, which didn't come often. "Late at night, when we weren't supposed to be out, I'd try to memorize the planets and constellations by color and shape—had to be right, you know me. But she'd just make up whatever she wanted—fairies, mermaids, unicorns. Then she'd really push it, throwing in kittens and puppies, spinning these wild stories that made no sense except to her. Drove me nuts. I'd call her an idiot and storm inside."

I couldn't stop myself from giggling. "That's actually kind of funny. I'm sorry."

"Looking back, yeah, it was," he admitted. "Of course, after I lost touch with her, I would have given anything to hear those stories again. Especially because after they sold us, I didn't see the stars for three years."

I sucked in a gasp.

"The floodlights," he explained quietly, dropping his gaze. "They were too bright."

God. And to think I'd *resisted* this, even playfully. I'd stay out here with him for *another* three years if I had to, to make up for every night he'd lost.

"You don't talk about her," I said softly. "You came all this way to find her, and yet you don't talk about her."

"I could talk about her all night if you got me going," he said. "But I guess I've learned not to. It's just another thing they can use against you. Family, I mean."

"How?"

He tilted his head up and stared intently at the sky like he believed he could see whatever was behind the clouds if he stared at it hard enough. "They sold her when they sold me. They didn't have to. She didn't do anything wrong. But they did, just to punish me. If they'd kept her, at least I'd know where she was. But they didn't even want me to have that." His eyes were glassy and far away now, completely lost in memories. "She'd had me and our mom her entire life, which is more than most of us get, and now, in an instant, she was alone. She was only eleven. Another thing I'll never forgive myself for."

"It's insane that you blame yourself for that, you know," I said.

"I know. But I do."

"She'll be okay," I said with conviction, stroking my thumb across his knuckles and squeezing. "Maeve is a survivor, I can tell. It runs in the family."

That was enough to get him to smile. "My mom used to say that, too."

I went silent for a moment. "I used to send him messages, too."

Confusion crossed his face briefly before it dawned on him: the *real* reason I'd started crying when I'd made my impassioned speech to Erica about his need to find Maeve himself. Not like I normally needed a reason to cry, but, well. I'd been holding the tears in for this for a long time. Frankly, the only thing I'd *ever* held them in for.

"Ethan?" he asked with careful curiosity as if he'd always wanted to ask me more about my brother but didn't want to open wounds. Nobody knew better than him about wound-opening, after all.

I nodded slowly. "Like every few days, for almost a year. And he never replied. We used to be best friends. We had our own languages, all the same references, the same sense of humor. But the pills stole all that. All he wanted was money, and if he couldn't get it from us, we—my whole family—were useless to him. And then Mom's drinking got worse, and Daddy seemed to give up, and nothing's been the same since then, and it won't be until he comes back. And I thought if I had just tried harder, said something different, I could have made things okay, but I tried and tried and—" The tears were falling, as usual, but I wasn't worried as much anymore about him thinking I was weak. He'd made it quite clear that that was far from the case. So I just let them all rain down.

"Hey, look at me." He tilted my chin his way and lightly wiped away a tear from my cheek with his thumb. I breathed, trying to focus on where his eyes would be in the dim light. I had been hypnotized by that brilliant color so often I could almost see it in my head, even with hardly any light. "That is too much of a burden for anyone. You alone cannot fix your entire family. They have to want to fix themselves. Granted, pop psychology isn't exactly one of my fields of expertise. But I'm fairly confident about this."

I nodded through my tears. "You're going to hate me for saying this, but you're so lucky that you have a sister who *wants* to come back to you."

"Oh, Lou, your brother wants to come back to you, too," he said, squeezing me tight. "I promise you he does. He just needs time."

I pulled the blanket around me tighter and burrowed into the warmth he offered. "We are so good at blaming ourselves for things that aren't really our fault, aren't we?"

"Yeah, we are," he said, sighing and resting his head on the back of the chair. "Luckily, we're good at other things, too."

"Like what?" I asked. "Bantering? Arguing? Getting into shitty situations and wriggling our way out of them?"

"Ah, that's just speed chess," he said, waving his hand. "You learned that from me."

"I did not." I raised my head again. "Remember when we first met in the bathroom, and my dad came in?"

"The showerhead story?" He rolled his eyes, making it clear where he thought it fell in the hierarchy of zany gambits.

"Hell yes, 'the showerhead story,'" I repeated mockingly. "Which saved *your* ass as I recall. And that was all me."

"All you?" He shook his head. "Ha. No. You planned, I executed."

"Fine," I said. "In that case, perhaps we should call ourselves, I don't know, a team?"

"The two of us vs. the world? Yeah, I like *those* odds."

"I've heard worse."

"I've heard better."

"Hey, a meteor." I pointed up to the sky at the path where the dot of pure light had appeared. Or where I thought it had appeared.

"Wait, really? I didn't see it."

"Well." I shrugged. "Sometimes I see things you don't."

HIM

"I won't always be broke, you know," she said delicately. "I just have to finish undergrad, get through medical school, and start my residency. I'll start making money then. It'll just take some time."

I braced myself. I already knew where this was going. I'd expected it all night, ever since Milagros told her story. But I'd pushed it aside, drunk on the fog of sex and weed and jazz and wine and her, letting her share every dirty thought she'd ever had, then letting me in to touch and feel it all. It was easy not to think about the future, in the face of the miracle happening right before our eyes. But now she was speaking of other miracles. Ones that flashed and were gone before even the most powerful telescope could reach them, like that one meteor on a cloudy night. Miracles I'd promised to try to believe in but couldn't yet.

"Erica and Milagros did it," she said. "We can, too."

Shit.

The fact that I didn't answer right away, and every second I didn't answer thereafter, made her panic just a little more.

"The truth is, I almost never think about freedom," I finally said.

I guess I shouldn't have been surprised by her reaction. But I was.

"But why?" she demanded.

"Why?" I repeated calmly. "Let's see. Because why waste valuable brainpower wanting something I don't have? Because surviving day to day is hard enough without torturing myself thinking about everything I could have if I'd only been born somewhere else or someone else? Because I never thought I would live long enough to ever get it?"

"Oh," she said softly. "Well, if you don't want to think about it, I'll just think about it *for* you."

"I appreciate that. But how long is it going to take to start your residency, anyway?" I was trying not to sound dismissive, but I saw her deflate anyway.

Shit.

"Ten years?" she said sadly, though the question mark was really just to soften the blow.

It sounded like a prison sentence, and in a way it was. My whole life was. One that personally—though no doubt I'd done a lot wrong—I didn't think I deserved. "You really think your dad's going to keep me around that long?"

"If he doesn't, I'll find you," she said. "Wherever you are. Whatever they ask. I'll find a way."

I paused, took a deep breath. "Lou, I'm going to ask you something, and please don't get upset. You know it costs money to buy someone's freedom, right? A tax equal to their last sale price. And that's on *top* of what you pay to buy them."

"I know."

"And how much do residents make at first?"

She sighed. "Honestly? Not much. Plus, loan payments."

"And do you know how much your dad paid for me?"

She closed her eyes. "Do you?"

I nodded slowly. "Yes," I said after a moment. "We aren't supposed to know, not in a private sale. But there's always a way to find out. And it's—"

"Don't tell me," she said quickly. "I don't want to know. Not only because I couldn't afford it, but because ... well."

"My worth is incalculable?" I teased.

"Let's put it that way."

I had one long curl of her hair entwined in my fingers now, like one of the living vines that grew up and down the walls, lush and vibrant under my touch. "You're so young."

Of course, she could have pointed out that I was young, too, but we both knew I was talking in terms of experience. And in those terms, I had about a lifetime on her.

And in that lifetime, as someone had helpfully pointed out, I'd already been lucky once.

"Look, Erica and Milagros beat the odds," I reminded her. "What about the ones you don't hear about? The ones lost to history? The ones with ruined lives and futures, the ones whose bones are at the bottom of mineshafts? Sure, Erica could help find Maeve and maybe even prove that she was freed, but then what about us? What happens after? Are we just going to go on like this? I hate to break it to you, Lou, but this"—I waved my hand, gesturing to the walled garden, the temporary Eden in which we now lay peacefully in repose—"this isn't what we're going back to. This isn't real. This isn't ours. It's not our cat or our piano or our pool. We don't have a pool. Well, you do. I just skim the bugs out of it."

"But we *could* have one someday," she said softly. "And *I'll* skim the bugs."

"That's very sweet, but it's not really the point. Look, I told you I'm going back to be with you for as long as I can. I made up my mind about that. But let's face the facts here. We kind of suck at this," I said with a rueful laugh. "Like half the people in your house already know, and more than a few outside of it, and it hasn't even been a month. How long do you think it's going to take your dad to figure it out?"

I hated how defeated she must have looked, but this was a kindness, I told myself. If she had to hear it, she might as well hear it now.

"And even if we get past that, at some point in the next ten years—hell, the next *one* year, there's a good chance I'll be on the run, in a mine, or dead, and even if I'm not, I'll still be a slave *somewhere*, watching you waste the best years of your life waiting for me. Waiting for a ghost because that's all I'm going to be to you by then. Do you understand? It's the same reason you can't come with me. I can't do that to you," I said, swallowing hard, "and I won't."

"We said we were a team," she said in the smallest, quietest voice I'd ever heard.

"To be a team, you need goals, Lou. You need the *chance* to set goals. To plan a future. And I don't have a future. You do. That's the difference."

She shook her head, blinking away tears again.

"In ten years, you'll be traveling the world, finding cures for exotic diseases, saving sick babies in far-flung villages, and meeting smart and amazing people you never even knew existed. Your people. People who can give you the beautiful life you deserve. Who can give you everything I can't."

"Fucking hell. You really are stupid."

I froze.

For the last minute, she'd been sitting silently, staring at the vine-covered wall, blinking the tears away. But now, she whipped her face around with the kind of ferocity I knew always caught people off guard.

"*What do you think I need?* Diamonds? A white horse? A castle? After all we've been through, do you think I'm just going to pack up and call it a day because you can't give me a fucking fairy tale? Do you *know* me?"

I opened my mouth, though I'd seen her like this enough times that I probably knew there was no point.

"You must not because if you did, you'd know what my fifth-grade teacher told my parents during the finals of the district spelling bee when I paused for eight minutes on the word *chiaroscuro*. I was just standing up there, rooted to the spot, dead silent. They said my eyes were as big as saucers. They thought I had broken down. That I was choking under the pressure. That I'd run off the stage crying because it was too hard. But I went home with a blue ribbon, and you want to know what he told them?"

"What?"

"To always ask for the language of origin," she said, grabbing my chin and wrenching it toward her to look me dead in the eyes, a kiss fierce and bold, as bold as I had once been with her. "And to never *ever* give up on me."

And I fell, collapsed bodily into her, my face in her warm, silky nest of curls, waiting there for me, despite the odds.

And I whispered the two words I'd *told* myself not to say. Even though they were the only two words at that moment I knew, without a doubt, to be true.

"I won't."

"You promise?"

"I promise. Like I said, I—"

"But you said you never think about freedom. You—"

"You didn't let me finish."

She stopped interrupting.

"Because the truth is, if it's freedom alone that could give me *this*, could give me *you,* I know it's not just half of me that wants it anymore."

She just sat there wrapped in a quilt with her freshly kissed mouth half-open in surprise, her eyes the same color as the starless sky. "No?" she whispered as if she didn't dare to breathe. As if she knew what I was about to say. And never expected to hear it.

"No," I whispered, never having expected to hear it myself. "It's all of me. Every single part."

HER

Milagros said she wanted him to have tried at least two Mexican dishes, so she made us all chilaquiles.

"She never makes breakfast for *me*," Erica pouted before walking us, just after daybreak, all the way back to where we'd left the car.

At that hour, the campus was quiet and mostly empty, with dew in the grass and rosy shafts of sunlight on the red brick buildings that lined the mall. The walk was all business: no run-ins, no hugging, and no getting caught. Before she left, though, Milagros slipped him a new burner phone, with both her and Erica's numbers in it. By the end of the day, with any luck, she said, he'd know *something* about Maeve.

She waved off our thanks, just as Erica had earlier. "Until next time."

Even with her neon blue hair, it was amazing how fast she melted away into the tapestry of campus, calling no attention to herself. She'd been a slave, after all.

"Think we can get back before the housekeeper notices we're gone?" I asked him once Milagros was out of sight.

"I can guarantee it," he said. "If you let me drive."

"What?!"

"Wait, hear me out," he said. "I know this is going to sound weird, but on our last drive, this car and I developed, like, this telepathic bond." He ran his hand lovingly along the glossy white hood of the Cadillac. "And it's telling me it doesn't want to *let* you drive it. The last time was just too traumatic. I'm sorry, but I'm only looking out for the car's mental health." He awaited my response, a smile playing on his lips.

"*God*, just when I thought you couldn't be any more full of shit," I said, even as he started laughing. "Besides, I told you, I don't normally drive like that. And I don't even know if you *can* drive."

"I can but even if I couldn't, I think I'd *still* feel safer. Plus, I won't tell if you won't."

I bit my lip, hating that I was even considering it. "I think one thing we can agree on after the past few days is that from now on, nobody is telling anybody anything. And anyway, it doesn't matter. It's illegal since I know for a fact you don't have a license."

"I had one in Europe."

I looked at him in surprise. "Wait, really?"

"No," he admitted. "Almost had you there. The truth is, I—we couldn't have licenses. We could drive with our owners' permission, though."

"Or without their permission, in your case, I'm guessing."

"That, too," he said. "Tell you what. I'll flip you for it."

"I don't have a coin." I crossed my arms.

"I found one just now in the grass," he said, digging into his pocket.

With a sigh, I held out my hand as he tossed it to me. I reached for it, fumbling awkwardly to stop it from bouncing under the wheel.

"Hey, careful with that," he said. "It's my life savings."

"At this point, that makes you about one cent richer than I am," I muttered, positioning it between my fingernails.

He called heads. It came up tails.

I looked up at him expectantly.

"Best two out of three."

"Really?" I raised an eyebrow.

"Why not?" he said. "Some smug little know-it-all recently told me that with every toss, the odds are the same, no matter what came before. And for some reason," he said as he opened the driver's side door, "I'm feeling lucky."

"That's funny," I said as I opened the other one. "So am I."

13

HER

We separated just inside the door from the garage with only a brief kiss, both of us having underestimated how difficult it would be to quietly go to our separate areas of the house.

Thankfully, the place was blessedly quiet and still, the mourning doves cooing in the cool morning breeze the only sound. The light wasn't on in the kitchen, a sure sign the housekeeper was sleeping in, just as he had predicted she would.

He'd lost the coin toss, but I'd lied and told him he'd won. And even though my head swam with potential worst-case scenarios when he started the ignition, I forgot them as soon as I saw the way the Cadillac's engine purred like a lover under his careful touch, the curious grin he stole as he tested the accelerator, the way he ribbed me for my musical tastes as I fiddled with the radio knobs, and the way the breeze moved through the golden strands of his hair as we followed the sunrise through the valley and down the nearly empty highway. How could anything about this be wrong?

We're not saying goodbye. It's not forever, I recited to myself, thinking of Erica and Milagros as I walked alone up the silent stairs to my room. *Sometimes it works out. Sometimes it works out. It's not forever.*

It may not have been forever, but when even a day seemed too long to wait, *not forever* sounded like a very long time indeed.

Last night, in the walled garden that we'd claimed as ours, we'd managed to see each other—no, to resee each other—in the shape of the people we would be if the world were not what it was. To feel and touch and taste what our imagined eternity could be.

But in the dawn light, there was hardly anything that wasn't uncertain, starting with what Erica and her associates would find.

You know that if it gets to the point where only I can help my sister, I'll go. And I won't think twice about it.

And why were those words echoing in my head and no others? Not his vow not to give up on me, not his assertion that I was his only dream. Not the way he had looked at me, proving it was true. Why couldn't I simply focus on what I had? The fact that he wasn't leaving *yet*?

Because he wasn't leaving yet. But he could. He *could*. And he could be sold on a whim, too, especially if my father's business interests played out even the least bit different than what he envisioned. And that was without Max Langer's scheming—or his attempts to thwart it—in play.

And if and when he left, I would have to accept that it might be forever. Because promising to agree to let him go was part of why I had him back.

It was only November. I still had my final exam to think about—and next semester, for that matter. Surely the fact that I had passed would be enough for my father to agree for the tutoring to continue. Yes, it was for an hour a day only, but we'd done more with less. And it was that thought that enabled me to at last close my eyes, even out my breathing, and sleep.

HIM

Turned out the garden was remarkably peaceful and relaxing when I wasn't working in it. That was my main observation as I reclined that night on the cushions of the sand-colored chaise in the outdoor "room" Louisa had introduced me to, staring down at the phone. The night, alas, was no clearer than last night had been.

It was Saturday, but it felt like Sunday. The fence was done, the housekeeper's list for me was only eight items long, and none of them involved grievous bodily injury. Plus, I'd gotten to *drive*. So aside from the fact that I'd heard nothing from Erica about Maeve's whereabouts, I felt very lucky indeed.

It kind of scared me. Because fallacy or no fallacy, it was hard to shake the notion that lucky didn't last.

That morning, I'd decided not to risk drawing more attention to myself by going downstairs. As odd as the housekeeper clearly found it to see me up earlier than her, especially on a day when I explicitly didn't have to be, it would be odder still if she'd spotted me stumbling downstairs at 6:45 a.m. Instead, the first thing I did was hide the new phone in a different, better spot, one I was sure nobody knew about—only to go retrieve it half an hour later, against my better judgment. After all, carrying it around was exactly how I'd gotten into trouble before, and that had only led to a three-day-long argument. I suspected the next time wouldn't go half so well.

I put the phone down and picked up the book of Roman comedies Louisa had given me. I'd been keenly interested once she'd told me more about them, but I was also secretly afraid they'd all read like Shakespeare. However, in a modern translation, the language was simple enough for even a foreigner to understand.

But there was something missing, and it didn't take long for me to put the book down again to stare at the phone, reminding myself of all the reasons why it was a bad idea to send Louisa a message, even though she was only upstairs and I didn't have a goddamn thing to say except that I missed her. Of course if ours was anything resembling a normal relationship, that wouldn't matter.

But it wasn't. And it did.

Before I could decide, the phone vibrated.

She was calling *me*.

I snatched up the phone and answered, "Hey," greeted only by silence. "Lou?"

The line remained silent, but from behind me came uneven, delirious laughter. Male laughter. And a second later, the phone was snatched right out of my unwary hand.

Fuck. No shit, luck didn't last.

"Is that what you're calling her now?"

I rose from the chaise slowly, keeping my eyes fixed on Corey, who snapped the phone shut, weighing it in his hand like some delicious morsel he was contemplating taking a bite of.

"I know she's not calling *you* anything, except 'here, boy.' Or maybe she just whistles."

Corey laughed loudly and merrily at his joke. This was his birthday gift to himself, it seemed. Coming here solely to torment the one person who had been in his crosshairs for weeks—and evidently, it wasn't Louisa.

The walking, talking thorn in my side wasted no time at all rubbing my stupidity and carelessness in my face, snatching up the Plautus book from where it lay on the chaise, holding it upside down by the spine. His face bore a bloated, rosy glow even in the rapidly dimming light. His wavy dark hair was disheveled; his polo shirt and once-crisp twill shorts wrinkled and dusty as if he'd fallen on the sidewalk somewhere along the way and picked himself up. He wasn't entirely steady on his feet. But he was steady enough.

Enough to make my heart start pounding a fast, eerie, familiar rhythm. I should walk away. I should find Louisa. I should find the housekeeper. I should—but it was already too late, surely. Corey had the book and the phone with its brand-new call record. That was more than enough evidence for anybody who had a mind to condemn us. What was I going to do, fight him for it? I'd never been *allowed* to fight unless someone was betting on the outcome.

"Did she give you this?" he demanded, stifling a hiccup. "Aw, a toy for her faithful German shepherd? Does she read to you over the phone? Oh, wait. You *can* read. One of your little party tricks.

Sure worked on my fucking boss." He lurched closer, half of his face coming into the weak moonlight. "But a dog wearing clothes isn't a fucking person, slave. Some of us haven't forgotten who—sorry, *what*—you really are."

Corey was drunk, but he was also lucid. The worst possible combination. Especially in free men who hated slaves who were smarter than them. A lot of whom, for some reason, tended to have violent streaks.

"He's allowed to have it." The door to the kitchen swung open and to my amazement, Louisa—dim moonlight crowning her face in a way a less skeptical person might have called holy—walked over. She pointed to the phone in Corey's hand. "Daddy gave it to him."

"Oh, so it was Daddy he nicknamed 'Marie Curie?'" he jeered. "The one who asked him to 'come over and give him a hand behind the dry riverbed?' Jesus, you're even more of a ditz than I thought if you think I'm gonna buy that."

Well, God bless her for trying.

"What are you doing here, Corey? Really?" Wordlessly, she slipped her shaking hand into mine. It was the bravest and stupidest and most all-around surreal thing she could have possibly done. And I squeezed it back. "You're drunk, and you're not wanted."

Corey looked her up and down. He had been her friend, but it seemed clear to both of us that his problem no longer even had much to do with her. He had zeroed in on a new obsession.

"Wanted?" He laughed again. "*Wanted*? Who is *wanted*, then? Him?" He jabbed his finger wildly at the air. He was confused, genuinely.

"Yeah," she said, her voice quiet but steady. "Him. Go home, Corey."

Something about us together, again, helped me find my voice. "With all due respect, man, haven't you humiliated yourself enough?"

"What happened to 'sir?' Oh." Corey chuckled harshly. "Oh. I guess since you're fucking her and I'm not, you think 'sir' is too good for me?"

"I think 'cocksucker' is too good for you, but I was trying to be diplomatic." I knew Louisa was smiling. Not so as to be seen. But when I briefly met her eyes, they showed it.

However, Corey was not smiling. "You fucking just can't keep your smart-ass mouth shut for a second, can you, slave?"

"You know, I get that response a lot," I replied. "Especially when what I said can't be argued with."

"Now," he forged on in denial, "I could hang onto this until Daddy gets home and tell him about your late-night sex chat, too. That might be fun. But the truth is," he said, tucking the phone in his pocket and tossing the book away to catch on the paddle of a prickly pear, where it lay open limply, its pages impaled on the spines, "I've been drinking, and honestly, I kind of just *really* want to beat the shit out of you. The problem is, you don't fight back. But hey, I get it. I wouldn't want to spend the rest of my life breaking rocks, either. Fortunately," he added with a nasty grin, "I don't have to worry about that. So I think I'll just take back what should have been mine." And now he looked at Louisa with interest for the first time since she'd arrived on the scene.

"*Yours*?" I repeated the word with a disgust I could almost feel on my tongue. Of course, the only thing I wanted to do at that moment was shove Corey balls-first into a cactus. And Corey, shitfaced as he was, knew it was exactly what I couldn't do. "Fucking hell. You know, you seem to have a real problem telling the difference between people and things?"

"Things?" Corey chuckled with derision. "Let me guess, you think you fall under the first category?" He hiccuped. "You and that bitch who fucked ten mutts a day before spawning you? The one who lived just long enough for you to watch her bleed to death out of her gaping hole? I don't think there's any word for that but *thing*."

A very old heat—one of guilt and shame and helplessness, one I'd spent almost seven years trying to outgrow and outrun and out-smart—flooded over me. *Fuck* this guy. Louisa was looking at me, but I didn't dare look at her.

"Yeah, that's right," Corey barreled on. "Thanks to my ex-boss, I know everything. I know your master chained you up and made you watch him fuck her right in front of you. They should have cut your balls off, too, because a man who can't protect his women isn't much of a man, is he?"

Even Langer had been decent enough not to bring that up. But decency had no meaning for Corey.

I couldn't bear to look at Louisa. Yes, she knew. But for some reason, hearing it from Corey seemed to negate all the comfort and compassion and forgiveness she'd offered me and all the progress we'd made. Like we were back to square one.

But to my surprise, nothing changed. She was breathing evenly. In fact, her entire mien was oddly calm. It's not as if screaming for help would improve the situation at this point, but the serenity in her eyes was almost eerie.

"You're wrong," she said.

"I don't think so." Corey laughed. His hand went for her arm. She jerked away reflexively, but he caught her in his grip just the same. However, the entire time, his gaze was fixed on me. Watching my eyes. Watching how they moved, strained and helpless.

"Keep it up," he told her. "Wait for your good boy to attack. As soon as he does, they'll put him back in a cage where he belongs. I mean, we all know his history. Which does tend to repeat."

"Lou—"

Corey flicked his chin behind him woozily. "And when they come running—I tell everyone—and poor pathetic Daddy can't save you from the auction block, I only hope you'll be lucky enough," he continued, his voice low and hideous as an infected boil, "to get a master who'll give you *exactly* what you deserve." He grabbed her and jerked her toward his face, his fingers leaving an angry red mark on her satiny white flesh. Flesh she had revealed to me last night; in trust; flesh I had spent all night kissing and marveling at an infinite array of miracles, the first of which that she had ever chosen to reveal even an inch of it to me.

But choice had nothing to do with the world we lived in, as if we could ever forget. And it wasn't the look, or the touch, or even the threat that made me ill. It was the fear behind her eyes, much as she tried to hide it, the fear I had once again failed to prevent.

The fear that there was no one left in the world who could help her. The fear that she'd be sullied, violated, terrorized, discarded, just like everything that had ever been precious to me. And that maybe the streak could never be broken.

But no. *No.* Like she'd said, it was fifty-fifty, every time. And for a slave, those were better odds than most.

My voice was as calm as hers had been. "Get your hands off her."

"Like I said, *what are you going to fucking do about it?*"

"How about *this?*" But it was Louisa who had spoken, and I had no doubt my eyes were just as wide as Corey's as we watched her duck out of his grip, wrench her arm around, and take aim with a four-inch-long red cactus spine, the one no one had noticed had been lying flat against her wrist. He froze for a second as the spine drove into the flesh of his cornea. His scream echoed in sharp ripples through the dry night air. He cupped his face with both hands, streaks of blood oozing into the grooves of his fingers. His open eye was wild and mad, his body shivering with rage.

"You little bitch!" he yelled as he staggered half-blindly toward her, fingers clawing through her shirt, digging into her skin, his breath heavy as he wrenched her breast tissue toward himself, throwing her down on the chaise so hard one of the legs collapsed. "You're going to regret that for the rest of your fucking life."

She screamed as one of his bloodied hands pressed down on her tenderest place with all the strength of his body weight as the other one tore brutishly at whatever fabric of her clothing he could get, intent on taking whatever he could take.

Unfortunately for him, he wasn't dealing with a helpless, trembling, chained-up child anymore.

A second later, I had Corey off her and on his feet. He growled and lunged, but I jabbed my elbow into his throat and followed it up with a whipping uppercut that sent him tumbling backward. But he recovered more quickly than I expected, hissing as he charged. With a snarl, he grabbed hold of my weak shoulder—the arm I'd almost lost—with a grip as sharp as white-hot metal teeth, twisting it back against its already-limited range of motion. I stifled a scream at the sharp crack of my shoulder bones reverberating, grinding against each other, followed by a faint sound of tissue tearing again, awakening the old wounds, the old scars, the old sorrows. *Not now.* I drew up my strength, my other fist slamming into his chest, propelling us both onto the sharp trunk of a dead paloverde. The thin bark cracked and splintered under our combined weight, shards of wood flying off in all directions like shrapnel.

Corey, enraged, rolled out from under me, slamming me back where I had just been. We were back up an instant later, with Corey throwing wild, desperate punches that I easily blocked, followed by aiming a knee to my chest. I stumbled back but countered with what I had left, delivering a punch to his stomach, followed by a knee to the solar plexus that sent him staggering, and finally a hook that caught him in the jaw and sent him crashing to the ground.

He roared, attempting to scramble away, but whatever was left of his energy quailed as I went to the ground after him, unleashing the kind of one-handed fury I hadn't had to use since some bored overseers had thrown a skinny thirteen-year-old farm slave into a bare-knuckled match against a kid four years older and a hundred pounds heavier, expecting a quick kill and an even quicker payout on their bets, only to find my barrage of precisely calculated blows to his brainpan raining down so quickly he could barely cover his face.

They never bet against Lucky Sevens again, and neither would Corey.

After I'd pummeled him into oblivion, Corey lay spent, still, chest laboring to fill his lungs, blood seeping into the earth like spring rain.

And everything was silent again. Time had stopped. I stood there for a second, unthinking, unseeing, my shoulder throbbing as hard as if Corey had left a knife buried in it. My body was still as tense as if I expected another blow, my hands balled into fists and spattered burgundy alternating with dirt and blood, mud and grit, wood and bark. Finally, with a shaking hand, I swiped some limp hair out of my face and turned to face Louisa. Her sheet-white face emerged out of the gloom. During the fight, she'd been helpless, even to call for anyone to come, knowing how unlikely it was to result in anything in our favor. But now, gingerly approaching Corey's prone body, she seemed—foolishly and yet fittingly for a girl who aspired to heal—preparing to aid the person who least deserved it.

"Should we—"

But a scream left the sentence unfinished. I spun around again to see Corey lurching toward her—barely seeing her except as the closest target for his rage—with a heavy pair of metal garden shears, discarded under a nearby sage bush, raised high above his head.

Like so many of my decisions that night, it was already made. I lunged for the shears with both hands, through the piercing agony in my shoulder, wrenched them out of Corey's grip, and brought them down on the side of his already bloodied head with a crack.

Corey toppled like lead, his head coming down on the top of a barrel cactus before he rolled off and hit the ground. Blood seeped out from his wound and stained the dust below him, the spines embedded in his flesh. He was still.

Neither of us looked closer. Did it even matter now?

I turned to her, shoulders heaving in exhaustion and adrenaline. But whatever thin wire had been keeping Louisa preternaturally calm until now had snapped.

She stood rooted to the spot, a veil of blind panic flooding over her face as rapid breaths rattled unevenly out of her chest. She wasn't even seeing me.

"Ah, shit." In another second, I would completely lose her. Rapidly trying to get control of my own breath, I cupped her face in my hand with a grip I was sure was too tight, but no less than what the situation called for, forcing her to meet my eyes. "Look at me, Lou. Stay with me. Breathe. We'll figure this out, yeah? But I need you with me, so you have to breathe."

And all of a sudden, she returned.

"Fuck, Lou." I exhaled and kissed her forehead in awe. "What *was* that?" I asked. "And here you thought you weren't good at anything."

"I'm sorry," she whispered. There were tears in her voice, but at least that meant she was present. "I'm so sorry. I shouldn't have—"

"No. I'm glad you did," I said, cutting her off. "It was either that or—well, the important thing is that you're safe. Yeah? That's all that matters."

"No," she cried. "It isn't because—" She tried to look at Corey again, but I jerked her chin back, keeping her focused on me and my words.

"It's all that matters," I repeated firmly. "Yeah? Like I said, we'll figure something out. We always do. Right?"

She nodded.

I pulled her terrorized, shaking body into the shelter of my own dirt- and blood-streaked arms, knowing that whatever comfort I could give her would only be a farce—a laughable mockery of what a free man could offer. What a free man wouldn't *have* to offer because he wouldn't be in this situation in the first place. I wondered, for the millionth time, why she hadn't taken off running a long time ago. Fuck, if I were her, I would have.

But she was braver than that. And smarter. So much smarter, in all the ways I wasn't. And when she looked into my eyes, even though I couldn't protect her from what she feared the most, there was still hope behind them. Hope, even as the walls we'd built to shelter each other were crashing down into the sea.

In truth, I hadn't believed it when I'd told her we'd figure things out. I'd said it, almost selfishly, just to keep from losing her. But now, her eyes were almost enough for me to believe that we could.

"You have to go," she said quietly.

"What?" I blinked.

"You have to go. Tonight. Right now. Back to Erica's. She'll know what to do from there."

"But I—"

"Take the car. The keys are inside. The GPS will take you to campus, and you can find your way from there. Daddy will still trigger the chip, but not until tomorrow when he gets back. I can come up with a story and buy you a little bit of time. We've done it before. I plan, you execute. Speed chess, right? Right?"

Her voice seemed to come from underwater. My vision blurred for a second, and she looked at me as if afraid *I'd* now lost the plot.

But I nodded. "You're right."

A breeze rattled, of all things, some terra cotta wind chimes from far off in the garden.

And that was it.

But still, we stood there, with no solace but in the cold of the desert night, no warmth but in each other.

We'd come back here because we thought that, if nothing else, it would buy us time together. But we'd got it wrong. If it had to be goodbye no matter what, then it should have been that morning. Properly, by choice. Like real people, instead of fugitives.

As my shoulders rose and fell, she gave me the only things she had left to give: her spine, brushing my bruised hand over it; her curls, to gather and let fall. She gave me her manicured hand—how could it still be so flawless after *that*?—to caress my ruined and throbbing shoulder, to trace my blood-streaked cheeks and jaw, brushing away the strands of hair she'd once thought shimmering, now dull and dirt-covered and matted to my face. And finally, she gave me her lips. And then she had nothing left to give, except time.

Time. How had it all come down to seconds?

Louisa pulled away from the kiss. "I—"

All at once, the floodlights snapped on, effectively blinding us. Harsh, naked fluorescent light, designed to lay bare all the hardest, ugliest parts of the world. This was the light of dealerships and auction houses, buildings made of cinderblock and steel, chains and cages made for animals, where no one, least of all slaves, ever went by choice. Where I always seemed to end back up, despite every good thing I'd ever found in this nonstop horror show I'd been forced to call a life. Where Corey had insisted I would end up again, and it was looking like he might be right.

I'd thought I wouldn't get lucky again—as if I'd ever *been* lucky. What kind of twisted fucking luck would give me this girl, only to lose her like *this*?

From the garage access door strode a figure, moving slowly, on a bad leg that, like always, he was unsuccessfully trying to play down.

The old valet.

Well, it was time to start praying. Just this once because if a god was good enough for Louisa to believe in, it was at least worth a try. And because dammit, he or she or it or they or whatever the fuck was up there owed me at least *one* favor, surely.

But the word on Louisa's lips—once she made out the figure behind the valet—stopped me before I could even begin.

"Daddy."

14

HER

For the second time in as many days, I woke alone, in terror, in darkness. Woke to find him gone. But this time, there was no chance he would appear at my bedside, amid the scent of flowering vines and smoke and starlight, coaxing my eyes up to the stars with boyish excitement. There was no chance he was seeing the stars wherever he was now. There was a good chance he never would again. This time, time was up.

But I wasn't alone. There was a hand on my back, a voice in my ear, humming.

The last thing I remembered was screaming at my father over sirens and the neon blur of ambulance lights. Saying something, *anything*, to explain the situation. But I'd been shaking, disoriented, barely coherent, and I knew it hadn't worked. He was already gone. My father had sent him away *first*, to get him as far away from me as possible. And then the housekeeper had put a blanket over me and hustled me inside, all while my father's eyes bored into me with sheer disgust—a look I'd *never* received from him before, and one that made it clear that shutting up and following the older woman was my one and only option.

I'd been useless and incompetent, in other words. Like so many times before.

Upstairs, I stood catatonically in the shower for twenty minutes, thinking almost literally nothing, until the housekeeper came in again to tell me to turn it off and get into bed. She slipped a T-shirt over my head and handed me hot cocoa, tea, and soup as if tricking me into believing any of those things could possibly help this nightmare. My whole body felt wrung out and squeezed dry, the red marks on my arms and breasts still lingering nastily against the white. And that was the point. Corey had come for one and only one purpose: to make me a thing without agency, to be used as leverage, to be marked and manhandled and misused. Me *and* him. Because that's what Corey genuinely believed we were. And whether he had lived or died, he'd proven it. He'd won.

And just as that thought crossed my mind, a hand was rubbing my back and a voice was humming a song with my name in it, one I hadn't heard in a very long time.

"Mom?"

Yes. My mom sat on my bed in that aura of golden lamplight that always seemed to follow her, even when I was a child. It bounced off her expensive jewelry, reflected off the crystal stemware she always carried around, chiming like her laughter. Sure, as always, she was several martinis in, but this was a side of her I thought she'd buried for good, along with my brother's love. And yet, wasn't it strange when the very last people you expected to try, tried so *hard*?

"Is he still as brave as you said?"

The question startled me, but my mother hadn't indicated that she even knew who *he* was. Maybe she didn't. Maybe she was pretending she didn't. Maybe it didn't matter because there was virtually no chance she would remember this conversation tomorrow.

So I stretched and leaned my aching limbs into her touch. "Braver."

She nodded and kept humming.

I closed my eyes. When the sound of the door opening woke me again, my mother was gone, but the housekeeper had returned—not with water, soup, or cocoa, but with a silent, beckoning gesture. Without hesitation, I rose from the bed and followed.

HIM

In the weeks since I had arrived in the house, I had attempted numerous times to engage the old valet in conversation—half out of sincerity, half out of cynicism, knowing that when shit inevitably went down, it helped to have fellow slaves on my side, especially the ones at the top of the heap. But I'd given up quickly. The guy simply had no interest in engaging with anyone except his master. It was as if doing shit like picking out Louisa's dad's golf visor was the only thing that made him feel alive.

But that night, I found that maybe my efforts hadn't been in vain. Because as the valet escorted me downstairs and into the windowless basement storage room I now occupied, he was gentle as he closed the metal cuffs around my wrists—new and shiny, like they lived most of the time in a drawer—and attached a short chain that he looped around the bottom of a metal shelf bolted to the wall behind me. There was nothing on the bottom of the shelf, but the top seemed to hold cardboard boxes and plastic tubs of odds and ends that were just barely visible in the light coming from the crack under the door. The old guy held a bottle of water to my mouth and let me guzzle half of it before leaving it behind to manage as best I could. There was more he could have done—like wash the blood off or give me some pain meds, you think?—but apparently, he was already on borrowed time, so he just shook his head and shut the door, switching off the light as he went. Which seemed cruel until I realized that the naked fluorescent bulb burning into my tender retinas all night would have been a kind of torture in and of itself.

Besides, what terrified me more was the way the valet had looked at me just before he pulled the string. Like he thought this was the last act of kindness I would ever get.

The chain was just long enough so that I could almost touch the bottom of the door, though not the handle. Meanwhile, blood from somewhere—my mouth? My eye? I wasn't even sure of all the places Corey had managed to make me bleed—had leaked out to pool on the concrete beneath me, a wet, sticky, viscous mass soaking into my torn clothing, itself covered in dirt and broken bark. And my shoulder had gone rigid, even the slightest movement sending a horribly familiar searing pain down my entire arm and well into my torso. And with the addition of the metal on my wrists, the old wounds beneath it throbbed again as if the restraints had ignited the memories of the decade's worth of scars they already bore. Ones that over the past few weeks, I'd almost managed to forget were there. Until Corey came along to make sure I never would.

If I'd been able to stand up or even move normally, I would have been rifling through the storage room for something to maybe pick the cuffs open with, followed by the lock on the door. It wasn't as easy as it looked, but—usually with the help of idiots who hadn't put them on correctly to begin with—I'd managed it a little more often than the average slave. Anyway, say what you would about the valet, he wasn't dumb. And he knew what he was doing—the things were on solid.

But that instinct was exactly why I was now in chains, on the orders of the very man who had insisted, upon our first meeting, that I *not* be chained.

My master had finally figured me out.

There was no sound in that room, no ticking clock, no day, no night. The highlight was when what might have been a cockroach or a rat scrabbled in the corner, then hastily left. The room wasn't freezing, but it wasn't warm, either, and I spent what *might* have been all night and most of the next day huddled on the concrete floor. Occasionally, when I was lucky, drifting off for mere seconds before jerking awake, shivering in terror and renewed pain, possibly feverish now, remembering the reason why I was where I was. At first, I'd expected, if not Louisa, then her dad or *someone* to come, but now I was almost willing to consider the fact that they—her included—had forgotten about me.

If she had, *well, congratulations, kid.* Maybe she could still move on from this nightmare and have a real life. That was better than considering the alternative—that she was somewhere alone, crying, hurt in soul as much as in body, with no one to comfort her. And that was my only regret, really. Not what I'd done—I'd do it again in a second. The regret was that she might still need me, and I wasn't there. It was the same regret I had about Maeve. The same regret I'd have for what remained of my life, it seemed. Either do nothing and watch as you lose the ones you care about the most, or fight back and lose them anyway, only more painfully for all of you. I should have learned it earlier.

"I'm sorry," I whispered aloud to both of them. To my sister, to my mother. And then to *her*.

I'd failed to save them all, and the most shameful part of all was that if anyone *should* have been able to do it, it was me. Save for freedom, I'd had almost every advantage anyone could ask for. But what were all the gifts in the world if I couldn't do the only thing that mattered?

And meanwhile, I'd die. Not in a mine, but here. Alone. Forgotten. Entombed alive in her own house.

Knowing that you fucked up her life as well.

Well, at least I had the mocking voices in my head to keep me company.

It was better that she didn't come, I told myself, curling up into a tighter ball for the fiftieth time to delude myself that I could actually sleep like this, in pain, exacerbated by discomfort and grief.

Louisa had never seen me in chains. She didn't seem to realize, innocent as she was, that it was practically my default state. But Corey, idiot that he was, did. He'd *wanted* Louisa to see me like this. He'd wanted her to see me for the animal, for the *thing* Corey desperately needed me to be so he could cling to the superiority he'd felt had been stolen from him.

So this was best. Hell, it was best that she forget about me completely. But if she decided to be stubborn enough to try to remember me, it was better as the real person we'd both found a way to pretend I was, for a while.

I didn't really hope Corey was dead, but … fuck it, of course I did.

Anyway, dead or alive, it didn't matter. The punishment would be the same.

I fell asleep shivering and woke up to a voice.

15

HER

"I told him what really happened. What Corey did. And I'll tell him again. I'll tell him until he listens. And everything I said the other day, about not giving up? It all still applies. Nothing's changed. Whatever happens. We'll figure it out. We always do." I spewed my every thought toward the crack under the door, without even a word of greeting, which seemed ridiculous anyway.

But I got no response. There was nothing in there. No light, no words, no movement. "Hey," I said, though cold dread had already gripped me, sending my heart rate into overdrive. "Are you there?" Surely he just had to be asleep. What if the housekeeper had been wrong? Had he been moved? Sent away? Surely he couldn't have been sold *this* quickly, though I didn't doubt Daddy had his channels. Or what if he was *dead*? What if my fucking father had let him *die* down there in pain and despair and—

"Lou," he said. "Are you okay?"

"Oh, God," I said, exhaling, my forehead touching the door, my long hair swinging in front of my face. "I'm fine. I brought you some—for your shoulder—" I pulled out the pain pills and bandages and slid them underneath the door, followed by the energy bar courtesy of the housekeeper, shoving it up against the too-small opening. "Goddammit, it doesn't fit." I tried forcing it, holding back the urge to scream or cry. "And neither does water or antiseptic or—"

"Lou, I feel like I've been saying this to you a lot lately, but calm down. Breathe. I'm not going to starve to death in the next five minutes." His words were normal for him, but his voice was not.

He's in pain. I'd known he would be, hence the meds, but hearing it in his voice was altogether different.

"Fuck. You sound awful."

"Thanks. You don't even want to know how I look."

"No, I mean, you need to see a doctor. And as much as I wish passing one semester of o-chem made me one, it doesn't."

"Not really a priority for your dad now, I wouldn't think. Anyway, this wouldn't exactly be the first time I should have seen a doctor but didn't."

Yes, and his body was a hastily rewritten palimpsest of scars and untreated wounds, but there was no time to point *that* out because I had just realized that it wasn't my imagination that every time he moved, I heard an unmistakable and sickening rattling. And then I knew. "He *chained* you?"

"Why wouldn't he, after that?"

He seemed surprised at *my* surprise, but—oh. Because he was a slave. And that's what happened to slaves who fucked up. He didn't have the liberty to ever forget that, but apparently, I, naïve idiot that I still was, did.

"Is Corey ..." he trailed off.

Did the mention of Corey have to contaminate even *this* conversation? But he should know, even if it didn't make any difference now. "He's in surgery. Nobody is telling me anything, but I think it could still go either way."

Whatever happened, there would be no further involvement from the authorities. My boy would be my father's alone to deal with. The police were always happy to help subdue a violent slave or capture an escaping one, but then they'd immediately hand them back over to their owner, who would be trusted to take the appropriate actions. It was a system that had proved remarkably efficient—except for maybe the slaves, but nobody ever asked them.

"And what about—"

"They found your phone and gave it to Daddy."

"Fuck. At least it was the new one, so he won't find much."

"I know. He took my phone, too. I was careful, though. No names or anything."

"Will you—"

Even now, even while almost literally helpless, asking for help with Maeve seemed as painful for him as removing a vital organ.

"I just told you, this doesn't change anything, including with Maeve. We'll keep looking." *Even if you aren't there,* was my implication. What I didn't add was that mere moments before my phone disappeared into my father's hand, I'd already had a message from Erica (well, Emma Goldman, which was what I'd saved the number under), demanding I call her as soon as possible. It could be good or bad news, but one thing was certain: he didn't need to be worrying about his sister more than himself right now. I could handle Maeve, and I could *almost* handle the guilt of not telling him. I had no choice, anyway.

His next words were the exact ones I'd been dreading. "You should go." Though the eagerness with which he'd responded to the sound of my voice indicated he might personally feel otherwise.

"I'm not leaving."

"I know you think it can't get much worse than this, but it can," he said. "And it will if you get caught here."

I groaned. "God, will you stop being so fucking noble for one second?! I want to put myself in danger on your behalf, dammit, and anyway, you're locked in a fucking closet so it's not like there's anything you can do to stop me. Plus, the housekeeper and the valet have my back," I said. "They'll signal if Daddy comes."

"They both know everything now, don't they?"

"Yup."

But like Corey being alive or dead, at this point, it was whatever.

"Maybe they could—" But he stopped himself as if realizing he couldn't put a fellow slave in that position. It probably went against some kind of unwritten code, and anyway, nothing they could do would really help, unless they knew how to deactivate microchips. My dad had probably triggered his preemptively. Even if by some miracle he could escape the chains and then escape the room, he wouldn't make it halfway up the stairs.

"They don't have the keys, and they're already risking a lot letting me be down here," I said. "They want to help you. They know what happened. But there's only so much they can do without putting their own asses on the line."

"I know, Lou. Believe me, I get it. Can ... can you tell them thank you? From me?"

"Of course. They're not going to believe what they're hearing, or at least that they're hearing it from *me*. But I think they're going to be hearing a lot of things from me they've never heard before." I paused. "All thanks to you."

"No," he said. "It wasn't me. It was in you all along. You just needed a little nudge."

"Oh," I said with a little laugh. "Is that what you're calling it?"

"I could call it something else, but this hardly feels like the time or the place for such language." He was cracking *jokes*? I'd sensed a change in his voice, a lift, from when I'd arrived minutes ago until now. There was still a weak rattle of pain in it, and I didn't want to think about what kinds of awful things must have been going through his head before I'd arrived. I just knew I needed to keep him this way as long as I could, so fuck if I was going anywhere, no matter what he said. Because I knew he didn't mean it, anyway.

"Maybe we could—" We prided ourselves on figuring things out, but how? Force of will? Magic spells? Have me run upstairs and try yet again to make Daddy see reason, and cut short our time together? For fuck's sake, we'd already vetoed every idea for a possible way out of this. "Tell me what you need me to do."

"I need you to stop panicking. I don't—" I don't want to remember you that way, was what he meant.

I swallowed. In a minute, talking was going to be a lot harder, so I'd better get the words out now.

"And for you? What do I need to do for you?"

A pause. Not something he got asked very often. He'd once told me that, in this very basement. *No one does anything for me, ever.*

"Just—just talk to me?" There was a question in it. Why was there a question in it? Because he still didn't believe that anyone would do anything for him? Well, fuck. In that case, I'd better find a way to talk.

"About what?" Not that I thought he'd be picky.

"Um. Tell me about your dog."

"Oh—okay." Where had *that* come from? Then again, it was an innocuous topic that had nothing to do with violence, rape, torture, or death, and so actually had a lot to recommend it right now. "She was an English setter, and she was mostly Ethan's. Daddy wanted her trained for duck hunting, even though he only went once a year. I'm not sure she ever actually got a duck, though she sure seemed to like eating them. Not to mention rolling in their rotting carcasses. But she was the sweetest, gentlest, most loving dog I ever knew ..."

At first, there was only silence on the other side of the door. Had I said something wrong? How had I fucked up talking about a goddamn dog?

"Artemis," he said finally. "Her name was Artemis."

"What?" I exclaimed. "Are—are you psychic?"

A rueful laugh. "If I were, as much as I'm enjoying this conversation, don't you think I would have been able to avoid being forced to have it? Her old collar and bowls are in here."

"Wait, Daddy kept those?"

My father had always given the impression that he'd found Artemis a disappointment, given how much he'd paid for her. Then again, how many evenings had he spent with her head resting on his lap in front of the fire pit? Not to mention, Ethan had loved her more than anything. And maybe, with his dog as with his son, my dad realized too late that he should have held on tighter to what he had while he had it.

And unwittingly ensured I wouldn't *ever* make that mistake.

If I could have used his name, I would have. I would say it and say it and say it and never stop saying it, not until the end of time, not until I couldn't anymore, not until I was dead and buried and earth and rain and snow covered up my lips. If I could, I would give up my *own* name in exchange. Of course I couldn't do that, but there was one thing I could do. I'd already tried last night. But now there was nothing to hold me back.

"I love you."

HIM

"Don't say that," I said automatically.

"Why not?" she demanded.

"Because it's easier?" I realized instantly how lame that sounded but also that I didn't fully want—or know how—to take it back.

Instead, I awkwardly scrubbed a hand over my face, chain rattling, and took a breath. "You know, people—well, people who aren't Erica Muller, anyway—believe slaves can only feel ... basic stuff. Fear.

Anger. Maybe some loyalty. A simple affection for people who are kind to them. And honestly? I never questioned it that much. I just went with it."

On the other side of the door, silence. Well, I couldn't have fucked that up any more if I'd tried. Then:

"That's insane."

"I know. But it sure made things simpler."

"So you just ... shut it off?" she finally asked, more curious than accusing, thank fuck. "Everything real?"

"I mean, yeah. I've stayed awake for days at a time, thinking about quantum theory, pondering the subatomic world, and somehow *that* was easier, and a lot less scary, than thinking about love. About what it actually means," I finished, not waiting to find out if she'd stormed away from the door in disgust yet. "I mean, look, let's be honest, if your life's never easy and you're never really safe, why the fuck would you make it harder by giving away your heart, too? If you're forced to give away every other part of yourself, why would you choose to let go of one of the few things you can actually keep?" I glanced away from the door, terrified of her answer. Terrified she wouldn't answer at all.

"Because some things are worth letting go of," she whispered. "Because you get so much back in return."

"How do you know?" asked stubbornly.

"How do I know? I ... I don't know. I just—"

"Believe," I scoffed despite myself. "Like faith. Like miracles. You just believe."

"Yeah," she said quietly. "I just believe. And, look, it's a privilege to believe. I know it is."

"It is, but ..." I swallowed. I couldn't believe what I was about to say, because I hadn't known it was true until a second ago. "I wish I could believe, Lou. I really do. I wish it so goddamn much."

"But you do," she replied instantly, to my surprise. "Look at your mom. Look at Maeve. You would die for them. You know you would. You almost did, a few times."

"But that didn't feel like a choice. That just ... *was*. Letting someone else in—*choosing* someone—that's different. That's something I always thought I wouldn't do. Couldn't do. Wasn't meant to." I threw my head back helplessly on the cold concrete, my voice cracking slightly. "Because the truth is ... this is what scares me most. Not the mines, not dying and my bones getting thrown down the shaft, more than watching everyone close to me be tortured and raped, more than reliving every bruise, every beating, every whipping, every cut and burn I've ever gotten, *all at once*. It's *this*. Saying it out loud. Letting someone in. And I don't know," I paused to forcefully swallow back everything that was threatening to pour out, "why it's like that. I wish I did. But it is, Lou. It is." I closed my eyes softly. "And that's why I don't know if I can believe. And *that's* why you shouldn't say it."

She paused long enough that I was pretty well convinced she was gone. "Well, I'm sorry," she finally huffed in an old, familiar tone. "But that's how I feel, and if I want to say it, I will. You don't get to tell me what I can say, or what I can feel, or what I can believe." She took a deep breath. "I love you. I love you, okay? And I don't want to hear another word out of you about it."

And amazingly, I laughed. "Well, shit. Of all the things to act like a spoiled princess about. You really aren't making this easy for yourself, you know."

"Hey," she went on, softer now, "when have you and I ever been about easy? Anyway, the truth is ... I've never said it before, either," she added. "To a boy."

In my mind's eye, I could see her blushing.

"You've never said it either, have you?" she asked. "To anyone."

"No," I admitted.

"Have you felt it?"

I closed my eyes. "I think so," I said with finality. "But I'm not exactly an expert on this kind of thing."

"Well, I'm not either, you know."

"I'll—I'll figure it out," I said quickly, suddenly realizing I might have just fucked up absolutely everything. She might *leave*. My only hope was that she could read between the lines of what I was saying—even if what I was saying wasn't *it*. "Just give me some time." I sat up and scrambled against the chain to get closer to the door as if I could somehow reach out and touch her—as if that weren't the very thing throwing me in here was meant to prevent me from doing. "I promise. Just, um, don't leave right now," I pleaded. *Or ever.* "Yeah?"

"I'm not going anywhere."

She said it without a pause. Like it had never even crossed her mind. I exhaled and collapsed back down onto the concrete.

"And," she continued, "it's okay if you're not ready to say it. Because ... because you will."

And God, if her beautiful face were minted on a gold coin, this would be the other side of it—why she wasn't just *a* princess, she was *my* princess.

And why I felt such relief, I would never know because as soon as she got word that her father was coming downstairs, she *was* going to have to go.

And then, eventually, so was I.

I leaned closer to the door, barely breathing. "Listen, remember back at Erica's? That conversation we had in the kitchen, when I asked you why you were there?"

"I remember."

"I knew I'd done nothing, *nothing* to deserve you there—for fuck's sake, I'm too much of a selfish, cowardly asshole to even choke out three little words—and yet, despite it all, you were there. And I just ... I doubted that I, a faithless man in a faithless world, could possibly have the love of someone with so much goddamn *faith*."

"Well?" she breathed, soft as a whisper. "Do you still doubt it?"

I shook my head slowly, forehead resting against the metal shelf, and whispered it like a prayer. "No."

My fingers dug into the shelf like it was the only thing holding me up. "Look, maybe ... I don't believe in souls. You know that. But I know you do, so if I've got one—if there's some piece of me that still exists on the other side of all this, of whatever I end up—then it's yours, *mäi léift*. And maybe ... maybe in some better world, one where I'm not shackled and you're not dragging around the weight of the privilege you didn't ask for and every goddamn person you couldn't help, maybe we get to find each other again. Not as what we are now. But as what we were supposed to be."

She hiccupped her next words, and I knew what that meant. Hell, I could *see* it—her face crumpling, her shoulders shaking, trying to stay quiet and loudly, exquisitely failing, like always. And I could never do the one goddamn job that mattered—

"I have an idea. Put your hand by the bottom of the door."

I obeyed instantly. The length of the chain was just enough. If I stretched out my good arm as far as it would go, trailing the bad one behind it, I could fit the rough tips of my fingers just beyond the surface of the door. And I was rewarded by warm, delicate, manicured nail tips against my own. It wasn't anything, really. But it was so much more than I ever, in all my years—exposed, boiling, freezing, starving, bleeding, chained, caged in dirt and mud and piss-filled holes—thought I would have, or ever deserve. I still didn't deserve it, or even understand it, but what I'd said was true: I didn't doubt it. Not anymore. I knew she would stay until the very end of the line, and that I would stop being so fucking noble and let her. Until the other side of the door was quiet, until one or both of us fell asleep on the concrete floor, or the housekeeper gave her the sign, whatever happened first.

She was quiet already. Could she already be lying there asleep, the tears on her cheeks frozen where they'd fallen? Could this be—

And then came a sudden, sharp, staccato giggle.

"What's so funny?"

"Here we are, talking without seeing each other's faces," she said. "Just like the first time."

16

HIM

Needless to say, when the door was thrown open at first light—or what would have been had there *been* any light—the face that appeared was not the one I'd dreamed of last night; the one serene image that finally allowed me—along with the pain pills, maybe—to close my eyes and sleep for a few minutes. Rather, it was one that bore just enough of a familial resemblance to Louisa to make it, unfortunately, impossible to hate. I'd tried.

Seeing my master, I scrambled to my knees, since that was as far up as I could get. It was agony kneeling on the hard concrete floor, and now I was weak and almost shaking from a day with no food, little water, and mere minutes of sleep. Pretty much everything hurt, of course, but my re-torn shoulder had swollen nearly double and frozen stiff. Even moving it slightly brought white-hot, searing pain, so I tried not to.

But Louisa's father didn't look well, either. Every ounce of vitality he'd regained in recent weeks had vanished. He was hollow-eyed, wan, and unkempt as if he'd slept fully clothed. If he'd also been bruised and bleeding, we wouldn't be too far apart.

After snapping on the bulb, he just stood there, looking at me, who, though my head was bowed, watched him through the sticky, bloody, matted strands of hair in my face.

At least I wouldn't be in suspense for long. So what would it be?

Oh. The swift backhand across the face. Solid choice.

The blow hit its mark precisely. Even in his disheveled state, Louisa's father, athlete that he was, was by no means physically weak, and I gasped as I struggled to stay on my knees. Shooting pain and the taste of blood filled my sinuses, blurring my vision and stealing my breath. I doubled over, placing my hands on the floor to steady myself; such an amateur, childlike thing to do. Wainwright-Phillips roughly grabbed me by my injured shoulder, hauling me back to my knees, and I bit back a whimper of pain at the stabbing of a thousand invisible knives. Gulping for air, I still averted my eyes. Why? As if it mattered now. It was just that they'd fucking trained me so *well*.

"I trusted you."

The phrasing surprised me. A slave's transgression, to an owner, was frustrating, infuriating, and occasionally even disappointing, but it was rarely a deep, personal betrayal. To my master, though, it seemed this was.

"After nearly twenty years, you *still* haven't learned your place," Louisa's father continued. "And I certainly haven't helped by being so lenient with you. I should have known something like this would happen when they said you were potentially dangerous. But I thought I knew what I was doing. I thought three years of hard labor in the fields must have taught you your lesson. I thought a hands-off approach would show you that I trusted that you could be a good slave, one who would make me proud. Obviously, I was wrong."

Well, yeah. He was. About pretty much everything.

"I've read that slaves can't change their fundamental natures and that once past the event horizon, can't be corrected. I didn't believe it. It seems I should have." He began to pace what little square footage the storage closet contained. "Did you think of me at all and the trust I placed in you? Did you think of *her*? What this would do to her reputation?"

What did he mean, did I think of her? Fuck, of course I thought of her. More often and more thoughtfully than her own father seemed to think about her most of the time. But *that* observation certainly wasn't worth sharing, at least if I wanted to keep all the teeth in my head.

"You of all people should know how hard she's worked to make a life for herself, one that I tried and failed to give her. You've seen it. You *helped* her do it, which makes it all the more mind-boggling to me." He paused. "So what do you have to say for yourself, boy? This is your one chance to speak, so choose your words wisely."

My vision was still blurry, my weakened hands digging into my thighs through the torn fabric of my shorts as if I just needed something to cling to while I rifled through the far reaches of my brain for anything I could possibly say that would help. But I didn't find anything, so I might as well tell the truth.

"I did, sir," I said. "Think of her, I mean."

Well, whatever Wainwright-Phillips had been expecting me to say, it clearly wasn't that. His stern mask, as it often did, slipped for a second before reappearing.

"The bottom line is, you violently attacked a free person and at the very least, your fixation on my daughter, whatever else it may be, is wildly inappropriate if not downright dangerous. Anyone else in my position would be trying to determine whether anything more than what I saw tonight happened between you. But frankly, I'd rather not know."

Except the way he said *I'd rather not know* sort of implied *I already know*. And really, how could he not? Up until now, he may have been oblivious, but he wasn't stupid.

"I wonder," he continued, taking a step closer, prompting me to try not to flinch. "When I told you I would see that you were rewarded, did I give you a reason to think I didn't mean it?"

What? Was he kidding? There was *every* reason to think he didn't mean it.

"I know you probably think I'm a complete idiot, but I'm not. I know you're far above what I've had you doing. I knew that when I bought you, and what I've seen of you, up until now, has only reinforced that. I had plans for you: greater responsibility; more autonomy; a better life. I wanted you to be happy here. I really did. But before I gave you that, I needed to be sure you could be trusted. You've not only violated that trust, you've lit it on fire.

"To be honest," he continued, "I blame myself for letting you be in such close proximity to her so often. I should have *never* let the two of you be alone unsupervised. But hindsight won't help mitigate the damage. The Killeens will not let this go. They are absolutely ruthless when they feel they've been wronged, and they want you on your way to a mine tomorrow, or they'll get the police involved. And you know what that means for Louisa if they do."

Of course I did. Just the same as she knew what getting caught meant for me. And we'd done it anyway because ... why? Well, for starters, because we were idiots. As if he needed to rub that in.

"And don't think quietly paying a fine is going to make it go away, assuming I can scrounge up that money somewhere. They've also threatened to use the civil courts." He meant they'd sue, something that never happened in Europe but did here, and if they did, they'd take him for all he was worth. And that would be the end of his deal with Langer, the end of any chance he had to claw his way back to the top. But amazingly, that seemed to be only his secondary concern.

"If they file suit, never mind the financial damage, this one incident will be blown up into things that have no basis in reality. They'll rip our entire family to shreds when we can least afford it, and worst of all, they'll publicly throw my daughter's life and future to the wolves. And above all, my first obligation is to her."

Funny that he should only realize that *now*.

"However, we both know that what they want would be a tragic waste of your gifts, and as angry as I am, I can't allow that to color my judgment." He looked away as if he were gazing out the nonexistent window. "Purely from a practical standpoint, the world is better served with you above ground, and my daughter—" He choked on the words. "My daughter has also spoken up on your behalf."

I squeezed my eyes shut. He didn't have to tell me that. He probably *shouldn't* have told me that. But for some reason, he had. When we first met, I had thought he almost deserved a chance. If nothing in the interim had ever happened, maybe that would still be the case.

"That's why I've worked out an alternative solution—courtesy of Max Langer."

My head hadn't snapped up so fast in front of one of my owners since I was a child. I forced my eyes down to the bare concrete again, my heart pounding so fast I was certain Wainwright-Phillips could hear it.

"Mr. Langer has offered to pay the Killeen boy's medical bills—for my family's sake, hopefully not his funeral costs—plus a significant sum in exchange for their keeping quiet and pursuing no further action. And in return, I'll lend you to Mr. Langer. Permanently."

The implications of this—what it meant for me, for Louisa, Maeve, and for the future—were almost incomprehensible after forty-eight hours of this funhouse of pain and anguish. And Wainwright-Phillips was *still* talking as if from the other side of an underwater tunnel.

"After all this, I doubt you'd be foolish enough not to rid your head of any further thoughts of my daughter, but if you are, rest assured I'll be confiscating her phone and computer and monitoring all her other communication channels. And don't forget I'll still have the capability to track your whereabouts. If I find that you've tried to contact her in any way, I can and will revoke the deal. The mines are *not* off the table. You're being given a chance to atone for the damage you've done to my family. If I were you, I'd work very hard to keep on Mr. Langer's good side. Do not squander this opportunity as you won't get another one."

He paused again. Oh, shit, I was probably supposed to say something. I opened my mouth.

"Do *not* thank me, boy," he cut me off. "This is entirely Mr. Langer's doing. You have him to thank that you're ever going to get another chance to see daylight. What you will *not* see is this house again or anyone in it, except for perhaps myself and then purely for business. Other than on paper, I'm completely washing my hands of you. Your future is effectively his to decide. And that's far better than you deserve."

I drew in a ragged breath. "Am I—"

"Are you going to be flogged? That's what you want to know, isn't it?"

Actually, it wasn't even near the top of the list.

"The answer is no. Not on my orders, anyway. And—" He cut himself off as he often did when he seemed tempted to treat me too much like a person. When he felt too compelled to say something like, *You've suffered enough.* Slaves could *never* be allowed to think that they'd suffered enough.

He looked at me expectantly. Wait, he was still going to let me speak?

"How much time do I have, sir?" I asked.

Of course Wainwright-Phillips would be appalled to know the one and only reason I was asking. To know that I was praying to something that yesterday I'd been convinced I didn't believe in for just one chance to say all the things to that fearless angel that I was too much of a coward to say last night. How could I have been so foolish as to think I'd ever get another chance to say them? To ask for more time? There was *never* any more time when your time wasn't your own.

"One of Mr. Langer's security team is outside the door as we speak. As soon as I leave, he'll show you to the car."

My vision blurred. I looked down at my hands and nodded.

All right, then. That's how it will be.

By the grace of whatever, I'd been spared the mines. And yet it barely registered. All I could think about was that Louisa was right. She'd entered my life as merely a voice, and she'd exited that way, too. And like countless times before, she'd been braver than me, braver than anyone ever gave her credit for, brave enough to say what I couldn't. And now, because of my cowardice and stupidity, she'd exit not only not knowing that I loved her but not knowing that she'd accomplished the impossible: proven, definitively, that I was capable of love.

At Erica's, I'd heard a phrase I knew I'd read before, and it soon turned out I had. Five years ago, soon after the professor had ensured my literacy was up to an acceptable level, he'd handed me a stack of books he felt an educated person should be familiar with and ordered me to read. Shakespeare and Dickens in English; Goethe and Hesse in German; Hugo and Dumas in French, plus—much to my frustration—*poetry*, in all of them. Because literacy, I'd quickly discovered, wasn't the same as comprehension, and I was pretty sure Louisa had caught onto that when we'd started exploring her bookshelf. It didn't help that there was almost no real Luxembourgish literature, as tiny as the country was. But as a teenage slave, lately erased from and restored to the world, I simply lacked the cultural context to understand it, in any language. It wasn't because of the inferiority of my *fundamental nature*, as Wainwright-Phillips had said, but simply that I'd been raised by those who already believed in it.

Maybe someday, I'd hoped, when I was older and wiser, I'd go back and the meaning would just fall into place as easily as the hydrogen and oxygen molecules did in those endless chemical reactions I'd spent thousands of hours poring over in the lamplight after the professor had gone to bed. Maybe someday was now.

And this was why my eyes, under my matted hair, scanned the room—the shelves—one more time. *Time.* As predicted, my luck had run out, but surely—even restrained, weakened, in pain—I was still good enough to find a second. Because that was all I needed for this.

Meanwhile, Wainwright-Phillips was preparing to sweep out of the room like he usually did. He stopped, though. Softened his voice. "Look at me, boy."

At first, it seemed he meant to grab and tilt my head up, as he did. Instead, he let me raise my gaze on my own. For a second, our eyes met.

"In this world, there are some things that simply cannot be, no matter how much we want them," he said. "I've come to understand that more than you probably know. And in time, so will you."

I dropped my eyes again as he paused, just for a second, on the knob.

"Good luck."

Then he was gone.

17

HER

I lay motionless on the bed as I had for most of the day and night. I was vaguely aware of the sun rising and setting and rising again, that the week had begun, and that I should be getting up, getting dressed, and going to class. Ha. It was as if my body refused to respond to normal stimuli, just as it unconsciously refused to shower or remove the clothes I'd worn for two days, as if even the last things I'd worn in his presence were a memory worth keeping. The housekeeper rotated in and out, her offerings and admonitions largely ignored. But at some point, as I knew it would, the door opened and it wasn't the housekeeper. And when it finally did, I squeezed my eyes shut. My ears. My mind.

"This is me looking out for you, Loulou. I know it doesn't feel like it."

"You know nothing," I spat into my pillow.

"Don't you understand? They were going to the police about you, and even if I could find the money to keep you off the auction block, which is no guarantee, they threatened to sue. A court case would destroy you publicly," my father said. "They have no compassion, no remorse."

"But they can't prove that I did anything."

"They can prove enough. And worse, they can suggest it. Don't you see? It's not about what you did or didn't do. It's what they can convince people you did. You could lose everything I know you've worked so hard for. I know the kinds of things they would say about you, sweetheart. Horrific, vile, disgusting things that would devastate you and devastate me to hear them."

"They could take all your money," I said, my voice flat. "That's all you care about. It isn't about me at all."

"Being homeless and destitute with no way to support yourself? That isn't about you?"

I could hear him coming closer.

"Those Egyptian cotton sheets you've been lying on for two days didn't fall off a truck, Loulou. That computer, those clothes, that roof over your head—nothing comes cheap in this life. I thought I taught you better than that. Then again, I thought I taught you better than—" He stopped himself before he crossed the Rubicon. "Than lying to me. Than going behind my back, to do things the world would never forgive you for."

"Things they'd never forgive me for, or things they'd never forgive *you* for?" I asked him coldly.

That seemed to take him aback, and for the first time, I turned my head, still resting on the pillow, to gaze at him. I was calm, clear-visioned, though my eyes still felt heavy and leaden with tears, shed and unshed.

He looked exhausted, which was no surprise. But more than that, he looked ... guilty? Devastated? Anxious? Confused? Like somebody who might listen to what I had to say, finally?

For the first time in a long while, I sat up. "He did it for me, Daddy."

"Loulou—" He fumbled for words.

"To protect me. I know it, and deep down, you know it. So don't you dare stand there and pretend you don't."

Something flickered like a lit match behind his eyes and then was gone.

"It doesn't matter why he did it, Loulou. He's a slave, so all that matters to the law is that he did it. And this isn't about him. This is about you and my doing what's best for you."

"You don't know what's best for me!" I shouted, leaping up from the bed. "Did you ever even bother to ask me what I want? No, you didn't. You never ask me what I want! Because if it isn't a fucking prom dress or diamond earrings or a trip to St. Barts, you don't care what I want! You just think it's the same thing you want! Well, it isn't!"

"Loulou, you're only eighteen. I don't think you know what you want, and I don't think you can begin to comprehend what you're up against. Now I'm asking you to please appreciate that I've been in this world thirty years longer than you have and that I know how it works."

"The only reason it works like this is because you allow it." My voice was icy, precise.

"Loulou, if you'd just listen—"

"No, Daddy. No. Listen to me." My heart was racing, the adrenaline coursing now. I'd never spoken to my father like this, ever. I'd never had to. We'd always seen eye to eye, mostly. The good daughter and her doting father. Simple, and now not. "A man risked everything to protect me, your only daughter, and in return, you've condemned him to torture and death. No, don't delude yourself. You aren't doing this for me. I don't need it. I don't need anything from you. He taught me—well, he taught me so many things, but above all, he taught me that I'm stronger than you think. And that I can handle so much more than anyone thinks. And whatever I have to endure—imprisonment, slavery, the worst slander and disgrace, no matter how awful, how vile—isn't worth a good man's life." My voice was calm, crystalline, almost oracular in its precision. "You're wrong, Daddy. It may take a hundred years, or it may take a thousand, but when the coming generations look back on us, you're the one who won't be forgiven. Not by the world and certainly never by me."

I'd grown up without religion, like most people these days, but I'd read the Bible as I eagerly read everything. And I had been not only astonished to find that I believed in God after all—not that God, per se, but *a* god—but that there were things in that book that were beautiful, things that people had taken comfort in for millennia for good reason, and that shouldn't have ever been abandoned or lost. And I thought of it now, of the Book of Isaiah, which talked of wolves lying down with lambs, babies, and snakes sleeping peacefully beside each other, and of a little child who shall lead them. At the time, I could almost believe all of it, except for that. The child I had been couldn't imagine leading. Wanting for nothing, there was nothing and no one to lead, no cause to fight for.

"Loulou." He cleared his throat.

I turned away. "Leave me alone."

"I didn't." The words, vague as they were, stopped me cold.

"You didn't what?" I whipped my head back.

"I couldn't—" He took a deep breath and I waited, heart hammering. "I didn't send him to the mines."

My pulse pounded in my ears. Auctioned, then. To a farm? A factory? A testing lab? Some other abominable house of horrors? "Then is he—"

My father's face had changed. Before, he'd been exhausted, a slumped, spent shell of a man. Now he looked pained; his face contorted as if this admission felt just short of a cardiac event. "I haven't auctioned him, either. I've sent him—somewhere where he won't be hurt. And Loulou?" He sighed. "I don't expect you to ever forgive me." He turned to go.

And suddenly, my body reawakened. Awash with the sense of—what was it? Time. Time. Time renewed; time regained. I sank into the mattress, the wave of relief that crashed over me pulling me under like the strongest tides.

Because I wasn't a child anymore. I wasn't helpless. And leading wasn't even half of what I was planning to do.

"Oh, Daddy, I—"

"That's enough." He managed to force some customary sternness back into his voice. And somehow, that was comforting, too. "I've already told you more than you should know. This is the last we'll ever discuss this. Is that clear?"

I nodded, blinking at my father. My tears of sorrow had retreated just long enough to reappear as tears of relief. Nothing more needed to be discussed. Because for today, it was enough to know that neither of my men was lost. Not yet.

HIM

On my second night at Langer's, I met the girls.

They were both gorgeous, though far apart in age. The first was no older than me and probably younger, with tawny skin and long black hair, athletic, almost tomboyish, with a loud, merry laugh. The second was older, maybe even in her thirties, though her face had a timeless, ethereal quality. She had pale skin, light blue eyes, and short, wispy, ash-blond hair that created a halo effect around her face. The first wore a tiny floral bikini; the second wore a white one-piece with gold accents and a plunging neckline that showed off the sides of her tits in a way that attracted every eye in the room but somehow managed to still look classy.

These girls moved playfully around Langer's thirtieth-floor rooftop hot tub like baby otters, the neon lights of the rooftop terrace and the surrounding towers lighting up their bodies in purple and orange and white. They made light, intelligent conversation. They laughed. They joked. They were not conditioned or submissive. They were not brainwashed. They wore actual jewelry, not a slave bracelet in sight. But still, something was wrong.

And worst of all, I was going to be forced to try to figure out what it was after three glasses of top-shelf bourbon, water jets massaging my aching body, a veritable buffet of prescription pain pills courtesy of Langer's private physician, and yet another cocktail in my hand.

"I knew you secretly liked the finer things," Langer had said earlier as he handed me the glass.

"Oh, it was never a secret," I said, to Langer's approving nod.

The problem was, I'd now wasted forty-eight hours on the finer things, and while I wasn't going to pretend I didn't prefer them to being chained up in a storage room thinking I was about to be sent to my death, none of it had brought me closer to Maeve, who the prospect of finding was the only glimmer of hope amid the smoking, bloody wreckage of the last few days. Or helped me forget about the girl who would have to get up and go to class today as if nothing were wrong, to sit at her desk and open her o-chem book at the empty desk next to the empty chair, one that probably looked as much like a memory—or like a dream—to her as it felt like to me.

It all still applies. Nothing's changed.

She was right, I supposed. Nothing had changed. Except for the fact that we were never going to see each other again.

There was virtually no chance she knew where I was. If her father was smart, he would tell her I'd been sold to the mines. If he was *really* smart, he would tell her there'd been a cave-in and I was already dead. Anything to lessen the chances she'd try to find me.

I wondered if she had found my message yet.

Across the hot tub, I locked eyes with the younger girl, who had been following my gaze. It stopped at her shoulder, where she wore a long, jagged scar, which she'd appeared to try to cover up with makeup the color of her tawny skin, most of which had now been washed away. She quickly turned. I felt my eyes glaze over as I collapsed into the not-unpleasant muddle of meds, liquor, and the rare privilege of being able to turn my mind off.

Forty-eight hours earlier, the owner of the city's most coveted downtown penthouse condo found me bruised, bloodied, and drugged-up, standing slumped in front of the elevator like a package of misdirected goods. My first stop had been to "Mr. Langer's personal physician" to get my wounds treated, and while the pain meds, steroid injection, and God knows what else the doctor had given me were verging on blissful, they were well on their way to knocking me flat on the floor.

Langer snapped his fingers in front of my eyes. "Holy shit, kid, anyone in there? Looks like Dr. Waxler sure gave you the good stuff. He always does."

"Yes, and I'm ever so grateful for your kindness, sir," I mumbled, staring at the floor.

"You can cut out that servile shit right now. I know you don't mean a word of it."

"Okay, then. Go fuck yourself."

"That's better." Langer crossed his arms. "So what the fuck happened over there, anyway? I leave you alone and you get yourself almost killed defending your lady's honor? Fucking hell. I thought you were supposed to be smart."

"Yeah, I thought so, too, so I guess that means we're both idiots."

"Well, you look like complete shit, anyway, so I assume you'll want to sleep it off before I give you the grand tour." He glanced around the bare entryway, looking puzzled. "You don't have any belongings or anything?"

I bristled. "For fuck's sake, I am a belonging. You and I both know that's the whole reason I'm here. Now if you don't have any more stupid questions, can you please just throw me in whatever dank, rat-infested cellar you have ready for me and just let me sleep off these meds before you get started on whatever unspeakable torture you've got planned? Thanks."

Langer gave me another bemused look. "Well, I hate to disappoint you, but this is a condo, so there is no dank cellar, and the exterminator I had in last week should have taken care of the rat infestation in your bedroom, but—"

"Hold on," I cut him off. "I don't understand."

"What, about the rat infestation, or—"

"About anything!" I growled through my mental fog. "You don't have to give me a bedroom. You don't have to give me any of the shit you offered. I turned down the deal. Remember? I'm only here as a slave, so just fucking treat me like one. It'll probably make both of our lives a lot easier." The irony of trying to order someone to treat me like a slave wasn't lost on me, but it didn't matter at this point. My body was bone-tired, my brain fuzzy from the opioids, and both were firmly refusing to play any more of Langer's bullshit mind games. Being ordered to scrub the floor might be a relief. At least menial chores never pretended to be anything other than what they were.

"Hey. Kid. Come inside, sit the fuck down—on the sofa, not the floor because apparently, we need to specify that now—and listen to me."

I obeyed, and as zoned-out as I was, I couldn't help but inhale a little as I stepped for the first time out of the alcove and into the massive two-story living room, which was mostly air, its floor-to-ceiling glass windows gazing imperiously down at the entire valley sprawled like a carpet in front of them, with those mountains, ever-unreachable, still winking on the horizon in a rosy haze. I collapsed onto the leather sofa, apathetically accepting that I wouldn't be able to get out of it ever again. I wouldn't look Langer in the eyes.

"When I told you I didn't want or need a slave, I meant it, and nothing has happened in the past week to change my mind. Everything I offered still stands. I know you think I'm a lying, cheating, amoral scumbag, and you're mostly right, but on this, I'm keeping my word. Are we clear?" he asked.

I nodded because what else could I do? If Langer was or wasn't keeping his word, I'd find out soon enough.

After that, he showed me to my bedroom suite, which, besides featuring the same stunning floor-to-ceiling view, was of a size equaling spaces I'd only ever shared with ten other people. Through it all, *Need to look for Maeve,* kept running through my brain. But so far, all I'd been able to determine was that she wasn't hidden in the shower, which was my next stop before I slept like a corpse in the bed for the next twelve hours, woke up with a start to face a flame-colored sunset hitting me in the face, took some more meds to quell the pain going off in my shoulder like an alarm, and, when I emerged from the bedroom, found a pile of packages deposited in the alcove. I got the suspicious feeling they were for me. In the kitchen, I found that Langer's personal chef had arrived—the only personal chef in town, or probably the country, who wasn't a slave—and was asking me what I wanted to eat.

"Uh." I'd been too tired to even think about food for hours and hours, and I stared vacantly at the guy for a minute and a half before answering with the first thing that popped into my head, something I'd barely known about a few days ago. "Tacos?"

And that's what I got.

A little later, Langer himself emerged from the bar area with a highball glass in his hand. "Well, that's a little better, but you still look like a fucking bear attacked you," he remarked, looking at me—still dazed, blinking, now well-fed but still wearing my torn-up and bloodied T-shirt and shorts—up and down. "I want you in the office at some point, and you can't show up like that. I'll send you shopping later, but for now, I took the liberty of having my personal shopper send over some stuff."

"What? Like clothes?"

"What, would you rather it be a leash and collar? Yes, like clothes," Langer said with an eye roll before making his way toward the door I assumed led to his study. Langer had a "personal" everything, it seemed, which allowed him to handle nothing himself while still orchestrating everything precisely. Oh, to be able to live like that. "In the meantime, I'll be finishing up some work. But the girls are on their way."

"The girls?"

He just smiled and disappeared.

Look around, a stupid voice in the back of my head told me. What the fuck was that going to accomplish? It wasn't like I was going to find my sister tied up and gagged under Langer's bed or something. Still, I managed to open up a few doors and poke around anyway. I'd need to know the layout of the place for the future, and it was something to do until I was lucid enough to figure out a more intelligent plan. Plus, I was curious.

It was also that curiosity that prompted me to cautiously approach the younger girl, who called herself Lemaya, in the kitchen as she cheerfully poured us drinks in the outdoor bar—bourbon for me (I'd never tried it before, but fuck, that stuff was good), champagne and raspberry liqueur for her. She explained that, for the time being, she worked for Langer's research and development division.

Wait. Lemaya? I knew that name. Had Maeve mentioned it? Shit, I thought for the hundredth time, if only I still had her messages to refer to. Because my brain sure wasn't any help right now.

"But I'm going to school to become a vet tech," she was saying meanwhile. "For now, I'm helping Resi out with her research. They gave me a place to live and pay all my expenses, and once that pays off, the company is going to pay all my tuition, everything."

"Oh yeah? What research? Drinking champagne in a rooftop penthouse?" I asked, trying to put her at ease with a smile. Thank God even on the meds, I could still do that. "If only that could be in all our job descriptions."

She melted a little, giggling, and slapped me flirtatiously on the arm. "Well, it's a perk, no doubt. She invites some of us here sometimes to hang out, and of course, for such a rich guy, Max is pretty chill. I like his vibes." She shrugged as if to ask, *any more questions?*

Yes, one. "Resi?" Another name I'd been hoping to hear.

"She's Max's head of R and D," she said. "We're helping disrupt slavery. They need my help because—" She caught her tongue as if she were afraid she'd told me too much.

Good. That meant there was something to tell. And that she *knew* there was something to tell.

And all at once I knew who she was: the slave girl who had been teaching Maeve English. The one who had suddenly disappeared.

I looked her up and down as she swallowed, raising her chin a little defiantly as if daring me to say something. There were always signs for those of us who knew what to look for: scarring, lack of eye contact, referring to people as "sir" who clearly didn't deserve it. She had the scars, at least. Of course, she hadn't done any of the rest, but maybe she'd been told not to. Maybe she'd been living like a free person for a while. Maybe she was like Maeve and her owners didn't want her but hadn't freed her, and that was why Max was using her for the chip experiments. But if so, what was she doing *here*? Max clearly wasn't doing any research in this penthouse tonight, other than maybe an experimental bikini probe.

Before I could decide whether to risk blowing my cover and asking her more, the door to Langer's study opened, and Lemaya's hair whipped around dramatically as she returned to the hot tub with her drink, as if she were passing the torch to him.

I just stood near the bar, which was silent but for the ice popping in my glass. Fuck the pills. Without them, I could have figured out a way to ask her about Maeve without getting either of us in trouble. But maybe I could ask the blonde when the time was right.

"Your sister isn't here," said Langer.

I wished I were as good at sneaking up on people as this guy was. I turned. He was dressed for the hot tub, with a towel over his arm. Rapidly, I looked back toward where Lemaya had disappeared, sorry she hadn't stuck around long enough to let me see the expression on her face when Max mentioned Maeve.

"What?"

"She isn't here," he repeated. "With Resi, I mean. I showed Resi her picture after you told me about her."

"I didn't tell you about her." I didn't think I had, anyway. I wouldn't count on the reliability of my memory right now.

"You mentioned a freed girl named Maeve, and I pieced together the rest." His eyes narrowed as if he were genuinely concerned about my sanity. "Remember, I told you to assume I know everything about you. Anyway, I'm sorry she's missing, and I'll see if there's anything else I can do, but right now all I can tell you is that she isn't with us."

He's lying, I thought immediately, because I always did. Maeve had *named* Resi in her messages. Whoever she was, wherever she was, she had to have Maeve somewhere. Even if it wasn't with the rest of the girls.

"Come on, Max. What are you really doing over there with those girls?" I asked even as I realized I was showing my hand yet again. I knew I'd regret it as soon as the words left my mouth.

"Just like Lemaya said. Employing them."

That sure wasn't what Maeve had implied. Then again, there'd been a language barrier between her and the other girls, and she had mentioned something about being paid. Fuck. And that still didn't explain why Langer said she wasn't here. She *had* to be here. Because the alternative—that I'd come this far and cost myself this much for a dead end—was unthinkable.

"Look, the booze and pills have you loopy right now," Langer said. "You're not thinking clearly. I can tell just by looking into your eyes. Later this week, when I give you a tour of the office and the labs, you'll see everything. And you'll understand you have nothing to worry about."

Nothing to worry about? As usual, I had one million things to worry about, but I couldn't remember what half of them were right now. And my shoulder was practically screaming for those water jets.

Plus, there was still the blonde to ask about Maeve.

And the time to do it might be now because as soon as I got in the hot tub, she started running her angel-soft fingers up under the new turquoise board shorts I'd taken out of one of the packages, while my traitor dick reacted predictably. Over her shoulder, I could see that Langer had joined us on the other side of the tub with Lemaya, who must have decided she liked more than his vibes, given everywhere her hands and mouth were.

Employing them. How stupid did Langer think I was? It was easy to assume from her enthusiasm that she was doing it all by choice, but I knew better.

"You're a million miles away, sweetie," the blonde said gently. The fingers that grazed my jawline and tilted my face toward hers were surprisingly soft, even though they came alongside stiletto-shaped nails the hue of glazed vanilla. And so were the fingers that zeroed in, somehow, on exactly the place between my dick and balls that I would have liked a girl's hand to be under the right circumstances—which these were anything but. "What are you thinking about? Or should I say, who are you thinking about?"

Something about the way she spoke made me think she already knew. Which was ridiculous. Wasn't it? Fuck these drugs. I was so off my game, and I needed to get her goddamn hand off my junk. It wasn't the first time a free woman had tried this kind of shit on me when she thought backs were turned. The problem was, sometimes they weren't.

Lost in shitty memories and a dearth of good ideas, I knew she could probably feel my heart rate increasing even through the haze of the meds.

"Shh. It's okay. I was a slave, too, a long time ago," she whispered. Startled, I followed her hand as she pulled back one side of her white swimsuit, revealing not only part of her nipple but a trail of burn scars on her torso, long and flat, like a cattle prod or even a clothes iron, winding all the way down past her waist. Now that I looked closer, I saw it. Cosmetic surgery or makeup had dulled some of it, but there was no mistaking what it was. Looking across at the entwined figures of Langer and Lemaya, a similar sight greeted me. *A real Michelangelo of pain*, Max had called the late Gerhard Langer. Whatever else he was lying about, it seemed he hadn't been lying about *that*.

What kind of topsy-turvy world had I fallen into where people with these kinds of scars ruled the goddamn universe from a thirtieth-floor penthouse? The one Langer was trying to create with Project White Cedar? I had a feeling I was going to find out.

"I take it you work for Resi, too?" I asked the blonde.

A weirdly joyful smile spread slowly over her face as she lifted her upper body out of the water, and it only took a second for me to realize my mistake.

"Tresa Hahn," she said, pointing to herself girlishly. "So sorry I never introduced myself. Of course you never introduced yourself, either." She giggled. "But I know who you are. There's no mistaking that pretty face. You look just like your sister."

My stunned reply was cut off, out of nowhere, by a pain as excruciating as any I'd ever felt as she sank all five of those glossy, pearly fingernails into my balls and wrenched them forward, jerking my whole body toward her. Tears leaked out of both eyes as I clamped down violently on my lip to bury my scream.

She pressed her forehead to mine, smoothing back my damp hair. "Oh, baby, I'm sorry," she whispered as I silently mewled through each eternal second. "I hate making bad first impressions. But you need to stop asking questions." She held me in her claws for one extra second before lazily releasing me, only to have my back hit like a brick against the tile edge of the tub, where I slumped, gasping.

"If you don't, remember this feeling because little sis is going to get something ten times worse."

18

HER

I stood at the door of the Cadillac, keys in hand, breathing in and out.

Why should *this* be one of my triggers, anyway? I'd been driving this car for over a year, and he'd only been in it twice. But I'd also been sleeping in my bedroom for *ten* years, and that didn't stop him from being the first thing I thought of when I saw my bed, my desk, my bookshelf, my chair, and oh, every time I opened my goddamn eyes. Fuck him for being so damn memorable.

Besides, what really mattered was that my dad had agreed to give me the keys back. The fact that he'd confiscated them to begin with was a joke because what the hell did he think I was going to do? Drive off a cliff in some dramatic final act of rebellion? It wasn't like I could go look for my boy—I'd need at least *one* clue as to his whereabouts to do that. But I *could* drive to campus, and on campus, I could find Erica, and Erica could tell me what she'd discovered about Maeve. And that was exactly what I planned to do now.

The confrontation with my father had been the catalyst; the chemical reaction, one might say, that had set me in motion. Now, to stay moving, to go *toward* something—to beat back the inertia that wanted to keep me in bed and shutting out the light morning after morning—was the only thing I *could* do.

I turned around when the door to the garage opened gingerly. The maid stood there, her hair pulled back in a swingy ponytail, brushing dust off the knees of her jeans from wherever she'd been kneeling earlier. She shrank a little when I met her eyes.

"Hey," I said.

"Hey."

Ugh. I supposed this was the two of us attempting to interact like normal people, but it was still awkward as hell.

"So, uh, I just came from the downstairs storage room."

Never mind the awkwardness. She had my full attention now.

"One of the paint cans fell off the top shelf. A mouse must have knocked it down or something. At least that's the story the house-keeper gave me. Anyway, I'm supposed to be cleaning it up, but—I think there's something you should see before I—"

I was out the service door before she could even finish the sentence. But before I disappeared, I stopped. Stuck my head back in. "Thank you."

The maid—who had flashed me that smug smirk so many times—responded with a smile. A real one.

HIM

In the very discreet back room of Max Langer's favorite men's clothing boutique—so discreet it had a separate entrance—the salesman draped a white linen suit jacket over an upholstered brown leather chair and asked for my opinion.

"He loves it," Lemaya said next to me, almost jumping out of her chair.

I shot her an alarmed glance.

"Don't worry, it's the desert," the salesman assured me flippantly. "We wear white all year round here."

Yes, as if making a fashion faux pas were my main objection. "Wouldn't it get dirty?"

"Oh, that," the man replied as if he'd suddenly remembered I was a slave he was being paid boatloads of money to pretend was an actual customer. He waved it off. "Remember, you don't work in the dirt anymore."

Throughout my life, I'd been able to get attention from women in just about any and all situations, including while bloody, dressed in rags, and covered in filth. But I had to admit it was much, much easier in a white linen suit tailored impeccably to my form, a floral shirt printed with green banana leaves, gold and amber pendants on delicate eighteen-karat gold chains, and gold-plated aviator sunglasses. At least if Lemaya and the salesgirls who kept poking their heads in just to gawk were any indication.

Look, I wasn't an idiot. I knew it was all just an elaborate illusion, a ridiculous charade—a dog wearing clothes doesn't make it a fucking person, as I'd so helpfully been reminded a few days ago—but it was easy to brush all that aside when the brand of bourbon they'd handed me to sip while I waited was the same brand that, a few weeks ago, a certain ex-employee of Langer's had smashed on the pool deck just to make me clean up. The same ex-employee who was currently in the hospital, hooked up to a brainwave monitor, being fed protein shakes through a tube, while his family debated whether to pull the plug.

Smugness was an unattractive trait, I knew. But still.

In any case, resolving to use the day to learn as much as I could without earning myself another "warning" from Resi, the first thing I learned was that I was surprisingly good at blowing offensively large wads of someone else's money, especially if the other person in question was someone I was still eventually hoping to destroy. And Lemaya was my perfect partner in crime. She may have nominally been a "research assistant," but her only "research" that day was to get me fitted for not only a half-dozen suits of all colors and patterns, both casual and business formal—plus a couple more bespoke ones to be delivered later—but dress shirts and silk ties in a dozen patterns and shades of light blue, green, and gold. Plus a bunch of other shit, including things that at first struck me as highly unnecessary—like sterling-silver tie clips and faux-snakeskin wallets—and then once she insisted I see and touch them, struck me as very necessary indeed. Look, no one had ever given me anything, ever, and who knew when

I would get this chance again? Hell, I was supposed to be dead right *now.*

Yes, Lemaya was good at what she did—and innocently flirtatious through it all. But then again, so was I because that seemed to be a way of interacting that we both implicitly understood. If she'd previously been a slave—a personal maid to someone rich, if I had to guess—she probably just saw that kind of thing, as *I* always had, as a survival mechanism. Anyway, her words suggested she was pretty sadly hung up on Langer, which wasn't surprising, even with the age difference—pale blue eyes, charm, and gobs of money would always be an irresistible trio for any girl. If only Langer weren't clearly a guy who threw away women as easily as the tissue paper on top of a cheap birthday gift, and if only warning her about that had any chance of making any difference at all.

Anyway, what I really wanted to do was to pump Lemaya for more information. I'd figured out she was Maeve's friend, and I was pretty sure *she'd* known all along that I was Maeve's brother, which meant we both had information the other sorely needed but that neither one of us knew how to get. Though she was bubbly and assertive, even demanding at times, she wasn't very forthcoming, except when she was gushing about Giza cotton shirts, Italian leather belts, or what she saw as Max's endlessly worthy attributes. Not to mention, if there was any chance Resi, not Max, was telling the truth and Resi did have Maeve, it was too risky to ask her—there was a non-zero chance that Resi had insisted Lemaya be assigned to the task to keep an eye on me, and that anything I said to Lemaya would filter immediately back up to her boss. And she was right to be wary of me, too. Maeve had thought she'd disappeared, but it was clear that she'd actually "graduated" to a far more privileged position than a vet tech. And she no doubt knew that appearing to sympathize with me over Resi was the quickest way to get booted out of it.

Of course we still might still find a way around all this, but the sharp ache down *there*, whenever I thought of my interlude with the blonde in the hot tub, was enough to make me think twice.

I was also happy to accept my first-ever manicure from Langer's (yes) "personal manicurist," but from his "personal hairstylist," I drew the line at giving my hair any more than a light trim or, God forbid, product. Yes, okay, maybe I was a little vain about it, but at least my hair, like very little else—including the money going to pay for all this shit—actually belonged to *me*.

And as for the pain? It was bad. I wasn't going to lie. The pills could no longer help, either, because I'd poured them down the toilet. I simply couldn't be off my game the way I had been the other night; not with this much at stake—but shit, it was hard to watch them go. No wonder Louisa's brother got hooked on these things—they were biologically engineered to make you never want to stop taking them. Come to think of it, if Louisa were here, she'd likely be flushing them away herself, informing me I was better than this, and demanding—as she'd once promised—that I get my fucking act together. And even though the thought made me smile, here I was feeling every ache, pop, and groan of my retorn rotator cuff. Which was what it was, according to Dr. Waxler, the first actual medical professional to ever bother to give me a diagnosis, five years after the original injury. Well, fuck it. There was ibuprofen in the bathroom cabinet, and that—washed down with a couple large bourbons, because there was no way I was giving up *those*—would have to do for now. I didn't *want* to endure pain, but I certainly knew *how*. And I would. As long as I had to.

I'd never made a habit of looking in mirrors—I got more than enough comments on my looks as it was, and counting new scars and bruises hadn't seemed like too worthwhile a use of my time—but the salesman urged me to now, and I blinked as the colors they'd chosen bounced off all the golden facets of my hair and eyes. Well. These people knew what they were doing, clearly. I locked eyes with Lemaya behind me, reflected in the mirror as she perched like a sparrow on the edge of her chair in her pleated leather miniskirt and heels. She followed my gaze down, to the rich fabric of my sleeve hiding the marred skin underneath, and the one accessory neither I nor she had chosen. And that the sales team—none of whom were slaves themselves, which I was sure wasn't an accident on Langer's part—had been discreet enough not to mention.

What would all my owners and overseers—the ones who saw my body only as a blank canvas for their sadistic handiwork—think if they saw me? Would Louisa—forbidden from even looking at me, and vice versa—even recognize the guy she'd met a month ago? Not like it mattered. She wasn't here to see this and was never going to be. She likely thought I was *dead*, or very soon would be. And here I was, the selfish prick in the gaudy suit who had left her to twist in the wind. Suddenly, the face in the mirror looked highly punchable.

I'd spent the last seven years with the knowledge that if I were to drop dead tomorrow, my sister was the only one on the planet who would care, the only one who would remember that I had ever existed. For a long time, I'd been *happy* about that, or at least content with it. I still wasn't quite sure how, but somehow, maybe due to what and who she'd already lost, Louisa had helped me come to understand that people—even slaves—weren't meant to live that way. And she'd given her all, risked her heart, said what I couldn't. And in exchange, she was getting—knowing her—tears, probably right this second. Sure, I may no longer be drugging myself to oblivion, but I was still getting comically expensive bourbon, bespoke tailored suits, and the promise of more cold, hard cash than I had ever expected to see in a lifetime. Did that seem fair? Of course not. But if Louisa were here, she'd remind me that it wasn't as if I had asked for any of it, and I'd know that she was right. In the moment, though, it didn't help much.

The message, I kept reminding myself, as pathetic as it was. A message couldn't comfort. It couldn't protect. It couldn't do my job for me. But for now, it was all I had.

———————— · ◆ ❤ ◆ · ————————

"Look at you!" Resi said cheerfully, walking around me slowly as if I were a marble statue and the glass-roofed central atrium of Langer Enterprises, a Renaissance art museum. The waterfall flowing down into the lush indoor garden provided a background of eerie tranquility to it all. "I can't *believe* the illusions they can create. Anyone would think you were a free man. I mean, if they didn't know where to look."

She giggled and directed her eyes toward the chain on my wrist. The one that, that morning, Langer had explicitly given me permission—if I chose—to cut off. He'd even directed me toward the tools with which to do it. But I had refused, and not because I thought it was a trick to get me in trouble. I'd finally accepted that Langer's tricks, whatever else they were, went deeper than such cheap chicanery. I'd refused because it would be a lie, to myself as much as anyone, and every time I looked at my bare wrist, I'd be reminded of it. But now, face-to-face with the veiled mean-girl sneer behind Resi's light blue eyes—almost level with my chin, thanks to her black-toed stiletto heels that matched her body-skimming nude pencil dress—I was starting to rethink my decision.

I stood motionless, trying to decide how to play this game. It was mid-morning, the atrium was empty, and she knew the layout of the office and everyone's schedules much better than I did. She knew no one was coming to interrupt her fun, especially not Max.

"But all in all, I think I like you best in the hot tub, crying and making those *adorable* sounds. Although I can't help wondering whether I'll get to hear them again. Or maybe you've decided to stop playing detective?" she quizzed me, that deceptively innocent tone back in her voice. She directed her eyes lower, to a specific spot behind my new gray wool suit trousers.

I moved back, eyes warily on her nails. Like I was ever again going to make the mistake of letting them anywhere near *there*. She saw where I was looking and giggled again, her light blue eyes dancing with amusement in the atrium light. "You do learn fast. I'll give you that."

"I know you're lying, Resi," I said, forcing calm into my voice. "You don't have my sister. Max told me that."

She laughed lightly and bounced a little on her heels. "Ah, the old calling my bluff trick. God, I *cannot* get over how cute you are when you think you're outsmarting someone."

Heat flowed into my face. Oh, that was a low blow.

"And by the way? When we're alone, that's *ma'am* to you."

I rolled my eyes. "If even Max doesn't want a title, what the fuck makes you think you deserve one?"

Lightning-fast, she reached up and grabbed a handful of my hair at the roots. With an iron grip, she jerked my head down to meet her at eye level. I struggled to swallow as she wrapped her weaponlike nails around my throat, her breath cool and cinnamon-like as her lips brushed my face. "Because I *do* deserve one. From you, anyway. And nothing Max says will change that."

"Fuck that. You think I'm not going to put it to the test?" I muttered, trying to jerk my head back against the sharp pain. I'd never had the occasion to throw a 120-pound woman to the floor, and as much as I wanted to, I wasn't going to start with Langer's head of R&D.

"Well, just try it. Go ahead. Tell him everything. See whose side he takes. He may own this company, but he's loyal to me in ways you couldn't possibly understand."

"I thought you said you used to be a slave," I choked out, indignant.

"I did," she said and released me nonchalantly, tossing her sleek, wispy blond ponytail, then directing the toes of her stilettos down the hall. "And doesn't that explain everything?"

———————— · ✦ ♥ ✦ · ————————

"I ask one and only one thing from the people who work here with me," Max Langer said as we walked side by side down a row of sprawling glass-paneled offices. Transparency seemed to be Langer's thing, at least when it came to decorating. Actually, his corporate headquarters, for all its brand-new crystalline trappings, was surprisingly intimate—besides Langer himself, it played host only to a couple of assistants, a small accounting team, an in-house legal counsel, one HR manager, security, and formerly—in the office at the end of the hall that I would soon be occupying—Corey. In fact, Langer currently had *no* other staff that worked in his core business on a daily basis. He kept his circle small, in other words. "Complete trustworthiness."

"Right," I replied, trying—as I had all morning—not to sound intimidated. Not to avert my eyes. To ask questions of anyone, at any time. Sure, I may not be here by choice, but that was no reason to *act* like it. "Then how do you explain me?"

An amused smile appeared on my boss's lips. "I have different requirements for you."

I nodded and flicked my eyes toward the people working on the other side of the glass. They didn't look up, but that couldn't shake the feeling that Resi—and Wainwright-Phillips, and Corey, and everyone who kept reminding me of the same damn thing—had left me with. That despite the trappings Langer had provided me with, I wasn't some up-and-coming corporate hotshot—or an engineer, or a rocket scientist, or even an intern. I was just—as always—a slave who refused to learn his place. And everyone who looked at me could see it. "Do *they* know that I'm, well—"

"Yes, they know," he cut me off. "And if anyone tries to treat you even the slightest bit differently because of it, you come to me immediately, and I'll handle it. But that won't happen."

It's already happened. And for the sake of my sister, I wouldn't be coming to Langer about it. Nor would I, as I'd found out to my dismay only a few minutes ago, be sneaking into Langer's office after hours and going through the file cabinets because there were none. Langer Enterprises had evidently completed its digital transformation, since everything the least bit proprietary was stored in a database locked down tighter than a bullion depository. Of course it wasn't like I hadn't expected to encounter something like this in the course of my search for Maeve. I'd even managed to teach myself some rudimentary coding (read: hacking) in the lab in Heidelberg, but my skills were nowhere near what I'd need for this kind of job, and I wasn't sure how much I remembered, anyway. Luckily, I was about to get my own computer and almost unlimited access to the internet, so I'd soon be able to dive back in. But like everything, it would take time.

I was gripped, not the first time in these past few days, by the cold of the void of ignorance, of having no way of learning whether Erica's team had found anything during their search of the two addresses. I was working totally blind.

Realizing I was probably supposed to say something, I remarked, "Well, that covers your office. And what about the rest of your companies? What about Orbital Dynamics?"

"They don't know you exist, nor will they," Langer replied. "That's for your own good—and mine, given my public views about slavery. It shouldn't be an issue, since you'll be reporting to me and only me, but if they, or anyone, find out I have a slave, even one that's not mine, it could compromise everything we're working on. And then you're back at Keith's mercy, and I won't be able to help you anymore."

I swallowed and nodded. "Ah. So I'm living proof that you're a gigantic fucking hypocrite, but I can't say anything, or I'm the one who's going to pay the price for it."

"Exactly. But it beats the alternative. And I'm not reminding you of that because I'm trying to hold it over your head. I'm reminding you of it because it's true."

It *was* true, but still. Fuck him. "What about Project White Cedar?"

"That's offsite."

I had a feeling I knew where the site was.

"Resi and the girls work there. In fact"—Langer glanced at his diamond-studded Rolex—"we're due there in a half hour for a tour. I've called for a car."

Good. I knew Resi would do her damnedest to make sure I didn't see anything even remotely interesting, but I sure wasn't going to make it easy for her.

We'd reached the elevator in the atrium—also clear glass—and Langer pushed the button that would take him up to his office on the top floor. "Before we go any farther, I just have one request."

"Which is?"

"For the sake of keeping me from going absolutely batshit insane, can you please give me something, *anything*, to call you? It doesn't even have to be a name. You can be fucking Superman if you want. Just *something*."

"No."

"Why the fuck not?" He didn't seem angry, just exasperated. "I know you're not supposed to have one, but I can tell you right now—as I tell everyone else who works for me—that here, you'll be doing a lot of things you're not supposed to be doing. Because that's the only way to win at the game I play. So give me a good reason."

"Because it wouldn't be my real name, legally," I said stubbornly. "And I don't want any name they can take away from me."

Langer groaned. "I'm going to wear you down on this, you know."

"Well, I'm going to have fun watching you try."

Langer actually laughed a little at that, which surprised me. The elevator dinged gently upon its arrival. Langer made to step on but paused on the threshold, holding the doors open. He looked back. "Ah, shit. I forgot one other thing. Your office."

"What about it?"

"I didn't have time to get it cleaned out. Corey's parents had the balls to call me up and demand I hand over everything in there, but I told them it's all proprietary. Naturally, they threatened to sue me, so I figured I'd leave it untouched, just in case." He recognized the look in my eye and shook his head. "Trust me, there isn't anything proprietary in there. I'd known for months that their idiot son couldn't be trusted with anything more than paper pushing. But my concern for the Killeens ended the second I finished signing their seven-figure check, which you'd think would be more than enough to get them to fuck off and leave me alone. Anyway, I'll tell the assistants to get on it, but—"

"Don't bother. I'll do it," I said quickly, not entirely sure why. Just a hunch.

He raised his eyebrows. "You sure?"

"Yeah, it's no problem." Let him think I was being helpful. "I'm used to cleaning, after all."

Langer forced his way onto the elevator and smirked as the glass doors closed. "Knock yourself out, kid."

19

HIM

Back in Corey's—*my*—musty office, I drew the shade and opened the window to let some light and air in. Blinking at the harsh sunlight, I closed the shade again partway. All the offices had a high-tech opaque screen that could be drawn over the glass paneling for privacy, but I couldn't think of a better way to broadcast "I'm up to no good" to the entire building, so I left it alone.

I turned to the desk with a strange anticipation. Langer had said there was nothing proprietary in there, and I had no reason to doubt that. Honestly, I didn't know what I expected to find by volunteering to do a menial chore, other than flashbacks to how I'd spent most of my life up to this point and the dubious opportunity to learn way more than I ever wanted to know about Corey.

A few minutes later, most of what I'd learned was that the dude was disgusting. The desk boasted a bobblehead of his college mascot and a couple of other pieces of tacky swag, plus a pair of douchey wraparound sunglasses and spare change, all mired in layers of sticky residue from whatever he'd been drinking—likely the bottle of cheap whiskey stuffed in one of the drawers—topped off with a pack of novelty playing cards with naked women on them, a gift from one of his classier friends, no doubt. Balled-up clothes that looked like he'd worn them to the gym. And cigarette butts because apparently, he'd been too lazy to even go to the window to surreptitiously smoke, let alone all the way downstairs. In the drawers and in a couple of cardboard boxes, I found untidy stacks of old gas station receipts, sales catalogs, and business cards. Obviously, the digital transformation didn't seem to have made it here. What kind of so-called engineer doesn't have a filing system, electronic or otherwise?

I quickly rummaged through the remaining drawers and shelves, scanning every page, front and back, to see if it was of interest before throwing entire stacks of paper and knick-knacks into a large garbage bag with the kind of vengeful satisfaction I'd never expected to get from cleaning. I supposed that would have to satisfy me.

And then, at the very bottom of the drawer, covered in papers from over a year ago, as if to make it look less conspicuous, was a tablet. I pressed the button, but it obviously needed a charge. Stuck on the other side, a sticky note read:

Hey, Cor, hope you enjoyed the lab tour! These codes should help you next time. Feel free to bring some friends. I owe you one. - R.

She'd written two four-digit numbers on the back.

And under *that*, in what I now recognized as Corey's handwriting, was a list of passwords.

HER

I had been surprised but not overly concerned when Erica had abruptly sent out a mass email canceling her office hours that day, or even when she hadn't replied to the email I'd sent her from the throwaway account I'd made in the university computer lab, asking her when and where we could meet. Or even when one of Milagros' fellow volunteer guides at the mirror telescope told me Milagros hadn't been in for a couple of days. And yet as I hung around the library trying to study, and more hours passed without a reply, the more uneasy—and guilty—I felt that it had taken me so long to get in touch with them, especially after the urgency of Erica's message asking me to call back re: Maeve. Then again, two days of wallowing in abject depression didn't seem like too much to ask after *that*, and I thought even the professor, for all her single-minded devotion to the cause, might have at least a *little* sympathy for me. Not to mention, I no longer had a computer *or* a phone. But as I approached that now-familiar little adobe house near the university, that feeling I'd had on the walk over—dodging what I knew intellectually were probably *not* suspicious looks from passersby—had only grown.

As before, the windowsills were lined with potted succulents, and vines cascaded down from a trellis on the wall. But that wrought-iron iguana, which before had seemed friendly and almost welcoming, now seemed to wear an unseemly grin that made me want to kick it over. I paused, my hand hovering above the brass doorknob, listening for any sign of movement inside. When no noise came, I took a deep breath, turned the knob, and stepped inside.

Not even the echoing of my footsteps on the tile could break the silence that blanketed the lush living room. I could almost hear the plants breathing. Millie the cat meowed a greeting from the kitchen, but for now, came no closer. Her food and water bowls, just inside the kitchen door, were empty. Should I take a look around or wait until someone came back? I wondered.

No. Neither. Because I didn't want to see it. I didn't want to see the plants; didn't want to see the cat; didn't want to see the hammock or, God, the *pool.* I didn't want to see them for the same reason I didn't want to wake up in my own goddamn bed every morning.

Look, I knew *I* was the lucky one, not him. But one thing was for sure: wherever he was, at least his memories were only in his head.

Back at home, the lid on the thick white eggshell paint in the storage room had popped off, its contents gushed to all corners, as if *someone* had rattled the bottom shelf as hard as they could to get it to fall. It was going to be a bitch for the maid to clean up, and since I had about fifteen minutes to spare before I risked being late, I did the right thing and helped her with it. The wooden stir stick that had been used to write lay mired in the thick paint, next to the words:

When You Are Old.

And that was it. There was no hint to his location, no hint of *anything*, really. I couldn't pretend I wasn't crushed. I'd offered my heart and said the words. And as much as I didn't begrudge him his fear—I'd never met anyone so equally terrified of love *and* being alone—it hadn't been easy for me, either. And all he could think to write to me, as the last thing he might ever get to say, were four words about me getting old? Yeah. Getting old without him, it looked like.

I felt heat rush to my face. No wonder Erica and Milagros weren't here. They had probably long since given up on getting any help from me and gone off on their own. And now, in Erica's silent living room, with Millie's tail swishing and the lacy drapes fluttering, here were the tears falling again. Right on cue.

Stupid fucking crybaby. What was I even doing here? His sister was stuck in some living hell and I'd promised him I would find her, and yet I'd done nothing but lie in bed and cry for the past two days. And I was *surprised* when he didn't say he loved me? I was a joke. I was making things *worse*. I'd started fucking up his life pretty much right from the moment we'd met, and clearly, not much had changed.

Millie gracefully leaped from the top of the pillow-strewn sofa to the bookshelf as if trying to bring my attention to that spot. Another memory: his startled eyes tearing themselves away from the page, slamming the book shut, caught in the act of ... reading poetry. As if that were somehow transgressive. Though for him, maybe it was.

Still, there was something about *that* memory in particular. Inspired, I ran my fingers along the spines of the old books, looking for poetry volumes, until I finally stopped at a thick one at the end. I grabbed and opened it, flipping through the pages until suddenly, I stopped dead and looked up. The air around me seemed to darken as if a cloud had passed over the sun, muting the birds and the distant street noises. The shadows of the room seemed to stretch and swirl as if a hidden figure stood just beyond the edge of my vision, watching my every move. And then the front door slammed shut.

HIM

After a month of trying, I was finally getting a glimpse inside the legendary 2481 Salt River Boulevard—and finding it a total bore. Lemaya had predictably been made the tour guide, her bouncy energy perfect for the job. At first, I followed her dutifully through the glass-paned doors of the lab—high-security and totally unmarked from the outside—where gleaming white countertops lined the walls and a collection of brand-new equipment hummed, more advanced than some of the stuff I'd used in Heidelberg, even. She moved swiftly around the room, pointing out each feature with care. But her words were predictably rehearsed, glossing over certain details, like where the other girls were who supposedly worked here and whether Resi was experimenting with microchips, the way Maeve—and later Erica—had suggested. And even though I hadn't had time to charge the tablet or try any of the passwords, I already had a feeling the tour I was getting was very different from the "tour" Resi had given Corey.

In fact, all Lemaya would tell me was that "we all have different schedules" and that they were working on "cutting-edge technology" and that "it was all very exciting." In other words, complete bullshit straight out of a marketing brochure. I tried every way I could think of to cajole her for more. Sure, I might be able to come up with an excuse to come back here in the next few days, but I couldn't count on it, and I was fairly confident that the other address Erica had found—the one that used to belong to Max's father—was not going to be on any tours Resi planned to give me. I had to do what I could right now. Half an hour later, though, Lemaya had had it. Even her bounce felt forced. It was almost as if she was telling me with her dark brown eyes: *for both of our sakes, please, just shut up.*

Langer, who'd been following along for the first five to ten minutes, had slipped out. *That* gave me an opportunity. Right now, I needed to get Lemaya acting—and talking—like a real person again. Luckily, that was *my* specialty.

"What do I think? I think that's the most beautiful pipette I have ever seen in my life," I said, directing my eyes toward the glassware she was holding with a teasing smile.

After a second, she giggled. "Isn't it, though?" she said, gesturing elegantly to it like a showroom model.

"No, but seriously, I do have a question I *know* you can answer. So you know how it is when a light bulb just goes off in your head and it's all you think about and you just have to get it down on paper before you forget? Is there maybe a quiet place nearby where I can go do that? Like, now?"

In a second, Lemaya's smile went from charmed to slightly terrified. And it wasn't *just* because Resi was hiding something, or *just* because I was Maeve's brother.

It was both. And probably more.

Better throw some puppy-dog eyes in, too. "Ideas are sort of how I'm earning my keep here," I said. "So if it slips away, Max's not going to be happy."

In a second, Lemaya's smile faltered, her eyes flicking nervously around the room before settling back on me, the laughter gone. There was fear there, a subtle shift I almost missed. I wondered what instructions she'd been given and how often she'd been told the consequences for breaking them.

Or been shown them.

"I won't let anything come back on you," I murmured. It was a promise I might regret making, the kind I might not be able to keep but was always fucking making. And we both knew that was what it was, but we also came from the same place, so we knew that sometimes you had to make it anyway.

She chewed on her lip. "I disabled the cameras in here," she explained, her voice low. "But still, you didn't hear this from me. If Resi finds out I told you—"

"She won't," I said.

Reluctantly, she continued. "Down the hall, there's a storeroom. It's quiet, isolated. No one goes there much. You can work there, but be discreet, please."

I nodded, keeping my voice even. "And Resi—"

Her eyes widened slightly, a silent plea. "Just ... be careful around her. More than you think you need to be. I didn't want to tell you anything, and I shouldn't be telling you now, but I'm doing it for Maeve."

"You taught her English."

She nodded. "Tried. I—she was—is—my friend." Her deep, dark brown eyes stayed fixed on mine. The eyes of someone that I could actually imagine my sister being friends with quite easily. No, I still didn't fully trust Lemaya, but for a second, for Maeve's sake, I was glad she existed.

"Do you know where she is?" I tried.

"I wish I did," she said, slowly shaking her head. "Just like I bet *she* wishes she knew where I was." But she lowered her voice even further. "I'll try to find out more."

I nodded and moved quickly down the bright-white hallway and toward an open door leading to a side room. Inside was a smaller laboratory, filled with buzzing machinery, and an even smaller room branching off from it. And in that smaller room were two figures. After a moment, I recognized Langer and Resi, standing close together, almost touching in a way that could have been friendly or supportive—but could have been any number of other things, too. I crept around the corner of a stainless steel lab bench, pressing my back against the cold metal surface. Peering cautiously around the side of the equipment, I could see them. I ducked back down behind the bench and strained to make out the words.

"Wow, this place is fairly humming with activity," Langer remarked sarcastically. "It's a thrill to be in such a fast-paced and productive environment."

So I was right. They may have lived at another address, but the other girls *should* be here now. And in their absence, the place was dead.

"All joking aside, if I were Keith Wainwright-Phillips," Langer went on, "and had my entire fortune wrapped up in this project—not to mention having my name on the deed for this warehouse, thanks to a suggestion from *you*—I'd be starting to get a bit, I don't know, concerned."

"*That's* who you're worried about?" Resi asked, keeping her voice tuned to that sweet, innocent frequency I was beginning to dread the sound of. "I've seen him around you. He's like a starry-eyed kid getting a chance to kick a ball with his football hero. I really don't think you need to preoccupy yourself with him."

"I wouldn't underestimate him. When he was a CEO, it took him only five years to turn some bottom-of-the-barrel insurance provider into one of the most valuable firms in the West."

"Yeah, by insuring companies whose slaves got hurt or killed on the job," she scoffed.

What the fuck? What, was she against slavery for everyone except *me*?

"He's coming around," said Langer, though he didn't sound entirely confident. "And, sure, I thought he was an idiot, too, at first, and he may have gone off the deep end recently, but he's not some neophyte, and he *won't* wait around forever. He's going to want to see some ROI, and soon."

"I thought Rocket Boy was supposed to take care of that," she sniffed, trying to regain her dulcet tones and not entirely succeeding.

"He will."

The statement could easily have sounded ominous, but instead, it sounded ... hopeful? Maybe even a little ... proud? Weird.

"By the way, are you *sure* you never had his sister working over here? Never saw her? Never even met her?"

"Yes, and why?" Her voice bristled, all the sweetness gone out of it in an instant. "What's he been telling you? I don't trust him. He's a snake."

I was flattered. I had no idea Resi thought so highly of me.

"He's not a snake. He's a kid who's worried because his sister is missing, and he can't fucking do anything about it because he's a slave. Anyway, I believe you, so calm the fuck down. This isn't about him, anyway. This is about you and White Cedar, and what I promised Keith that it would deliver. That *you* would deliver."

"I am delivering," she said, her voice heightened. "And I told you I could deliver it faster if you'd give me access to the books."

"And I told you you're crazy. Do you think I need the revenue service on my ass? I'm already paying a slave cash under the table, and that's just for starters. The last thing I need is *you* fucking around in the books for no good reason."

"But ... but ..."

I could swear Resi was about to cry. She even gave a sniffle. It was all a sham, I was sure. She was a better actor than *I* was. And all of a sudden, it hit me like a shelf full of beakers falling on my head. *Resi could manipulate Max.* Not only manipulate but maybe even lie to him.

Well, shit. I'd really have to kill her now because *I* wanted to be the only one doing that.

"I just feel like sometimes you don't trust me," she went on. "Sometimes I wonder whether you even *care* about me."

"Care about you?" Langer's voice bore an entirely different tone than I'd ever heard from him before. Wait, this guy could actually be sensitive? Caring? Sure, it was far from the *most* surprising part of this conversation, but it was certainly close. "Do we really have to talk about how many times I've bailed you out of trouble? Kept you from becoming a slave again? Kept you—"

Another long sniff as if she were feigning dabbing at her eyes or wiping her nose. "I know."

One thing Resi had told me *was* true: there was history here. History that went back a lot further than the hush-hush bailout in Belgium that Erica had discovered. History between the two of them alone, history I could only begin to guess at. In any case, it weighed a lot, as history often did. And whatever it was, it seemed to have sparked a level of trust in Resi that was completely irrational for Langer and dangerous for everybody else.

"Don't lose sight of why we're doing this, *Schatzi*," said Langer. "This is about so much more than money."

Resi didn't respond, but a moment between them passed, a moment I couldn't see but only guess at. A hug? Something else?

"I need better security at the lab and at the house," Resi spoke up in a slightly more robust voice. "For the past two nights, the cameras have picked up someone prowling around out there, and to top it off—" she cut herself off as if she'd suddenly decided she didn't want him to know about whatever other problem she'd been about to describe. "Never mind."

But it was enough. Dread hit me like a pair of soft, cold female fingers on the skin of my throat. I knew instantly who the prowlers were—well, not their names, but pretty much everything else. These were Erica's people, the ones that "specialized in this kind of thing."

And whoever they were, I had no doubt that Resi had the means to trace them back to Erica—and by proxy, Louisa. Maybe she already had.

But, like so many times before when someone close to me was in danger, I was helpless. My nails dug into my palms with the kind of frustration and rage I knew tragically well.

Fuck Wainwright-Phillips, I thought, not for the first time. My master wouldn't think he was so clever when his daughter ended up *dead* because the one person who could warn her had been rendered incapable of contacting her.

What's more, I now knew Resi was lying to Max about Maeve. *But still, where the hell is Maeve?*

"Who do you think the prowler is?" Langer asked.

Resi paused as if she knew. "It doesn't matter. Leave that up to me. But if you want ROI, then please make it so I don't have to waste my time playing rent-a-cop anymore."

Langer sighed. "I already got you Obadiah. What more do you need?"

"Everything—everyone—you can get me."

"Consider it done. In the meantime, what can I do to take care of the immediate problem?"

"Nothing," Resi replied softly. "I'm taking care of it now."

HER

I dropped the book on the floor. Instinctively, I knew it was just the wind that had blown the door shut. But my heart was still racing, and I recalled enough bad movies to know I should run straight out of there. But before I could, I forgot about the door. Because suddenly, from the pool area, came a faint sound, and it wasn't Millie.

Fuck. All of a sudden, Erica's message from two days ago came rushing back with a new and horrifying clarity. Maybe it hadn't been news at all. Maybe it was a *warning*. I *never* should have come here alone. What if—

"Erica?" called a thin, foreign-sounding female voice, at once so familiar—and unfamiliar—it set me trembling from within, like a response to the echo of some distant dream.

I ran as fast as I could out to the pool. There, curled up in the woven hammock, pale skin dappled with watery sunlight, lay a thin, petite, bleary-eyed girl with a blood-soaked bandage on her arm. As she raised her bruised body, her pixie-ish golden hair was pressed flat against her cheek as if she'd been sleeping on it for days.

Mother of mercy. That face. That hair. Those *eyes*.

"You are Louisa, yeah?" Maeve asked in slow, careful, halting English. "Where is my brother?"

—————————— · ◆ ❤ ◆ · ——————————

Well, friends, it seems I've done it again. Sorry.

But hey, we'll see Maeve—yes, and *him,* of course—again soon in *Never Lost (The Unchained #2),* coming this summer. Turn the page for an excerpt!

In the meantime, much more awaits you at my website, where, if you haven't read it yet, you can download *Riven,* an 80-page spicy forbidden romance prequel novella featuring two characters we'll soon (re)meet in *Never Lost*— when you sign up for my newsletter by scanning the QR code or visiting EverlyClaire.co m.

Can I also tempt you with a bonus spicy scene, one that took place in the shower the next morning at Erica's house, before they drove home? No? Okay. I guess don't sign up, then.

Of course, you can unsubscribe and keep the free book, but if you stick around, you'll also get ARC opportunities and exclusive giveaways, and be the first to find out about every new release before it happens. If you like dark worlds, forbidden love, and charming, protective bad boys with a habit of getting chained up, come connect with me!

FROM CHAPTER 1 OF NEVER LOST

HIM

That evening, I got a call from one of the assistants telling me to go down to the parking lot. I did, just as a silver Porsche convertible—gleaming so bright in the evening sunlight that it hurt my eyes—sped from around the corner and up the circular drive. The arrival of the car surprised me. The identity of the driver did not.

I just stood there, staring at the model, blinking. My mouth was probably hanging open, but I didn't care.

"Is that—"

Max Langer raised his dark sunglasses and nodded. "It's a nice day and I've had my eye on this one for a while, so I got it for a twenty-four-hour test drive," he explained. "Get in."

I had no specific reason to object other than spite, and my feelings of spite toward Langer, at this point, weren't nearly as strong as the almost supernatural draw I was feeling toward this car. My hands were practically shaking as I removed my suit jacket and shoved it in the minimal space behind the two black leather seats, rolling up the sleeves of my shirt. I wasn't exactly nostalgic for my old castoff clothes, but one thing was certain: in the desert heat, keeping cool in jackets and dress shirts—no matter how awesome they looked—was a lost cause.

Of course, it also occurred to me right away that this might be an opportunity to get answers. I had used the rest of my time at work that week to look for them, firing up the tablet that I'd left charging, and experimenting to see which of the passwords worked where. Some of them didn't work, which I'd expected. Some of them revealed files behind additional security that I'd need to try to hack into. And some unlocked some files so huge that it would take days to make any sense of them. Many appeared to be financial. Resi had wanted access to the books and been shut down, so it wouldn't surprise me if she—and Corey—had been working on finding another way in. Unfortunately—though calculus had come easily—finance, for someone who had never had any money, had been easy not to waste time on trying to understand. So before I got much further, I had to go to school.

Good thing I'd always wanted to go to school.

As for Lemaya, by the time I got back from my spying expedition, she was gone, and I hadn't seen her all week. Of course, Resi ordering her to be imprisoned, tortured, and/or killed because she'd allowed me to sneak away from the tour wasn't the only possibility, but it was definitely one of the likelier possibilities.

Fucking hell, was there any woman I'd ever interacted with whose life I didn't end up ruining?

I sank into the seat, hoping Langer couldn't tell that I'd never been in a convertible before. He didn't say anything as he slammed on the gas pedal and I savored the sound that beautiful German engineering made as it roared to life. Another thing I could get used to, but shouldn't. And then, as suddenly as a pair of screeching tires, I stopped. I wasn't going on any joyrides. Not today. "Max, wait. I—" I bit my lip.

"She's fine."

"What?"

"Keith's daughter. Curly Sue. Loulou. That's what he calls her, anyway; I forgot what the hell her real name is." He glanced over.

"Louisa," I said faintly, burying my head in my hand and sinking into the soft leather seat as he pulled out onto the highway at top speed. I kept my eyes on the pavement melting away beneath the tires as saguaros flew by against the backdrop of the ever-distant mountains. "How do you know?"

"I talked to him this afternoon. I know you think I'm lying because you always do, but I'll even show you the message he sent me. He mentions her by name."

"No," I said weakly. "I don't need to see it."

So Resi's claws hadn't reached Louisa. Yet. I felt the tight knot of dread in my chest that had been my companion since that afternoon fade by a few degrees. Maybe for a few hours, I could have only two people to worry about instead of three.

"And I'll ask about her again tomorrow."

"He'll get suspicious," I muttered, hating to admit that Langer was again offering the worst thing in the world he could possibly offer to someone who had long ago vowed to kill him: kindness.

"No, he won't. Besides, I see you pining over her every damn day like the lovesick teenager you are while failing to offer any better ideas. And, anyway, I'm good at this shit."

"What, deception and subterfuge? Yeah. I noticed."

He smirked. "I'd tell you to look in the mirror, but you wouldn't recognize yourself in those clothes."

Funny guy.

"Anyway, a less self-aware person would expect a thank you." Before I could scoff in outrage, he continued. "But I don't. Because as much as I've tried to create the illusion that you're here by choice, you're not, and to expect you to be grateful for that would make me as delusional as Keith. But I will take this opportunity to point out that you've yet to successfully catch me in a single actual lie. To you, anyway."

"You're wrong."

Langer whipped his head around so fast I was surprised the convertible didn't go flying off the road.

"You keep telling me my sister was never here, but you're wrong."

Eyes on the road again, he paused before answering. "I know."

Now it was my turn to whip my head around. "What the fuck, Max? You knew and you didn't tell me?"

"I didn't know until today, and I'm telling you now," he said irritably. "Anyway, it doesn't matter anymore, because she's gone. She left. Okay?"

Even the roar of the engine seemed to quiet as I sat silently suspended in a wind tunnel of horror. "Gone? When? Where?"

"I don't know."

"You don't know? Do you know what this means? What I had to go through to get—" I groaned and ran both hands through my hair in frustration, unable to even form sentences. I was back to square one. Below square one.

"I fucked up, okay? I'm sorry. Resi lied."

"No shit, she lied, and thanks to you, now my sister could be anywhere." For the first time, I twisted in the seat, turning my entire body toward Langer. "Fucking hell, Max, how tightly does this woman have you by the balls? Why do you believe everything she tells you unquestioningly? You're fucking her, aren't you? Because that's the only explanation I can think of that makes the least bit of sense."

"I'm not fucking her."

"Then what? What is this all-important, all-consuming history between the two of you that nothing, not even the truth, can come between?"

Wordlessly, he swung a hard right down a dirt side road, one that seemed to lead clear out into the middle of the desert, and I had a feeling, not for the first time recently, that I'd just made a huge mistake.

· ✦ ❤ ✦ ·

We'll find out soon what exactly Resi's deal is, but how about in the meantime, leaving me a review? Positive reviews and recommendations keep authors writing the books you love. They're the single most powerful thing you can do for us (yes, even more than buying the book, and they're free!) You can find a link to my books on Amazon or Goodreads by scanning the QR code or visiting linktr.ee/everlyclaire.

I love to chat, so don't be afraid to connect with me on my website at everlyclaire.com, via email at everly@everlyclaire.com or on your social media of choice. Find all my social links at linktr.ee/everlycl aire.

ABOUT THE AUTHOR

Everly Claire is a full-time writer living on a palm-fringed, white-sand beach on a Caribbean island (really, you should try it!) When she's not writing, she spends her time on a boat or on a beach (always with a fruity cocktail in hand), getting nerdy (and kicking ass!) at trivia night, and/or dreaming up more hot scenarios and dark twists involving protective, wounded, charming men you aren't allowed to touch (but we all know you will, anyway).

ALSO BY EVERLY CLAIRE

The Unchained Series

Suggested Reading Order

Never Broken (Louisa and [Redacted] #1)

Riven (Bex and Riven #0)

Never Bound (Louisa and [Redacted] #2)

Never Lost (Louisa and [Redacted] #3, coming summer 2025)

ACKNOWLEDGEMENTS

Well, it's been a little over three months since *Never Broken* launched, but it's amazing how things can change—and I'm not only talking about the book. Believe it or not, I did most of the work on preparing *Never Bound* while preparing myself to start a brand-new job on a brand-new island (and let's face it, a brand new life) in the Atlantic Ocean. And given everything else I was dealing with, I was so, so grateful to have these people in my corner:

Nigel, my partner in many things, looked after my book and more importantly, looked after *me,* when I didn't have time to do it.

My amazing PA and proofreader, Brianne Matheny, is my anchor to dry land, in so many ways.

Kate Malden aka LittlePerilStories, is the undisputed number one fan of this series, a soon-to-be-debut author you need to read, and the friend and unpaid therapist I don't deserve.

My beta readers who continued on to book 2: Adele, Annie, Ana, Havilah, Jamie, and Ritika, are the critics and cheerleaders I needed to keep going.

My brilliant editor, Emily A. Lawrence.

My gifted cover designer Najla Qamber and her colleague Nada Qamber delivered a flawless work of art once again (and happily humored me as I requested the 20th redo of [Redacted]'s hair).

My ARC team and Rule Breakers street team, which in the past few months has grown from a dozen or so fairly unhinged folks willing to take a chance on a new-to-them author to over 100 stunningly enthusiastic fans of The Unchained, believe in me and my stubbornly off-trend, off-market writing more than I believe in it myself most of the time. They've created beautiful content, bought multiple physical copies of my book, and hyped me up to anyone who will listen. When I think no one else could ever possibly be interested in my writing, they're what keep me going when I want to quit. Thank you from the bottom of my heart. I wish I could acknowledge you all by name.

My PR team: Jane at Torchlit Ink, stepped in when my last PR person dropped me abruptly and I had a breakdown on social media because I really thought I was going to have to delay my ARC campaign. Shannon at R&R Book Tours for once again setting up an amazing tour. And of course Amanda at Book of Matches Media, who did so well for Book 1. Thinking of you and wishing you healing. Layla at Bound to Love PR, for helping me up my social media game and sending my reel views into the stratosphere while I focused on writing and putting out this book.

My family: my parents and David, Rachel, and Nora. I love you.